Holding Her Breath

Nicole Green

Genesis Press, Inc.

INDIGO LOVE SPECTRUM

An imprint of Genesis Press, Inc.
Publishing Company

Genesis Press, Inc.
P.O. Box 101
Columbus, MS 39703

All characters in this book have no existence outside the imagination of the author and have no relation whatsoever to anyone bearing the same name or names. They are not even distantly inspired by any individual known or unknown to the author and all incidents are pure invention.

ISBN-13: 978-1-58571-439-1
ISBN-10: 1-58571-439-9
Manufactured in the United States of America

First Edition

Visit us at www.genesis-press.com
or call at 1-888-Indigo-1-4-0

Dedication

To everyone who reads this book.

Acknowledgements:

First I would like to thank the members of the Lovestory group from the Internet Writers Workshop for welcoming me into their group. I must also thank my first readers: Jen, Judy, Lauren, and Pepper. Their input was invaluable.

To the Virginia Romance Writers, thank you. I have learned so much and met so many wonderful people through this group.

And most of all, thanks to my readers. I couldn't do this writing thing without you.

Chapter 1: No Place Like Home for the Holidays

Whitney didn't know what the big deal was. All the potholders looked the same to her. But why stress out her holiday-mode mother more than necessary?

"Okay, Mom, these?" Whitney held up the red and green potholders. She was tired of digging through the giant drawer full of miscellaneous kitchen gadgets, aprons, potholders, and other such things. Especially after having been pricked by unidentified objects hidden deep within the drawer twice already.

"No, Whitney." Jo, her mom, heaved a sigh, temporarily blowing her bangs off of her forehead with the upward puff of air. "I'll do it. Just come stir this pot for a minute."

Whitney switched places with her mother, going over to stir the pot of goo thickening into gravy.

"Don't stir too fast," Jo called across the kitchen while digging through the drawer of mish-mosh wonders.

"Mom, I think I can stir gravy."

Jo put her hands on her hips before giving her daughter a playful smile. "This from the girl who burns water."

They laughed. It was true. Whitney wasn't the world's greatest cook. Her brother and sister had inherited the cooking gene, not her. Maybe it was the sort of thing that skipped the eldest daughter.

"Are they still out in the woods?" Whitney asked. Her stepfather, brother, and some of her cousins were out hunting deer.

"I guess so," her mom said.

"It's a wonder they haven't frozen to death yet," Whitney said while staring down at the bubbling, thickening liquid she was stirring.

"Yeah, they should be back soon, though. It's already dark out there." Jo rushed over to the pot and peered inside. She set a pair of blue and white potholders featuring smiling snowmen on the counter next to the stove.

"I really am capable of this," Whitney said as her mother bumped her out of the way with a small hip check and took the wooden spoon from her.

"Hmph. You ain't gonna burn my gravy up. You know how Shorty loves this stuff," Jo said. Shorty was Whitney's stepfather.

"Where'd you find these?" Whitney said, picking up the potholders. "I swear I never saw them in the drawer."

"Don't swear, and they were right in there, plain as day, honey."

Whitney's BlackBerry vibrated on the counter opposite the stove and she went over to check the screen.

"I wish you would put that thing away for one night," Jo said. "It's Christmas Eve. They can let your family have you for one night, can't they?" Jo poked at the gravy with a long, wooden spoon.

"How do you know it's work?" Whitney felt too guilty to open the email from Gibson and Grey, the law firm she worked for, after her mother's comment. She set her BlackBerry on the counter.

"When is it not work, oh daughter of mine?" Jo opened the oven door. The mouth-watering aroma of baking bread that had filled the kitchen already became even stronger. Homemade yeast rolls were one of Jo's specialties, although Whitney and her siblings often said that everything was their mother's specialty.

"I have friends. They call," Whitney said with a defensive little shrug of her shoulders.

"I know that," Jo said. "But you know what all your friends are doing right now? Helping their mothers prep Christmas dinner and get a good Christmas Eve meal on the table for their families." She lifted the lid on a pot. "Only those bloodsuckers you work with are on their phones right now trying to make more money instead of being at home with their families." Jo bustled around the kitchen making sure dough was rising, meats were defrosting, and spices and other dry ingredients were lined up for the baking she had to do after dinner.

"I'd help if you'd let me," Whitney said.

"I didn't mean it that way." Jo laughed. "I don't want you burning my house down or my turkey up. The others will be back any minute. Everything's almost ready. We'll eat soon," she said. "You just keep me company, honey. And help me get ingredients and stuff ready for the cooking I'll do after dinner. That's plenty."

Whitney grinned. Her mother was the only person who could get away with comments like that. "Okay. Well, I've set the table. I made the lemonade and the sweet tea. Sodas are in the fridge. And I stuck a pitcher of water in there, too. What's next?"

"Run over to the pantry and get me a can of—" Her mother's voice broke off at the sound of the front door slamming open, soon followed by loud male voices and boisterous laughter. "Y'all take off them boots before you make one more step or I'll kill you!" Jo shouted toward the sound of the voices.

"Of course, dear honey pie!" Shorty shouted back.

Whitney grinned. She couldn't imagine two people being better matched than her second stepfather and her mother. Jo said Shorty was living proof that the third time was the charm.

Jo rolled her eyes, but her face flushed and she smiled. She told Whitney she still got jittery and flutters started in her stomach when Shorty walked into a room. Whitney wondered if that would happen for her one day, but she wasn't too worried about it. She wasn't even thirty. Not quite yet, anyway.

Shorty and the others walked in wearing their hunting gear—camouflage coveralls in shades of pale brown and tan along with their orange hats. On their feet they wore only socks, ranging from white to gray to black depending on which man those feet belonged to.

Shorty, Whitney's half-brother Devon, and two of her cousins stood hulking over the counter and sniffing around the kitchen, talking about how hungry they were and how good everything smelled. Devon's father was Whitney's first stepfather. Shorty was her second stepfather. The cousins were her crazy aunt's children.

"Umph, I can't wait to get into that gravy. When are we eating?" Shorty said, starting toward Jo.

Jo held up her hands to keep him where he was. "Don't you take another step in my kitchen all nasty with the woods on you like that. You know better." She pointed him toward the doorway. "We won't eat 'til y'all wash up."

Shorty laughed. "Yeah, I knew better, but my stomach led me in here anyway." He nodded to the others. "All right, y'all, let's wash up so we can get down to business."

The group of hunters walked toward the half bath on the first floor. Shorty branched off toward the master bedroom, which was also on the first floor.

Whitney smiled after them, thinking of how those were the things that made her so happy to come home and visit. That was why, despite her crazy schedule, she always made it home for the holidays. She wished she could've been there more often, though. Gibson and Grey kept her busy working sixty- to eighty-hour work weeks, so she didn't have time to go anywhere much besides the office.

The front door banged open again and Whitney heard Aunt Cheryl's voice. "Umph. Jo, why you burnin' that gravy in there for?"

Whitney's smile faded. And then there were those things that made her visits a little less pleasant than she would have liked.

Whitney started to ease out of the kitchen.

"Don't you dare leave me alone with her. I'm about to strangle that woman the way she's been acting lately, and I need a buffer," her mother called across the kitchen in a loud whisper.

Whitney groaned, but stayed put. She leaned against the counter near an empty muffin tin and a package of brown sugar.

Aunt Cheryl walked into the kitchen, put a hand on her hip, and leaned back a little. With a small upturn of her lip, she said, "What y'all been doin' in the kitchen all day? Don't look like much to me. But no-body wanted to come over to see Miss Margaret with me. I see how it is." Miss Margaret was a family friend.

"How is Miss Margaret?" Jo asked, trying to diffuse the situation. She was always trying to put out the fires her sister set.

"Oh, she's just fine. Asked about y'all." Aunt Cheryl fussed with her wig as she spoke. That year's Christmas wig was a black bob with burgundy highlights.

Of course Aunt Cheryl hadn't told them she was going until the last minute. Whitney had the sneaking suspicion she'd gone to see Miss Margaret in order to keep from helping with Christmas dinner. The sisters took turns preparing Christmas dinner, and it was Jo's turn that year.

"I'm going over to see her day after tomorrow. After we get Christmas out of the way," said Jo.

"Where's our dear sister at?" Aunt Cheryl said. "Shouldn't she be helping you with this? And our brother's no-count wife?" She sniffed around the kitchen.

"Brenda is at the store," Jo said. "We ran out of milk and I forgot all about cranberry sauce. And Larry and his wife are on their way. She's bringing some banana bread with her."

"Mmph." Aunt Cheryl scrunched her nose. "I ain't touching that loaf of brick. That stuff could kill a water buffalo. No, sir, I don't have a strong enough stomach."

Whitney's mother signaled to her. She walked over to the counter and started chopping the scallions on the cutting board that her mother had set out for her.

"Whitney, girl," her aunt said.

Whitney pasted on a smile. She knew her aunt was about to start in on her, and she was not looking forward to it.

"It is so good to see you. We don't see you enough," Aunt Cheryl said. "I still want to know when we gonna see some babies from you. We need some more cousins in the family for my grandbabies and Larry's. You gettin' up there, ain't you?"

"I'm still trying to get my career off the ground." Whitney's chops of the little green tubes on the cutting board became more staccato.

"All I'm saying is you're almost thirty now, ain't you? And your mama has yet to see her first grandchild." A smirk hovered around the corners of Aunt Cheryl's lips.

"Women have babies well into their forties," she said.

"Don't you and your Aunt Brenda hope so?"

Whitney smiled and kept chopping.

"Speaking of Brenda, I can't believe that woman finally got married. Look at what she chose, though." Aunt Cheryl rolled her eyes.

"Don't start, Cheryl," Jo said. "It's gonna be a long night if you get started in on that." She looked up from the kitchen sink and wiped her hands on her apron.

Aunt Cheryl raised her eyebrows at Whitney's mother. "Jo. You know I'm going to speak my mind. Always have. Always will."

"There's a difference between speaking your mind and being obnoxious," Jo said.

Aunt Cheryl opened her mouth to respond, but just then the front door opened and voices filled the hall again. Two squealing children ran into the kitchen followed by their laughing parents, Whitney's Uncle Larry and his wife, Janet.

Whitney hugged both of them after they entered the kitchen and greeted everyone.

"How are y'all? It's so good to see you," Whitney said. She hadn't seen them since she'd gotten into town a couple days earlier.

"I see how it is. I ain't get nary a bit of hug when I walked in here earlier." Aunt Cheryl cut her eyes at Whitney.

Whitney forced herself not to groan. She hadn't seen Uncle Larry or Aunt Janet since the summer. She'd seen Aunt Cheryl almost every moment since she'd arrived home two days ago. It was always easier to just apologize. "I'm sorry," Whitney said, walking toward her aunt with her arms outstretched.

Aunt Cheryl stepped away from Whitney. "Naw. I don't want one if I have to ask for it."

Whitney turned back to Uncle Larry and Aunt Janet. "How have you two been?"

"Great. Settling into the new house and trying to keep up with them." Uncle Larry nodded to the young boy and girl hopping around the kitchen and begging their aunt Jo for cookies.

They made her think about having kids one day. Not that those were at the top of her priority list. Making partner was the most important thing at the moment.

"They're so sweet," Whitney said.

"Yeah, you wanna take 'em back to D.C. with you and see if you still think that?" Janet asked. The three of them laughed.

Janet called out to her children. "Brianna, L.J., come say hi to your cousin."

Four-year-old L.J. and six-year-old Brianna ran over, shouting Whitney's name. They were a lot younger than Janet and Larry's kids from their previous marriages. Both of them had been married before. In fact, they'd met through a divorce support group.

Brianna and L.J. each took a side and wrapped themselves around Whitney's legs. She unwrapped herself from their grips and squatted down. She put an arm around each of them.

"How are you guys?"

"Good!" they shouted.

"You been good this year?"

They nodded vigorously.

"Then what's Santa bringing you?"

L.J. gave his answer before his sister could open her mouth. "Toys and candy and all the presents in the world."

Whitney laughed. "Really?"

"Whit, why don't you take Brianna and L.J. to get washed up for dinner? We'll be ready to eat as soon as Brenda and Glen get back," Jo said while handing Janet an apron.

"Okay," Whitney said, glad to escape the kitchen. She took a tiny hand in each of hers and led her cousins toward the half-bathroom.

By the time Whitney was done helping her cousins wash up for dinner, everyone else had arrived and made their way into the dining room. Whitney took a seat at the table and looked around at her family assembled there.

Brianna and L.J. sat at a card table a few feet away with Aunt Cheryl's grandchildren, swinging their feet from where they sat in their folding chairs. They merrily swirled mashed potatoes around their fingers.

That was the only place in the world she wanted to be. It was so good to have all of her family in one place. Almost all of them, anyway.

Whitney's paternal grandparents were in New York. She wasn't looking forward to calling them for Christmas the next day. It always took so much out of her to keep her patience while talking to them. Grandmother was always finding new ways to insult Jo while ostensibly paying her compliments.

"...Yo, Whitney?" one of Aunt Cheryl's sons called with his hands cupped around his mouth. Apparently, he'd been trying to get her attention for a while.

Whitney shook her head, bringing herself back to the dinner table. "You ask me something?"

"Oh, I just wanted to know what you gettin' for Christmas." He looked at his brother, and the two of them snickered.

"I don't know. Why?" She knew whatever he had to say was going to be stupid.

"Mom said she hopes you ask for a man 'cause you sure need one." He tittered. He would've punched his brother in the arm, amused by the supposed cleverness of his own lame joke, if Cheryl hadn't been between them. She just knew it. He said, "You know, 'cause you still single. You know, 'cause Devon just got engaged. Even Alicia has a man."

"Funny," she said before taking a sip of eggnog. "Really."

The front door banged open and a voice called out, "We're home."

12

"Finally," Jo muttered. "I was wondering if they went to mine that salt themselves." She craned her head toward the living room.

Whitney turned to see Alicia walk into the dining room. Alicia was Whitney's sixteen-year-old half-sister, Jo and Shorty's child.

Alicia kissed Whitney's cheek and bent over her chair to give her a hug. They chatted for a minute before Alicia went around the table saying hello to everybody else. Whitney thought about what her cousin had said while she watched Alicia make her way around the table.

Whitney didn't have any trouble finding men. And she might not have had any trouble keeping them, if she could find the effort to put into a relationship. She had precious little free time, and she preferred to spend it with her friends rather than with the losers who always came on to her.

She was still busy making a name for herself at the firm. Later, she always told herself. She had plenty of time to worry about things like love and marriage and all of that. So Devon was engaged. And one of Aunt Cheryl's sons was married and the other one had a long-time girlfriend. So what? Like Aunt Brenda had told her, she wasn't in a race to the altar with anybody.

She smiled at the memory of Devon's proposal to his girlfriend over Thanksgiving. Her smile faded when she remembered the look on Devon's face earlier when she'd asked where Trina was. He'd spat out that she was with her family for Christmas. He'd made a point of mostly avoiding her after that. Whitney liked to help people with their problems. Devon called that being nosy.

She sat back, picking at her string beans. Her appetite had dulled a little even though her stomach had been growling when she first sat down to her mother's perfect meal.

Hopefully Christmas Day wouldn't be too wild. Something always went wrong, though. And it usually happened when stepdad number one and his girlfriend stopped by on Christmas night. Jo tried to remain civil to him for Devon's sake, but it was always iffy when those two saw each other.

Chapter 2: But It's Christmas Eve

"I'm moving out." Kelly put her hands on her narrow hips and delivered the news to Chace. Kelly was the only reason he'd moved to this place that wasn't even a dot on the map.

"What?" Why was she saying this? On Christmas Eve. They were supposed to be exchanging presents before heading to her parents' house for Christmas carols and eggnog. Like last year. And the year before that. The big Weiss tradition.

"Chace, I can't do this anymore."

"Can't do what?" They hadn't had any big fights. He wasn't aware of anything he'd done to piss her off. Anything he'd done wrong at all.

She put her hands over her face and shook her head. "I've been seeing someone."

Chace dropped into the chair he'd just risen from. "What do you mean, seeing someone?"

"Hank."

"I don't understand." He didn't want to understand. Hank was a lawyer in town and Kelly's boss.

"Remember how I told you I wanted to move back here from Richmond to be closer to my family?" She took a deep breath. "Well, I also wanted to be closer to Hank. We've been seeing each other off and on for three years now."

"But we've only been together for two." Chace felt sick.

She crossed her arms over her chest and stared away from him.

"Hank's married."

"I know," she said. "But he's finally going to leave his wife for me. He's telling her right after the holidays. But I can't live this lie with you anymore. I'm going to stay with my parents until after New Year's."

Did her parents know what she'd done to him? And he'd thought they liked him.

Chace stared at the presents under the Christmas tree. That was why she'd barely let him touch her lately? Was hardly ever home? Never wanted to go out anywhere with him when she was? Because of balding, ancient Hank?

"Chace, you have to know I didn't want it to be this way. Hank and I had called it off before I met you. I really liked being with you, and I'll always care about you."

"Is it the money, Kelly? Is that why? Because Hank is a big, fancy lawyer and I'm just a freelance photographer with a crappy day job? Because I'm not afraid to follow my dreams and try to be what I really want to be?"

"Hank and I…we have a very special bond. When I'm with him—don't make me say these things. I don't want to hurt you."

"Uh, you don't want to what?" Her words were a brick to his stomach. Two years. And it was going to end like that. He stared at the shiny red wrapping around the box that contained her present. He remembered being so excited about finding the right frame for the photo of her grandparents on their wedding day. The photo that he and Kelly's mom had spent hours digging through old shoeboxes full of photos to find. The perfect prelude to a New Year's Eve or a Valentine's Day proposal. He hadn't yet decided which. Now he wouldn't have to.

Kelly cleared her throat, breaking the uncomfortable silence. "Amy is coming over to help me pack. I want to get out tonight. Make this as quick and painless as possible."

Chace had to laugh. "This isn't ripping a bandage off a scratch, Kelly. Nothing about this is quick and painless."

"Don't. This is already hard enough." She walked over and put a hand on his shoulder.

He shrugged away from her. "Don't touch me. Ever. Again."

"I do lo—"

"I swear, if you say it? I'll put my fist through a wall," Chace said, standing up and walking over to the wall near the balcony as if readying himself to carry out his threat.

Kelly ran a hand through her long brown hair, settling it back behind her shoulders. There was a knock at the door. Kelly went to answer it. Chace folded his arms over his chest and leaned against the wall.

Kelly opened the door and a petite blonde with a round face and short hair walked into the room. Kelly's friend, Amy. She dragged two boxes in with her that were almost bigger than she was.

"Hi, Chace." Amy gave him a sympathetic smile. The kind of smile you'd give someone if they'd lost their best friend.

"Hey," Chace said, kicking at the carpet with the toe of his gray sock.

Kelly took the boxes from her and set them on the couch. "Did you bring more?"

"Yeah, there are some more in my car. I brought those crates you asked about, too. I found them in my garage." Amy handed her car keys to Kelly.

Kelly nodded and headed out of the door.

Amy walked over to him. She twisted her wedding ring around her finger and looked up at him and down at it alternately. The look she gave him reeked of guilt. Amy was the only person who knew Chace had planned to ask Kelly to marry him.

"Did you know?" he asked.

"I knew about him, but she told me that it was over." Amy looked over her shoulder. "She said she'd broken up with him for the last time, and she was all about you. Otherwise, I would have told you when you told me you were going to ask her to marry you. I swear." She looked up at him with pleading brown eyes, as if willing him to believe her.

Chace nodded, letting his brown hair fall into his eyes as he looked down at the carpet.

"She told me this morning that he told her he couldn't live without her. That if leaving his wife was what it took to get her back, he was going to have to do it. I'm sorry."

He looked across the room. "Yeah. Me, too."

"Really, you're better off not being in this mess." Amy put a hand on his arm.

"Would have been nice to have a warning about the kind of mess I was in."

"I couldn't—I couldn't say anything. Kelly made me promise. We've been friends since first grade."

He nodded, swallowing thickly. He knew it wasn't Amy's fault. The one he really needed to blame was downstairs getting boxes out of Amy's car. He walked over to the bar counter that bordered the kitchen and slipped on his shoes. He grabbed his keys from the counter.

"Where are you going?"

He shrugged. "Somewhere. I can't be here and watch you two pack up her things."

"But what if we don't know what belongs to who?"

"She can take whatever she wants. She's already taken the most important thing anyway," Chace said. He shuffled toward the front door. He grabbed his coat from the back of the sofa on his way there.

"I'll text you when we're done."

Chace shrugged and walked out to the breezeway. When he heard Kelly's high-heeled black leather boots clicking past, he didn't even look up.

"I still want us to be friends," Kelly said.

Chace kept walking, pretending she hadn't just said something completely idiotic so he wouldn't have to get even angrier.

Chapter 3: Christmas Cheer.
Sort of.

Whitney woke up early Christmas morning. The first thing she did was go to her window. She hoped for a white Christmas even though she didn't really expect one. She closed her eyes and pulled back the curtains. When she opened her eyes and saw the frostbitten lawn, she sighed. No snow. Just a cold, gray morning.

It was cold near the window. She shivered a little and reached for her fuzzy yellow robe, which was draped over the post of her four-poster bed nearest the window. She heard her personal cell phone ringing—she'd promised to turn off her BlackBerry on Christmas Day after Jo threatened to hit her over the head with a rolling pin—and she went over to retrieve it from her night stand. Erika. Of course.

"Hi."

"Am I the first person to wish you a merry Christmas?" Erika asked.

"Yes, you are, Erika dear."

"Good. I thought you probably hadn't left your room yet. I bet I woke you up."

"Maybe."

"I don't know how you get up for work in the mornings 'cause you sure don't get up if you don't have to."

Whitney grinned. "Why should I get up for no reason? And I was awake, for your information."

"Yeah, uh-huh. When did you get up, then?"

Whitney rolled her eyes, but laughed before answering. "About five minutes before you called."

Erika laughed. "See?"

"Yeah, yeah. You know me too well. How are things with the fam?"

"Great. They all asked about you."

"Same with mine. They miss you for some crazy reason," Whitney said. "It's been forever since you came down here with me."

"Yeah, I need to go down there soon. How's that brother of yours?"

"He's good. And engaged."

"I know. And you know I'm kidding. For now. He knows where to find me if they break up."

"Sure," Whitney said. Erika and Devon were both huge flirts.

"Aunt Cheryl riding your last nerve yet?" Erika's tone indicated that she'd guessed the answer to that question.

Whitney tapped her fingers against the window pane as she answered. "Oh, she's well past it. Again with the man and the marriage and the babies and all that. As usual."

"You know, she might almost have a point. A year is a long time to be single."

"You should talk. You're almost single. And your boyfriend lives with you."

"Hey. Don't you start on A.J. It's Christmas, after all."

"Ha. Right. Anyway, the only thing on my mind right now is making partner. You know that." Whitney was on the partnership track at her firm and making good progress toward that brass ring.

"You know you're going to get it."

"I sure hope so," Whitney said with a sigh, thinking of her supposed mentor who was overseeing her progress on the partnership track. Kim. That woman lived for Gibson and Grey, and she didn't have much patience for things like mentoring. She only did it because all junior partners were required to mentor senior associates on the partnership track.

After Whitney got off the phone with Erika, she tightened the belt of her robe around her waist, slipped her phone into her robe pocket, and followed her nose down to the kitchen. The scent of cloves blended in with the scents of vanilla and ginger.

Jo had probably been in there at least since five that morning like she was every Christmas. Jo's hair was covered with a red scarf, and she wore a purple sweat suit that had streaks of flour across it. The apron she wore hadn't saved her outfit from the streaks. She was wiping her hands off on a dish towel when Whitney walked over and kissed her cheek.

"Merry Christmas, daughter," Jo said.

Whitney hugged her and laughed. "Merry Christmas, Mother."

"Grab that apron and start chopping the vegetables for the stuffing," Jo said, nodding to an apron hanging from a hook near the pantry door.

Whitney grabbed the apron and tied it around her waist. "I talked to Erika this morning. She said to wish you a merry Christmas."

"When is she coming down here again?"

"I don't know. She said she hopes soon." Whitney diced a stalk of celery as she spoke.

"She still with that no-good A.J.?"

"You know it." Whitney picked up a knife and began chopping onions. Her mother didn't like A.J. any more than Whitney did. He didn't treat Erika with enough respect, even if Erika refused to see it.

Whitney prepared vegetables and her mother baked, sautéed, and measured. All the while, they talked about Shorty's business, Devon going back to school, and Alicia wanting a new car.

Brianna ran into the kitchen, shouting that it was time to open presents. Whitney put down the knife and wiped her hands on the front of her apron. She scooped the girl up in her arms so that she could no longer run circles around the island in the center of the kitchen.

"Presents, huh? I guess you think Santa left you something." Whitney tickled the little girl under her chin.

She giggled. "Of course he did," the little girl said with an adorable lisp. Her two front teeth were missing. She put a tiny fist on her non-existent hip.

"Oh, really? And what is it you think he left you?" Whitney said.

The little girl's big, round eyes widened and so did her toothless grin. She clapped her hands together. "Lotsa cool toys!"

Whitney laughed. "Is that so?"

She nodded vigorously. "Just wait. You'll see." She started squirming to be let down. "Let's go. We have to get everybody and open up presents!"

Whitney set the girl down. She grabbed two of Whitney's fingers. Her little cousin dragged her around the house, harassing the rest of their family to get up so that they could all open presents.

Least happy was Whitney's sister, Alicia. Alicia had crept back in the house only a few hours ago. Whitney, a light sleeper, had heard it all.

"What were you doing out until three in the morning?" Whitney kept her voice low so that only Alicia would hear her.

"None of your business." Alicia groaned and pulled a pillow over her head.

"Whit, 'Leesha. We gotta open presents," their cousin said.

"Go ahead, Brianna," Alicia said. "We'll be down in a minute."

"We're right behind you," Whitney said, smiling at her little cousin. "You're doing such a good job waking everybody. Keep up the good work."

"Okay, but I'll be back in fifty-five minutes if you don't come downstairs," she said in a serious tone.

"Okay," Whitney said. The girl skipped out of the room. Whitney turned back to her sister. "So you're not going to tell me where you were?"

"Nope."

"Do our parents know about you going out any time you feel like it?"

She shrugged and yawned. "Dad wants to believe I'm always up to no good because I'm hard headed. Why disappoint him?" Alicia pushed back her covers and slowly swung her feet out and over the side of the bed.

"Be nice."

"He's always trying to boss me like I'm Brianna's age or something. He needs to get it in his head I'm not a baby. He still trying to tell me where I can go and what I can do." She rubbed her eyes, muttering about people waking her up in the middle of the morning.

"He's your father. He cares about you," Whitney said, wishing the father nature had given her had cared half as much as Shorty did.

"Whatever. Tell him if you want. He'll yell. I'll yell. It's our routine," Alicia said before standing and stretching. She wore shorts with candy canes on them and a matching camisole. Alicia had always been rail thin. A combination of being a picky eater and taking after Shorty's side of the family saw to that. "Last night wasn't the first time I ever snuck out, you know."

Whitney had curves her sister always complained about with envy. She went to the gym, but she wasn't obsessed with it like some of her friends were.

Alicia yawned, slipping on a flannel robe. "We better get down there before Brianna has a fit."

Whitney followed her sister downstairs. A large pot of coffee was brewing in the kitchen, and it smelled too good. She reached for the coffee maker as her mother scooted her in the opposite direction.

"You know better. Coffee in a minute, but we better go open these presents before these children eat us alive."

Whitney grumbled, but stumbled to the family room, knowing her mother was right.

Shorty put a CD in the stereo in the entertainment center. Moments later, Christmas-themed jazz filtered out of the speakers on low volume. Her family was sprawled around the living room. Everyone was half asleep except for the kids, who were almost sitting underneath the Christmas tree. They were arguing about who would get to open the first present. Half the adults in the room had cameras aimed at the kids.

Uncle Larry, Janet, Aunt Brenda, and Glen sat on one side of the room. Aunt Cheryl, who was in a sour mood and frowning already that morning, sat on the other side with her sons. Uncle Larry's and Aunt Janet's older kids from their first marriages hung in the background. Whitney's favorite cousin, Uncle Larry's eldest child Melinda, wasn't there yet. She was getting into town that night, having wanted to spend half of Christmas in New York with the people at the homeless shelter at which she volunteered.

"Okay, everybody. Presents," Jo said, clasping her hands. She hurried over to the kids and helped them hand out packages wrapped in colorful paper decorated with snowmen, reindeer, and Santas.

"How long do you think this is going to take?" Devon muttered from where he was standing next to her.

"Why, you got somewhere you gotta be, Grinch?" Whitney said with a playful smile. When she saw his face, her smile faded. He narrowed his eyes at her.

"He's been like this for a week," Alicia said. "He can't get along with his girl."

"Stay out of my business," Devon snapped, walking away from them and going over to stand next to Uncle Larry.

Whitney heard squeals of delight and turned her attention back to the present opening. Wrapping paper was briskly ripped off of packages. Toys came out of shiny boxes. Soon, the living room was filled with the lights and sounds of new toys, shredded wrapping paper, and some very happy children.

After tearing through the gifts everyone had bought for them, the children started insisting everyone else in the room open their presents. Brianna and L.J. had made gifts for each family member. Brianna hand-delivered Whitney's to her.

"What's this?" Whitney took the package.

"Won't know until you open it, silly." She giggled.

Whitney smiled and turned the lumpy package over and over in her hands. The red and gold wrapping paper was wrinkled and secured with masking tape. She opened it and found inside a hair tie glued to a piece of cardboard with her name written on it in multi-colored crayons. Around her name were various drawings—a briefcase, a cell phone, a square with circles on the bottom that was apparently a car since the word "Lexus" was written on it, only it was spelled "Leksus."

"Did you make this all by yourself?" Whitney squatted down next to the little girl.

"My brother and me made it." She looked over at L.J., and both of them burst into giggles. "It's for your

lawyer desk at work. My teacher has one on her desk.
You need one, too."

Whitney felt a pang of guilt as this made her think
about work, but only a small one.

"Thank you. I'll put this on my desk as soon as I
get back to work." And Whitney fully intended to put
the homemade craft next to the marble, black and
gold nameplate that sat on her desk at the office. She
hugged Brianna and kissed her cheek. "This is the best
present anyone's ever given me."

Brianna smiled shyly and ran over to Aunt Janet.
She wrapped her arms around Janet's legs.

When it came time for Jo to open presents, she
told Whitney hers was too much, but Whitney insisted
it wasn't. It was a simple gold and emerald necklace
and earring set. Emerald was her mother's birth stone.
Anyway, nothing was too much for her mother. Jo had
given her so much—the love of two parents before,
during, and after her second marriage. The love her
absent father had never given. Even though Shorty
was like the father she'd never had, she knew she and
her mother would always share an extremely special
bond.

For Shorty, and for Jo just as much as it was for
him, Whitney had gotten a new laptop. Jo always complained that theirs kept freezing up on them, and their
desktop computer was pre-historic.

"A Mac!" Shorty crowed. "I was in the Apple Store the other day looking at this very one."

Devon snorted. "Always gotta show us up, huh? I bet that necklace costs what I make in a month," he muttered to her. "And I don't even want to think about what that computer cost." He plucked at one of the low-hanging ornaments on the tree.

"This isn't about you. This is about Mom and Shorty and Christmas," Whitney said.

"This is about you feeling guilt for running off to the big city and only coming around here once or twice a year." Devon glared up at her.

Whitney turned away from him, sensing that he was trying to pick a fight. "Mom, what did Shorty get you?"

Jo held up a box wrapped in silver paper. She darted a suspicious glance at her husband. "That's a good question."

"Go on. Open it." Shorty was grinning, looking quite pleased with himself.

Jo ripped the paper off the box and stared down at it open-mouthed. Then she looked up at Shorty, narrowing her eyes a little. "What is this? What have you done?"

"Go ahead and open up that box, and you'll find out." Shorty looked at Whitney. "This woman has to question everything to death."

Jo opened the box, closed it, opened it again, and then handed it to Shorty. She shook her head. "Now you know I don't know what to do with that."

"What did he get you?" Aunt Brenda asked, walking over to them.

"A doggone smartphone. What in the world would I look like with one of them things?" She snorted. "I barely know what it is."

Devon jumped up and went over to them. "Mom, please. You'll love it if you just give it a chance. I helped pick it out. Look, we even got a pink holder for you."

Jo shook her head. "Y'all know better."

"But, Mom. It has email, GPS, internet, all that stuff."

"Son, what good is that gonna do me? I just started getting comfortable with text messaging." Jo eyed the box that Shorty kept trying to give back to her with suspicion.

"It's just like mine," Shorty said. "You'll love it. Here, please take the thing out of the box." He tried to hand her the phone.

Jo shook her head. "I can't fool with no phone smarter than I am. It gets smarter than me, time to leave it alone."

Whitney walked over and put an arm around her mom. "They're really not that bad."

Jo snorted. "Huh. So *you* say."

"Really." She laughed. Then, she attempted to explain the basics of using the phone to her mom.

After presents were all exchanged, and the smartphone lay lonely on the mantel in the family room, Jo headed back to the kitchen to work on the finishing touches for dinner. She'd prepared all her desserts the night before, and her turkey and ham were coming along nicely. Shorty kept the Christmas music going.

Whitney was allowed to boil the potatoes for the mashed potatoes—under supervision, of course—while Jo started the macaroni and cheese. After that, Whitney took a break so she could grab a shower. Hot water was a precious commodity when they had a full house.

After showering, wrapping and drying her hair, and checking her email to make sure she had nothing urgent from work, Whitney stopped procrastinating. She finally called her grandparents.

Her grandmother answered the phone. "Hello, Whitney dear. Merry Christmas." She called for Whitney's grandfather to pick up a second phone on the line.

"Merry Christmas, Whitney," her grandfather said.

"Merry Christmas, guys."

"How is everyone there? I do wish you would have come to Manhattan for a Christmas visit, sweetheart. It has been so long since you've done that."

"Everyone's fine," Whitney said, not responding to the second half of her grandmother's comment. Whitney had only been to New York a handful of times for Christmas since college. The holidays were always frostier up there, and it had little to do with the temperature. She didn't like standing amongst her grandparents' friends as they played the one-up game with each other. It was always about how much money a person had, who they were linked to in society, whose parents had done or owned what.

Whitney had never cared much for that sort of thing. That didn't stop them, though. Her grandparents always made sure they mentioned that Whitney worked for one of the largest law firms in the country with several of the most impressive practice groups in the world, including their real estate, tax, intellectual property, and international law groups. Whitney was a member of the intellectual property group.

"We're going to Marge's house tonight," her grandmother said. "She's asked your cousin to be her campaign manager. Now what do you think about that?"

Sometimes it seemed like all her grandparents cared about were connections and appearances. Whitney did as much as she could to keep them happy, but she had to draw the line somewhere.

"That's great." What was a good excuse to get off of the phone that didn't seem too obvious?

"Marge's son still asks about you. All the time."

"Good," she said. "We're having a feast for Christmas dinner tonight. You should see the spread that Mom made. It's incredible."

"How's your mother?" Her grandmother asked in a clipped tone. It was clear that she felt obligated to ask the question. Jo didn't have any warmer feelings for Whitney's dad's parents than they had for her.

"She's fine," Whitney said. That was about all they would want to hear, so she left it at that.

The way Jo put it, the only good thing she'd gotten out of the situation with Whitney's father was Whitney. Whitney's grandparents hadn't wanted anything to do with Jo at first. Jo didn't like the way they'd insinuated that she'd gotten pregnant on purpose to trap their son. They believed that Jo had ruined their son in the process. However, Whitney's grandparents had wanted to get to know their grandchild after she was born. Jo was glad that Whitney had a relationship with her paternal grandparents even if Jo could barely stand them. Jo and Whitney's grandparents were now civil to each other, but that was about it.

"I'm glad she's well," her grandmother said before turning the conversation back to society talk.

Whitney's father had dropped out of college and left the country with some of his junkie friends. He and his friends had left for Mexico right before Whitney was born. Whitney or Jo would get a letter from him occasionally, but that was about it. As far as Whitney knew, his parents—her grandparents—never heard from him at all. Then again, they had kicked him out of their house and told him to never come back right before he left for Mexico. Their behavior seemed kind of harsh. They set high standards for their children and grandchildren—maybe a little too high—and they didn't tolerate disappointment.

But they were still her grandparents, and she knew they loved her. Despite everything, they meant well. In their own, short-sighted and vain way. As much as she resented her grandparents' judgmental nature, she still wanted to make them proud. That was why she put up with them making her take her father's spot. And why she put up with some of the outrageous things they said and did.

Whitney listened to her grandparents subtly put down the Joneses and criticize Jo's choices a little while longer before she told them she had to go. After that, she helped her mother and Aunt Brenda finish cooking while listening to Aunt Cheryl complain and tell them everything was burnt or bland. Aunt Janet gladly volunteered to keep the kids under control. She'd beat both Whitney and Aunt Brenda to volunteering for the job.

By dinnertime, Whitney's nerves were frayed from her aunt picking at her all day about finding a man, not spending enough on her Christmas present, and everything else she could think of.

Then Cheryl started in on Aunt Brenda. "Where'd you say your so-called husband is?"

Aunt Brenda pasted on a smile and her eyes flashed only a little. Whitney caught it only because she'd been looking for it. "Glen is spending a few hours with his ex-wife and his daughter. He'll be back after dinner."

Cheryl snorted. "He left you here? On Christmas Day? To be with his ex-wife?"

"He and Margaret are still good friends. Just like Jo and Quinton are."

"You better watch it."

"I think it's good that they can still be friends," Brenda said, her pleasant tone just as fake as her smile. "Some people let old wounds heal."

Aunt Cheryl raised her eyebrows. "What is that supposed to mean?"

Jo stepped in. "Dinner is almost ready. Who's going to help me get all this food on the table?"

"Let's do it," Whitney said, reaching for a casserole dish.

"Some people," Aunt Cheryl said. She muttered the rest of whatever she had to say under her breath.

Whitney looked over at Aunt Brenda, and they rolled their eyes.

When Whitney walked past Aunt Cheryl, her aunt said, "Girl, you pick up some weight? You never gone catch a man if you don't watch how heavy you get.

Can't keep eating Jo's cooking all day. I don't care how good it is."

Whitney laughed off the comment before continuing to the dining room with the casserole dish. She made a mental note to take an extra helping of everything on the table.

∞⁘∞

After Christmas dinner, they all went to the family room to sit and talk and have pie. Whitney was going to need something stronger than eggnog if Aunt Cheryl didn't go home soon.

Uncle Glen was back from visiting with his ex-wife and daughter. He'd told Whitney all about his little girl's reactions to her presents.

"How's Christmas been here so far?" Glen asked.

Both Whitney and Brenda looked at Cheryl and then back at him.

He laughed and put his arms around Brenda, hugging her close. "She seems to be behaving herself better than she did last year."

"That doesn't take much," Aunt Brenda said. She rested her chin on his shoulder.

He rubbed a hand over the back of his pale, bald head. "Yeah, well, you gotta take what you can get when it comes to her."

"True," Whitney said. They laughed.

Glen squeezed Brenda tightly. Whitney smiled across the room at Jo and Shorty standing in front of the fireplace with their arms wrapped around each other. Even if it took three tries, Jo said he was worth every try. That seemed to be true. They just seemed to fit, as if they should have always been together. The room was filled with love. For the most part.

Aunt Cheryl had put on a Barry White Christmas CD and the soothing sounds of White's baritone filled the air.

"That's right. Nobody knows what good Christmas music is around here. Especially him." She nodded in the direction of Uncle Glen. "This the wrong Barry for you, Glen? You want us to put on some Barry Manilow? Do he even have a Christmas album?" She chuckled at her own bad joke. She was the only one laughing, though.

"I like Barry Manilow. He has some great music," Jo said.

"I bet you do," Aunt Cheryl sneered.

"Are you trying to ruin everybody's Christmas?" Jo said, tensing. "You can't even take one night off from being rotten and nasty, can you?"

"You know what I have to say about you and your mouth, Jo." Aunt Cheryl sat back against her chair.

"Hey, c'mon everybody. What happened to the Christmas cheer?" Glen forced a laugh.

"I think we all know the answer to that," Brenda said while staring down Cheryl.

"Well, we need to get it back. How about some Christmas carols?" he said. He looked around the room.

"Know any good ones about Scrooge?" Jo asked.

Aunt Cheryl made a nasty crack about Glen's singing voice.

After that they sat around talking tensely about Christmas, trying to ignore Aunt Cheryl's barbs for a while. When the doorbell rang, Whitney jumped up and beat everyone else to answer it, glad for the distraction; Aunt Cheryl was managing to kill all the Christmas cheer slowly but surely.

Whitney pulled open the door to see Quinton standing there with his girlfriend, Dawn. He wore a battered leather jacket and she a shabby parka. She was bone thin and could never keep still. If only Quinton would leave Dawn at home. It didn't seem right for her to be there, especially since there was a lot of suspicion she'd been the reason he'd left Jo.

Quinton was Devon's father. He and Jo had tried to remain friends and had succeeded for the most part.

"Whitney! It's good to see you." Quinton threw his arms around her.

"You, too, Quinton," she said. He was okay on a surface level, but that was it. He'd never been reliable. At least he hadn't been for Whitney's mother.

"Everybody in the family room?" Quinton stepped into the house. He took his girlfriend by the hand and led her in that direction.

"Yeah." Whitney closed the door and followed them.

"Hey, Jones family. My, ain't it good to see you? Jo, you looking good, girl." Quinton interrupted all conversation, bringing everybody's attention to him.

There were scattered hellos and smiles around the room.

"Quinton, Dawn, it's good to see you two," Jo said.

"Something sure smells good. You made your usual feast, huh?" Quinton rubbed his stomach.

Jo smiled. "Y'all eat yet?"

"Not really."

Of course they hadn't. Dawn didn't cook, and Quinton sure wasn't going to. Quinton should have to pay for a plate. That would be a good start on the back child support he owed Jo. Jo had a good heart. Sometimes, too good. Jo said the key to a good life was learning how to let things go. But there was a difference between letting things go and letting people walk all over you.

Jo started across the floor. "I'll make up a couple of plates for y'all." She paused and turned to Whitney. "Honey, can you come help me?"

"Sure, Mom." Whitney followed her mother into the kitchen. She went over to the counter to pull out a couple of the paper plates they'd used earlier to make Christmas dinner dishes easier on themselves. She put two of the white plates with holly leaf borders down on the counter.

Her mother rushed up to her, grabbing her elbow. "I forgot to get them a present. It must have slipped my mind. I double-checked my closet." She shook her head. "There's nothing under the tree. What am I going to do now?" Jo's eyes were wide with worry.

Whitney tapped the paper plates against the counter. "They didn't get you anything. Don't worry about it."

"You know me. I have to worry about it." Jo took the plates from her. "I always get everybody something even if it's just a little trinket. I need you to run out and get a gift for them."

Whitney wasn't going to object to escaping the house for a while, and she wanted to help her stressed-out mom. There was only one problem. "Where am I going to find a present this late at night on Christmas?"

"The 7-11. I don't know what, but they've got to have something in there. I don't care what it is. Bring me anything. Anything halfway decent. And drop it in a gift bag. Don't come back in here with a white plastic bag from 7-11." Jo tried to drop a twenty in Whitney's hand.

Whitney shook her head and pulled her hand away. "I got it, Mom."

"Take this money, child."

"No," she said. "This way, it can be from all of us." She folded her mom's fingers around the twenty. "I won't come back without something. I promise."

"I know you won't." Jo patted her hand. "I can always count on you, baby."

Whitney walked to the hall closet to get her winter coat, wondering what in the world she would find at 7-11 that would make any kind of suitable Christmas present. It was a good thing she was the tenacious type.

∽≫∼

Whitney was about to step onto the curb by the 7-11 when a man ran into her. Well, stumbled into her was more like it.

"Hey, watch it…" Whitney's voice trailed off when she caught sight of the most startling ice blue eyes she'd ever seen. Her breath was literally taken away from her when he put his hands out, spreading his fingers against the shoulders of her jacket—whether it was to steady himself or her, she wasn't sure.

She felt a sudden surge of warmth. It burned in her throat, her face. And she found she was unable to look away from those unfocused glacier-like eyes. They were the palest shade of blue she'd ever seen, yet they made her feel warm all over. There was such an intensity in his face, his gaze, that she felt as if he had become the world. She had no idea why she suddenly

43

felt so lost in this stranger. Even odder was the thought that she wanted to be lost in him forever.

He was probably even more attractive when he wasn't sloppy drunk, but he wasn't bad that night. His brown hair fell just below the collar of his black fleece jacket. He was a little taller than Whitney, so that if she were to press herself to him, her head would get buried in his shoulder. Not that she was thinking of doing anything like that. He wasn't too skinny, but he wasn't bulky with too much muscle, either. He was solid. Well, physical appearance-wise anyway.

After seconds that seemed to last hours, he said, "Sorry. I didn't see you there."

"Really? I was right in front of your face," Whitney said, backing away from the odor of his alcohol-soaked breath. She didn't mean to be rude, but the drunken fool had nearly knocked her over, she hadn't had the most fun Christmas Day, and she didn't have time to find him intriguing and attractive.

"Oh, yeah, well, again. Sorry." Chace's eyes moved to his hands on her shoulders, making both of them acutely aware of the fact that they were still there. He pulled his hands away from her and she felt her cheeks roasting. At least she could blame the sudden rush of blood to her face on the cold.

"It's okay. Just watch where you're going from now on," Whitney said.

"Sure thing. Oh. Yeah. I'm Chace. You?"

"Whitney," she said. "Nice meeting you, Chace."

"You, too, Whitney," he said with a crooked grin that made her heart skip a beat. She bet that grin had gotten him far with the ladies and would continue to. But there was no way it was going to work on her. "I'm usually not this much of a loser. I wish you hadn't met me this way."

Whitney nodded, wondering if his words were true or not.

"Have a beautiful night. You're so beautiful. Christmas is beautiful. Merry Christmas, Beautiful Whitney."

"Merry Christmas." Whitney fought a smile.

Chace saluted her and staggered over to Tim, who was sitting on the curb. Tim was something of the town drunk. He handed a brown bag to Chace.

"Thanks for watching my stuff, man," Chace said to Tim.

"Any time," Tim said before nodding a greeting to Whitney.

Whitney waved to Tim before hurrying into the 7-11. She needed to find a present and get away from the riff-raff. Even if the riff-raff was kind of sexy.

Whitney wandered up and down the aisles of junk food and trinkets and maps, unable to concentrate on the task at hand. Her mind was full of Chace. She couldn't stop herself from making excuses to walk past the large windows and the glass doors at the front of the store to catch glimpses of the back of his head and occasionally his profile as he talked to Tim.

Whitney hadn't had these grin-inducing, fluttery type of feelings for a guy ever. She'd had crushes. Been attracted to plenty of guys. But none of them had the impact Chace had on her. And not just because he'd nearly knocked her down.

There was something about him. She knew next to nothing about the man and, still, she felt like he was the type of guy who could make a girl forget everything else in the world. And it had to be nice to forget everything for a while except for something bright and beguiling like Chace's smile. Not that she had any idea what it was like to be able to forget the world. She'd never really wanted to. She considered herself a pragmatist, and she liked being one.

But maybe it wouldn't have been a bad thing to lose herself just once. For a little while. What she'd felt outside a few moments ago had been thrilling in a scary sort of way. For some reason, she couldn't stop thinking the ridiculous thought that she'd been asleep for twenty-eight years until Chace had awakened her outside by putting his hands on her shoulders and looking into her eyes.

She hadn't realized she was standing at the window, staring at the back of Chace's coat until someone walked into the 7-11, setting off the door chime. Whitney shook her head slightly, bringing herself back to reality. Chace turned toward the store and she hurried away from the window, hoping he hadn't seen her staring.

She had to concentrate. She was there to get a gift for her stepdad—ex-stepdad? She never knew what to call him since everything seemed awkward, and she usually just went with his first name. Anyway, she needed a gift for him and his girlfriend. She wasn't there to ogle some stranger she'd shared a momentary weirdness with. Maybe she was just horny. That was it. She hadn't had sex in over a year and Chace was hot. Just hormones. That was all.

Whitney walked past the wine, Boone's Farm and Sutter Homes and the rest of the wide selection. So many choices. Yeah. Right. Not that she could get alcohol, anyway. Quinton was a recovering alcoholic, and Whitney didn't think his sponsor would appreciate that gift.

Next, she went down the trinket aisle. She spied a few Christmas-themed trinkets. She ran her fingers lightly over a deck of playing cards, thinking of nothing in particular. Trying not to, anyway. It was a shame. She couldn't even concentrate on one simple task. It wasn't like she had many gift choices in front of her. It shouldn't have been so hard.

She sighed, scanning the magazines in front of her with half-interest. She wanted to go back outside and talk to Chace. Escape her family for the rest of the night and see if she could figure out what about him had jolted her so much. She knew all of that was out of the question, though.

She glanced up at the bored-looking cashier. She needed to get out of the store. Above all else, being close to Chace for too long would lead to her doing stupid things. Yeah, it was time to go.

Whitney walked up to the counter and smiled at the yawning cashier. "Do you have anything I could give as a Christmas present?"

"Talk about your last-minute shopper." The cashier laughed at himself as if he'd cracked the funniest joke ever told.

"I can't argue with you there." She forced a smile. "So, do you have anything?"

"We have some Christmas CDs, uh, a few holiday things over in the back there with the souvenirs. Not much, though. Sorry."

Whitney nodded. She'd noticed those "holiday things" he'd mentioned. A baby bib informing the reader that "Grandma Got Run Over By A Reindeer," a Frosty the Snowman pen, a couple of dusty snow globes, some Christmas candy in dented boxes, and a red and green "Season's Greetings" baseball cap.

"Thanks," she said.

"No problem."

Whitney circled the store again, forcing herself not to look outside even though her eyes sought out Chace independent of her will.

A few minutes later, she carried an armload of junk to the front of the store. She didn't have time to be selective and there wasn't much to select from anyway. She had to get away before she did something stupid like ask Chace if he had anywhere to go for Christmas and invite him home with her if he didn't.

She dumped a flashlight, copies of *Jet* and *People* magazines, several packages of gum, a snow globe, batteries, a generic Christmas card, the Christmas baseball cap she'd seen earlier, and a gift bag onto the counter. Reaching for her purse, she wondered if everything would fit into the bag. The only gift bag she'd been able to find that even remotely looked Christmas-like was a red medium-sized one. Looking at the bag and her stash again, she picked up the magazines, took them back to their shelf, and then went back to the counter. That was better. It would probably all fit now.

After paying for her purchases and stuffing everything into the gift bag, she left the store. Her traitorous eyes strayed in the direction of where Chace sat on the curb next to Tim. Tim waved and said hello to her and wished her a merry Christmas. She returned Tim's greeting, and then Chace turned toward her. He caught her eye and smiled.

He lifted his brown bag to her in a wave. "Merry Christmas, Beautiful Whitney."

She smiled. Her family issues shouldn't make her be rude to this guy who may have just been having a bad day. After all, he hadn't done anything but run into her, and he'd already apologized a million times for that. It wasn't his fault she was trying to avoid being attracted to him because it was crazy to think she could feel a connection with someone moments after seeing him for the first time in her life.

She waved to him. "Merry Christmas, Chace."

Maybe it was her imagination, but she thought that his grin widened and his face brightened a little.

She walked to her car, a smile playing at the edges of her lips.

Chapter 4: And As He Watched Her Walk Away...

Chace watched Whitney walk to her car. He knew the smile on his face was a goofy one even though he couldn't see it. She had the sexiest walk. She had the most sexiest everything. Beautiful Whitney. The word didn't even do justice to her. He'd probably never see her again, though. He didn't know anything about her other than her first name. Slowly, it dawned on his alcohol-soaked brain that Tim had said something to Beautiful Whitney.

Chace turned to Tim. "You know her?"

Tim nodded. "That's Whitney Jones. Jo's child. Known her all her life, I reckon."

"Whitney Jones." Chace said the name slowly, letting the syllables roll around his tongue. He was drunk, sure, but he knew perfection when he saw it. For a moment, looking into her eyes, he'd almost forgotten all about Kelly and the giant mess that had brought him there—drinking malt liquor on a curb outside 7-11 with Tim. On Christmas night. Tim could always be seen around town with a paper bag. Mostly right out in front of that 7-11 where they were sitting.

Chace stared at the car she'd gotten into. "How come I've never seen her around?"

"She's not here much. Lives in D.C. Works at some big, fancy law firm. She doesn't come home much anymore." Tim took a swig from his bottle and wiped his mouth.

"What else do you know about her?" He wanted to know everything about that woman. Whitney Jones.

"Oh, not much. She went to college at some fancy school up north. Harvard or one of them. Then she went to Howard Law School. Now she's making the big bucks."

"She married?"

"Not that one. Far from it. I've never even known her to bring any man home with her when she comes to visit."

"Hmm." Chace watched the sleek black sedan pull out of the parking spot in front of the store and glide onto the road. He'd caught her watching him from the store a few times. He'd thought about going in to say hi, but, even in his inebriated state, he realized he hadn't made the best first impression on her, and he didn't want to freak her out.

"What you thinking about, boy? I know you not thinking about Whitney. Didn't you say you had a girl?"

" 'Had' is key. She left." Chace upended his bottle and chugged down half of what was left in it.

"Aw, you young kids. Always breaking up for nothing. Y'all probably be back together by tomorrow."

Chace didn't say anything. He hadn't told Tim why he and Kelly had broken up.

"You know I'm right, boy. I'm always right. I've seen it all, know it all, just about."

Chace felt something special for her already. The thought struck him as odd. Love at first sight? Nah. That didn't exist in real life. But didn't some people say they just knew? Wasn't that what his brother had said about his wife? Chace hadn't "just known" with Kelly, but eventually things had started to click with her. Kelly. Oh, Kelly. He buried his face in his hands and moaned.

"You all right, boy? You not gonna be sick all over my curb, is you?"

"No. I'm fine." Chace looked up and smiled at the man with coarse, curly gray-black hair, a mustache that reminded Chace of a gray broom that had seen better days, and kind brown eyes.

Chace sighed. "You know where she lives? Whitney?"

"Boy, you think you gone over her. That's just the liquor messing with you."

It wasn't. He'd felt a connection with her he didn't know how to explain. He had to see her again. He didn't know how he'd make it happen, but he had to. "Tim, it's not the alcohol. Really." He put down his bottle. "Please. Just tell me where she lives. I promise not to do anything crazy like just show up there."

"Her family don't live in town. Live out near Bedford's farm somewhere. That's all I know."

Chace nodded, drawing his knees up to his chest and staring at the spot where Whitney's car had been parked.

His cell phone rang and he took it out of his pocket and stared down at the screen. He pushed a button and held it to his ear. "Hi, Cliff."

"Bro, were you going to call to wish anybody in this family a happy Christmas?" Cliff had taken to saying things like "happy Christmas" ever since he'd married his British wife.

"Mom and Dad are in Maui. They'll call when they get around to it. You know how they are when they go on one of their vacations. And I was getting around to calling you."

"Dude, it's nine o'clock at night. Exactly when were you gonna call?"

"I dunno."

"Are you drunk?"

"Maybe."

"What, you and Kelly boozing it up for the holidays? Shouldn't you be at her parents' place right now?"

"Kelly and I broke up. Yesterday." The words didn't feel right on his tongue. They felt kind of heavy. And dead. But they seemed to hurt a little less than they had before he'd run into...Beautiful Whitney.

"You what? Whoa. Really? On Christmas Eve?"

"That's what I said."

"What happened exactly?"

"I don't want to get into it right now."

"Ethan's gonna love this. He never did like her."

Chace groaned. "Yeah." He didn't want to even think about telling Ethan, his best friend. Ethan often referred to Kelly as 'devil without the blue dress.' He didn't want to hear the I-told-you-she'd-break-your heart crap Ethan was going to give him. Luckily, Ethan was in New Zealand at the moment. Chace had wanted to go on the trip, but Kelly had guilted him into staying at home and getting serious about his career. Or rather, the career she'd picked out for him. She hadn't considered his career path a real one. They'd had a huge fight over it.

"The kids loved their presents from Uncle Chace," Cliff said.

He grinned. One thing had gone right that Christmas, at least. Well, really, two, but he wasn't going to bring up Beautiful Whitney. There wasn't even anything to tell. "That's good. I'm glad."

"And Emma asked about you."

"Tell everybody I wish them a 'happy' Christmas and give 'em big, fat, sloppy kisses for me."

"I definitely will. Hey, man, you coming up for New Year's?"

"Maybe." Being around his brother so soon after what had happened would make him more miserable. Their dad had retired, and Cliff had taken over the family business and started turning a huge profit with it.

He was almost certain Kelly wouldn't have left him if he'd been more like Cliff. Stable income. Big house. Cliff had done everything he was supposed to. He was the typical provider. Chace had tried that route, but it wasn't for him. He knew he'd made the right decision, but he couldn't help but second guess himself that night. The second guessing would only get worse if he went to Cliff's house for New Year's Eve.

"Really try, man. We miss ya. Ethan's out of town. You don't have any family down in Podunk where you moved to for—uh, anyway, you should come visit. Emma and I are going out that night. We have a sitter. Come with, it'll be a blast."

"I'll think about it. I promise."

"Do."

"Okay, I gotta go." Chace rubbed his thumb and index fingers across his eyebrows.

"All right, but call me sometime, okay?"

"I will. Catch you later, Cliff."

"Bye, bro."

Chace tucked his phone into his jacket pocket.

"Family problems?" Tim's eyes crinkled at the edges when he smiled.

Something like that, sure. "You know it."

Tim slapped his knee and laughed. "Don't I? Boy, don't I ever."

Chace smiled, only half-listening to what Tim said next. His mind went not to his family, not to Kelly, but to Beautiful Whitney. And the grin she'd flashed at him before walking away. The image was lodged in his mind and he hoped it stayed there.

Chapter 5: A Train Wreck, or Another Jones Family Christmas

Once Whitney got home with the present, she could tell things were going sour. It was inevitable with the whole family together. Whitney slipped the gift to her mom who handed it over. Quinton and Dawn thanked them. Not long after, the feature film *Jones Family Drama* started.

Aunt Cheryl rolled her eyes and crossed her arms over her chest. "I don't know why you still buy him presents. He owe you money."

Whitney's mother's smile grew thin. Aunt Cheryl had been chipping away at her all day. Jo didn't like people analyzing her relationship with Quinton. They were still friends. It was Jo's choice to stay friends with him and her mistake to worry about if it was one. That was what she always said.

"What, Jo? You know it's true," Aunt Cheryl said while glowering at Quinton.

"It's none of your business either way. You know I don't like you talking about my family like that." Jo took a deep breath.

"Quinton ain't none of your family anymore."

Jo shook her head. "He's Devon's father and he'll always be family."

Aunt Cheryl smirked at Shorty. "What you think about that? Your wife calling that no-good scum family?"

Devon's jaw tightened. Whitney put a hand on his shoulder, but he shrugged away from her.

The living room grew silent except for the occasional crackle of logs in the fireplace. Shorty and Jo refused to switch to a gas fireplace.

Shorty put a hand over Jo's and she patted it with her free hand.

Aunt Cheryl said, "I don't know why he's still here. He don't never come 'round unless he want something. And that thing he brought in here with him. Was probably laying up underneath her before he even thought to leave you."

"What did you call me?" Dawn whipped her head around in Aunt Cheryl's direction.

"I called you what you are." Aunt Cheryl dismissed her with a sneer and turned back to Jo. "Well?"

"I asked you to leave it alone." Jo balled her hands into fists.

"Weak. Just like you always been," Aunt Cheryl said.

"Don't you say another word about my parents," Devon said. "Either one of them."

"Don't sass me, boy." Aunt Cheryl pointed her index finger at Devon's face as she spat out the words.

Jo said, "Devon, please, just stay out of it."

"Mom," Devon said, his nostrils flaring. "You've been taking this crap off her for years, and I'm sick of it even if you aren't." He jumped up from the sofa.

One of Aunt Cheryl's sons stepped forward. "Hold up, Devon. Don't disrespect my mom like that."

Devon didn't back down. "Why don't you tell her to get her mouth under control, then?"

Aunt Cheryl started defending her son. Soon after that, the whole living room erupted into a shouting match until Shorty wolf-whistled for silence.

Melinda, Whitney's favorite cousin, walked in right at that moment. "Did y'all know the front door was unlocked?" she said. "Can you believe I'm just getting here? My plane was late." Her voice trailed off when she realized the tension she'd just walked into. She set her large black handbag on a nearby end table. "Family, you at it again? It's Christmas. Come on."

"You know how this family is. Can't nobody get along for one day." Jo ran out of the room with her hand pressed to her mouth. Whitney knew her well enough to know the tears were coming. She started after her mother.

Shorty stepped in front of her. "Let me. She's been really upset all day. Your da—dang aunt."

"What did she do this time?"

Shorty's nostrils flared and he rubbed a hand over his bald head. "I'll tell you later."

Whitney watched Shorty go after her mother, wondering what Aunt Cheryl had done or said most recently. It was always something with that woman.

"We're not staying anywhere we're not wanted. Get your stuff," Aunt Cheryl said to her sons. They and their families did as Aunt Cheryl told them to do. She stormed out, commanding them to follow her, talking about being insulted, some people never having good sense, and being tempted to turn her back on all of them. Whitney had to wonder if it would be a bad thing if she did.

The rest of the family watched them leave with Aunt Cheryl leading the way. She was still shouting after the front door slammed behind the group. After that the gathering slowly splintered off, people mumbling about being tired or making excuses about getting home before it got too late. Soon, only Aunt Brenda, Glen, Melinda, and Whitney remained.

"Whitney, what can I say about her?" Aunt Brenda said with an apologetic shrug. Glen ran his hand up and down the center of Aunt Brenda's back.

Whitney laughed humorlessly. "What can anyone?"

"I certainly don't know." Aunt Brenda hugged Whitney and Melinda and kissed their cheeks in turn. "All right, girls. That's enough excitement for me for one night. We're going upstairs. Goodnight." They were staying at Jo and Shorty's house during the holidays.

Whitney and Melinda wished their aunt and uncle goodnight. Aunt Brenda grabbed Glen's hand and the two of them headed for the doorway.

Whitney looked down at her cell phone. "It's still early. Not even eleven yet."

"You want to go out?" Melinda asked.

"What? Now?"

"Yeah. Isn't that bar in town run by Jewish people? I'm pretty sure they're open on Christmas night. It's probably the only thing open in this place."

"You're right." she said. "Let's do it. I can't argue with needing to get out of this house for a few hours."

"Let's change and meet back down here in a little bit."

Whitney paired a mahogany wool sweater dress with black tights. She pulled her thick black hair away from her neck and pinned it up. Then she met Melinda by the front door. Melinda wore a mustard yellow tunic paired with skinny jeans and matching mustard boots.

The bar they went to was one of the only places open on Christmas night besides the 7-11 and a couple of Chinese restaurants. They caught the end of Christmas karaoke. By the time they had ordered drinks and staked out a table, the DJ came out and started playing '90s hits—the warm-up songs.

Melinda told her about school—Melinda was getting her Masters of Social Work—and Whitney told her about life at the firm.

"How's Ulrich?" Melinda asked once they were seated with their drinks. Ulrich was another fifth year associate at Gibson and Grey. Melinda and Ulrich had met one weekend when Mclinda had come down to D.C. from New York to visit Whitney.

"He's good. Still hasn't settled down yet."

"I hope that's not a hint. 'Cause you know how I feel about long-distance relationships," Melinda said.

Whitney sipped her drink. "Maybe it was, maybe it wasn't."

"You're such an instigator."

She grinned. "I know."

Whitney was shouting over the music to her cousin when she saw him. Her heart dropped. She'd never thought she'd see him again. Chace was propped up against a wall nearby, talking to some girl. The girl gave Chace an exasperated look and then walked away.

"Somebody needs to be cut off," Melinda said after following her gaze.

"I know him," Whitney said, squinting at Chace in the darkened bar. She knew it was him. She'd all but memorized his face in the 7-11 parking lot.

"Huh?" Melinda's eyebrows knitted together and she frowned slightly.

"Long story." Whitney didn't want to get into explaining that one.

Chace spotted her. He gave her a shaky wave and then pushed himself off the wall. He stumbled toward them. She couldn't believe her heart was actually beating faster. What was this effect this weird, drunken stranger was having on her?

"Beautiful Whitney. We meet. Again." Chace lurched forward and this time, she put her hands on his shoulders to steady him instead of the other way around as it had been at 7-11.

She smiled. He was charming in an obnoxious kind of way. "So we do."

"You know, fate might be trying to tell us something," he said, holding her gaze with his.

"Like what?"

"Ask me again when the world isn't spinning." He gave her a lazy grin that almost made her knees buckle. Then he closed his eyes, swaying gently back and forth with the music. He hummed so loudly that the noise could barely be called a hum.

Whitney asked, "You have a way home?"

"My car's…somewhere around here. It's back at the 7-11 I think. Only a couple blocks away."

"Oh, no. You're not driving. We'll take you home."

"We will?" Melinda raised her eyebrows.

"We will," Whitney said.

"Can't he just take a cab?" Melinda murmured, moving her head close to Whitney's so that Chace wouldn't overhear.

"He could, but he seems like a nice guy who's had a bad day or week or something. I just think we should help him out," Whitney murmured back.

"Oh, really?" Melinda's voice was full of suspicion.

Whitney shrugged, pretending not to catch the meaning behind Melinda's tone. "Really."

"And just how much help do you want to give him?" Melinda raised her eyebrows.

Whitney rolled her eyes. "Shut up, Melinda." She turned back to Chace. "You ready to go?"

"I'll go anywhere with you, Beautiful Whitney," Chace grinned, leaning against her arm as they headed for the exit. "Whoa. I am really, really drunk." He said the last word as if amazed at just how true it was.

"Looks like he wants any 'help' you want to give him," Melinda murmured close to Whitney's ear before moving to Chace's other side. It seemed he was going to need help from both of them to make it much further.

Whitney smirked, but said nothing. They stepped out into the chilly night air. Whitney was glad to have Chace so close and she told herself that was just because it was freezing out. Still, she couldn't deny that she was a little disappointed when he pulled his head away from her shoulder.

She had to stop running into him before something crazy happened. It was scary because she'd never felt this warm and shocking thing before, but she couldn't say it was unpleasant. That would have been a lie. And that fact made what she felt even scarier.

❧

After they helped Chace fall into the backseat of Whitney's car they closed the door after him.

"What if he throws up back there? Aren't you leasing this thing?" Melinda asked as they slid into the front seats.

"He'll be fine. Plus, the seats are leather. Almost anything will come right off them. Unless he bleeds back there or something, and I don't see that happening." Whitney turned the key in the ignition and pulled out of the parking lot and onto the road.

Melinda turned to the back of the car. "Where do you live?"

"The Gateway Apartments. Number…two…thirty…four," Chace said, mumbling into his arm, which he had thrown across his face.

Whitney drove to the Gateway Apartments, which were not that far from Main Street, where the bar was. Melinda kept throwing her glances that said Whitney was crazy, but Whitney just grinned, shook her head, and kept driving. She wouldn't have felt right leaving the nearly incoherent man to find his own way home.

Besides, she couldn't get that image out of her head from the 7-11 when she'd first seen him. And some irrational part of her wanted to stay with him as long as she could since she would probably never see him again. Then again, hadn't she said the same thing at 7-11? But really, why or how would they ever see each other again after that night?

When they parked in front of Chace's building, they helped him out so that they could all walk up the exterior stairs to the second floor landing. Then, they walked to the door of apartment 234.

Whitney and Melinda stood at the door while Chace fumbled through his keys with slow, clumsy fingers.

"Here. It's one of these." Chace slurred his words, handing Whitney the key ring. She tried each key until she found one that fit the lock. She turned it, unlocking the door. Whitney and Melinda walked inside, nearly dragging Chace between them. Her purse slipped down her shoulder to her elbow, and she let it fall to the floor because it was easier than trying to catch it. She would pick it up on her way out.

"You know, you guys really didn't have to do this." Chace's head hung forward. "It's really sweet of you. You're nice. Both of you. Really. I wish everyone was as nice as you."

"Which way is the bedroom, Chace?" Whitney asked.

"That way." He pointed straight back.

Whitney didn't know whether to be flattered or offended that he hadn't taken her question the wrong way. Looking down at him, she decided that he probably wasn't even capable of taking it the wrong way that evening. Then again, even though she didn't know much about him, he didn't seem like the garden variety lecherous jerks she usually attracted in bars and clubs late at night. The more she thought about it, the more she really thought Chace had just had a bad day. She could sympathize with that. Hers hadn't been great, either.

He leaned against her, settling his head onto her shoulder. His breath was warm against her neck. Her heart fluttered for a moment. She had a sudden, strong urge to sleep next to him all night so he could leave his head right there. Disturbing. Good thing Melinda was there so that she would have to be rational.

"Beautiful Whitney," he whispered. She moved a little faster toward the bedroom. The quicker she could get out of there, the better.

She flipped on the overhead light and they helped him stumble across his bedroom. Walking him over to the bed, she noticed a photo on the nightstand as he fell facedown onto the dark brown comforter. The picture showed him with a laughing brunette. The combination of the photographer's mastery of his or her art and the woman's beauty almost seemed to make a spotlight shine down onto her photographed face. Her oval-shaped face, thin and highly arched eyebrows, and creamy complexion combined in a very flattering way. She and Chace were holding each other by the elbows. Her face was turned slightly toward the camera and her head was thrown back in laughter, but Chace was staring at her with a huge grin on his face.

Whitney wasn't surprised there was a girlfriend in the picture. What did surprise her was that the girlfriend was nowhere to be seen at the moment. She wondered where the woman in the picture was that night. Looking closer, Whitney noticed fine, spidery cracks in the glass of the frame. As if someone had punched it with a fist.

She heard a groan from the bed.

"Chace?" Whitney called.

Chace rolled over and placed his hands over his face. She noticed thin, red scratches on the back of his right hand. He muttered something unintelligible.

Whitney forced herself to take her eyes off those scratches. "You gonna be okay?"

Another unintelligible mutter.

"I'm going to get you some water. I'll be right back."

Melinda followed Whitney to the kitchen. "Can we leave now? This is creepy, being in some strange dude's house."

"What's he gonna do to us? He's barely conscious." Whitney looked into his fridge. It contained only a pitcher of water, a couple containers of takeout food, some wilted vegetables, a few beers, and a whole lot of Slim Fast. Whitney grabbed the pitcher and closed the door.

"I'm not worried about that," Melinda said. "What if he remembers just enough of this to say we drugged him and robbed him or something?"

"What? That's crazy. You worry too much. Even if something outrageous like that were to happen, he wouldn't have a clue who we are or how to find us. If he remembers anything, he'll probably be embarrassed and he'll hope he never runs into us again," Whitney said, heading back to the bedroom with a glass of water. She set it on the nightstand and looked down at him. His head had fallen to the side, his wavy hair across his face. He was fast asleep, his lips slightly parted. She had a sudden urge to run her fingers across them and took a physical step backward as if she might not be able to stop herself from touching him otherwise.

He was out cold, lying there in his dark jeans, sweater, and even with his jacket still on.

"Should we turn him on his side so he doesn't choke on his own vomit if he throws up or something?" Melinda said. "He's pretty drunk. I mean, maybe we should have taken him to the hospital or something."

"Oh, now you're concerned."

Melinda snorted. "Yeah. If he dies, we were the last people seen with him."

Whitney laughed. "I think he'll probably be fine. He's just really, really drunk. Like he said earlier."

"Okay, then. Let's get out of here." Melinda walked back out into the living room. Whitney looked back and smiled at his sleeping form. One foot hung off the bed now, but other than that, he hadn't moved since Whitney had gone to get the glass of water for him. He'd started to snore.

She walked over and put his foot back onto the bed. She spread a throw blanket over him. She thought briefly about leaving him a note, but no. It was better to just go.

She met Melinda, who was impatiently tapping her foot halfway out of the front door, in the living room. "Whit, let's get out of here already."

"Okay, chill out." After grabbing her purse from where she'd left it by the door, she followed Melinda out into the breezeway. They went down to Whitney's car and drove back to Whitney's mom's house. Melinda was bunking with Whitney instead of at Uncle Larry and Aunt Janet's house.

They got out of the car and Whitney checked her purse for her cell phone after she locked her car out of habit. Melinda started to walk toward the house, but she stopped and turned when Whitney didn't follow her. "Whit? What are you doing back there?"

"Shoot," Whitney said, pawing through her bag.

"Huh?" Melinda raised her eyebrows.

"My phone. I don't see it anywhere." Whitney frowned.

Melinda groaned. "You must have left it at that drunk boy's place. Wanna go back and get it?"

Whitney slowly shook her head. "We don't know that it's there. I don't remember seeing it since the bar. I could have dropped it at the bar, in the parking lot, or anywhere."

"We could at least go see."

Whitney shook her head, rubbing a hand across her weary eyes, which stung with fatigue. "You know what? It's late and it's been a beyond crazy Christmas. I just wanna get in the bed right now," Whitney said with a sigh. "I'll worry about it tomorrow."

She was just glad she'd left her BlackBerry at home where she couldn't lose it. If Andersen tried to reach her on that thing and wasn't able to, the world might collapse. She dreaded going upstairs to turn it back on now that her mother's Christmas BlackBerry ban was officially over to find out if he had tried to call or email her or not.

Chapter 6: When You Wake Up, I'll Be Gone

When Chace opened his eyes in the morning, he immediately closed them again. Everything felt like sandpaper. His eyes, throat, tongue. Just—everything. He tried opening his eyes again. It was a little easier the second time.

He concentrated on thinking back to the night before. He remembered Tim and the 7-11. Making a fool out of himself at karaoke. Kelly, of course, before all that.

But most of all, he remembered Beautiful Whitney. He smiled, turning his head to look at the untouched glass of water on his nightstand. And then down at the throw blanket covering him. She'd done more for him in one night than Kelly had done for him in months.

Whitney. He tried to remember every detail about her. The way her sweater dress had clung to her shapely body. The warm brown of her skin. Her round face and soft brown eyes. Her black hair with brown highlights pulled away from her beautiful face. The slight slant of her eyes. The scent of her when his head was on her shoulder. Soft and sweet and woman. Just like all the rest of her.

He pulled himself to a sitting position on the edge of the bed and yawned, pushing the throw blanket aside. He pulled his cell out of his pocket and glanced down at the screen. He had several missed calls. Two numbers he didn't recognize. He'd probably been giving out his number at the bar like a fool. He doubted either of them were Whitney. He would have remembered giving her his number. He was sure of it. Besides, if she hadn't thought he was an idiot at 7-11, she had to think it for sure after bringing his sloppy-drunk butt home.

His stomach dropped when he realized that the other missed calls were from Kelly. She'd also sent him a text saying that she'd meant it when she said she still wanted to be friends and she hoped he didn't hate her. Muttering unflattering things to himself about her, he tossed the phone on his bed, stood, and stretched. He shrugged out of his jacket and let it fall to the floor along with the rest of his clothes. First things first. Alcohol was coming out of his pores. He reeked. Maybe he could at least wash some of it off.

After his shower, Chace walked into the living room wearing one of the large fluffy white towels Kelly had bought at a white sale. He was surprised she hadn't taken her precious linens and stuff with her, considering her obsession with that Martha Stewart kind of crap.

He flipped on the television, going for the satellite radio stations, when he noticed something lying on the floor by the front door. He walked over and discovered it was a cell phone. He peered down at it, furrowing his brow. He then picked up the slim, metallic flip phone and opened the shell. It must belong to Whitney. It sure wasn't Kelly's.

He flipped through the contacts, noticing that she had ICE, or In Case of Emergency, numbers in her phone. He scrolled down to the one labeled "Mom" and pressed "send".

After two rings, a woman answered in a deep yet feminine voice. "Hello?"

"Hi, my name is Chace. I'm calling from Whitney's cell phone, I think? Are you her mom?"

"Yes, I am. Misses Jones, but call me Jo. Oh, you angel. She's been carrying on about that phone since she woke up this morning. Hold on a minute. I'll go get her for you."

Chace heard Jo set the phone down. He heard her calling for Whitney. Thinking of the way he'd acted the night before, he started to worry about whether she would want to see him again. He shifted the phone from one ear to the other. While he waited for her to come to the phone, he tapped his fingers against the back of his couch. There were some shuffling noises in the background, and then he heard the phone being picked up again.

"Hello?" Whitney's voice came through the phone.

He grinned, her voice warming him all over. "Hi. This is Chace. I think I have your phone."

"Yeah, that's what Mom said. And from the caller ID, it looks like you do. Thank goodness. I was so worried it was gone forever and I'd have to get a new one. I don't know what I would have done about all the phone numbers I would have lost. Who keeps a paper address book anymore?"

He nodded even though she couldn't see him. "Yeah. Exactly."

"So how should I go about getting it back from you?"

His grin widened as the perfect answer to her question popped into his head. "I'll bring it to you. Just as soon as you tell me where you want to meet for lunch."

After a brief pause, Whitney said, "Lunch?"

"Sure. That is…unless you have plans already?" he said, silently asking her not to say that yes she did, and with her boyfriend.

"Not really. Just some after-Christmas shopping, but we're not going until this afternoon because my sister can't seem to get her lazy butt out of the bed today. Um, so I guess. I guess that would be fine. Where do you want to go?"

"That's what I asked you," he said with a chuckle. "Any place is fine with me."

"How about It's Just Coffee?" Whitney said.

"Sure. You want to meet…" he looked around his apartment for the time and realized Kelly had taken the clock that had been in the living room. He picked up the remote and hit the channel info button to bring up the heading at the top of the screen that listed the time. It was almost eleven. "At noon?"

"I'll be there," Whitney said.

"I'll see you soon," he said.

She said, "I'll see you in a little bit, Chace."

He liked the way she said his name. He smiled. "Bye, Whitney."

"Not 'Beautiful Whitney?' " she teased.

He laughed, his face burning at the thought of his behavior the night before. "Bye, Beautiful Whitney."

"Bye."

He hung up the phone. Thoughts of Whitney danced in his head.

After throwing on a pair of jeans, a beige sweater, and his favorite brown flip-flops, Chace walked over to his computer. He decided to try to get Ethan on Skype to pass the time since he couldn't leave yet. If he did, he'd be sitting at the coffeehouse, which was a five minute walk away, alone for almost an hour and looking like a loser. But he couldn't just sit around and wait for it to be noon. Besides, he hadn't called his best friend for Christmas yet.

Chace logged in and looked for Ethan's name in his contact list. Ethan wasn't online. Then Chace realized it was five-thirty tomorrow morning in New Zealand. He sighed and sent Ethan an email telling him to Skype him later that day. Really, it was just as well. Chace didn't feel up to talking about Kelly yet, and if he talked to Ethan, he knew it would come up. Right now, he wanted to focus on good things. Like lunch with Whitney.

After that, he decided to play around on the internet to kill time and occupy his mind until it was time to go. After Kelly tried to call him twice more, he put his phone on silent and slipped it into the opposite jeans pocket from the one where he was keeping Whitney's phone.

Chapter 7: It's Just Coffee

Whitney didn't know why she was so jittery as she pulled her car into one of the spots in the small parking lot of It's Just Coffee. She was just meeting this guy to get her phone back. He was just a guy. Who had her phone.

So what if she'd worn her most flattering jeans—an indigo boot-cut pair that fit her curvy form well. And she had chosen to wear her gray sweater, the one that was perfectly snug without being too tight. And she'd taken the time to curl her hair so that the haircut she'd recently gotten at her favorite Dominican hair salon in Silver Spring, Maryland did what it was supposed to do. She just wanted to look nice, that was all.

She walked into It's Just Coffee and saw him right away. He was sitting at a booth near the back. A pair of brown flip-flops rested on the floor, but he had crossed his legs one over the other so that his feet were tucked under them, and were between his thighs and the dark cushion of the booth seat. She suppressed a smile and walked over to him. She dropped her purse into the booth seat across from him and slid in next to it.

She grabbed a menu and looked up at him. "Hi."

He grinned, flashing white, perfect teeth. Even his pale blue eyes seemed to smile, and she wondered again how he could make eyes that were such a cold color seem so warm. "Hi."

She took a sip of water from the glass that had been waiting for her on the table. Condensation had started to pool around the glass and on the dark surface of the table.

"I asked for water for us. I hope you don't mind," Chace said.

"That was nice. Thank you." Whitney set the glass back down.

"Should I go order for us?"

"Sure," Whitney said, thinking about how different he was sober. He was convincing her more and more she'd been right about him the night before. He'd just had a bad night.

After she gave him her order, he slipped his flip-flops back on and went up to the bar. He talked to a tall, thin black man wearing black skinny jeans and a slim-fitting gray T-shirt with the It's Just Coffee logo in the upper left hand corner. The man nodded and punched some numbers into a cash register. Chace said something with a grin and they both laughed. When he came back to the table, he was holding two muffins.

He held one out to her. "He just gave me these. You like blueberry?" He sat down across from her.

"Sure." She smiled, taking the muffin. "You, uh, wear flip-flops in December?"

He shrugged. "Yeah. I wear flip-flops any time I can get away with it. Unless there's snow on the ground or a really good chance I'll get frostbite, the flip-flops come out."

"Okay." She laughed.

"Oh. Before I forget." Chace reached into his jeans pocket and pulled out her cell phone. He slid it across the table to her.

"Thanks so much." Whitney picked up the phone and put it in her purse.

"No problem. I'm kind of glad you lost it at my place, actually."

"Why is that?"

Chace looked at her in a way that made the rest of the coffeehouse fade away. "Because I was wondering how I'd see you again."

"Oh." Whitney nearly knocked her glass over when she reached for it so that she could take a sip of water.

Chace smiled, dropping his eyes to the table. "I mean, I didn't want your only, lasting impression of me to be as a stumbling, drunken fool."

"Well, it won't be now. You really saved my life." Whitney patted her bag, which now contained her cell phone.

"Good." Chace's eyes burned into hers again.

She gave him an awkward smile and looked around the coffeehouse at their surroundings. Focusing in on a landscape portrait by a local artist, she said to Chace, "Who's that girl? In the picture on your nightstand? She's really pretty."

"Someone from my past," Chace said, and his voice seemed to lose a little of its warmth.

She turned her attention back to the table, but focused on Chace's hands instead of his face. "Sorry. I didn't mean to pry."

"It's okay. You didn't. It's a legit question. I'm not seeing anybody." Chace's voice was quiet, yet it demanded that she look up at him. The sound of it drew her eyes to his face. "Not since the day before yesterday."

He looked so sad for a moment that Whitney wanted to reach across the table and hug him. Then he put a smile back on his face. His eyes were no longer smiling, though.

Just then, their number was called, and Chace went to get their food. He came back to the table balancing two cups of coffee and their food expertly.

"Wow, you're good at that." Whitney reached for her plate, and he set it in front of her. "I should have probably offered to help you, though."

"Thanks." Chace winked at her. "And it's okay. I used to be a server. I know a few things."

She nodded, grabbed a spoon, and started idly stirring her coffee. Just what else did he know?

Chace had ordered a veggie spinach wrap and espresso. Whitney decided on an egg salad sandwich and her normal caramel latté. Wherever she went, she got that coffee place's variation on it, but It's Just Coffee made the best she'd ever had in River Run.

"I love this place. I come here every time I'm home," Whitney said, breathing in the smell of coffee and listening to the whir of the espresso machine.

"Yeah," Chace said. He'd picked up his wrap, but hadn't taken a bite yet. "Kelly turned me on to this place."

"That the girl from the picture?"

He nodded, looking at his food instead of at Whitney. "She left the day before yesterday. On Christmas Eve. Said she…well, it's not important what she said." Chace put down his wrap.

"How long were you two together?"

"Two years."

"That's a long time," Whitney said, feeling that had been stupidly obvious to say, but she hadn't been able to think of anything better, and the silence was too awkward.

"Yeah. I thought we were happy." Chace put his wrap back onto his plate without taking a bite and gripped his coffee mug between his hands. "It's not a good feeling. Having your heart broken." He tapped the mug against the table.

Whitney knew nothing about that. She guessed there were some benefits from moving too quickly through life to pay attention to things like romance.

"I don't think I'd ever really been in love before her," he said. "I cared about other girls, but it wasn't the way—it wasn't like with Kelly. You know?"

Whitney slowly shook her head, twirling her spoon between her fingers. "I've never been in love."

"Never? Not once? The guys have to be all over you."

Strangely, coming from Chace, that didn't sound like empty pick-up line type flattery. She gave him a small smile. "Not even once. I've never even been in a serious relationship."

"Really?"

"Never found time. I mean, I was in a million clubs and organizations and sports and stuff in high school. I was really involved in college, too. President of the College Democrats, on the debate team, I started my involvement with Big Sisters back then, and I had a lot of other stuff going on, too. Then, law school and more of the same. And now, I'm working at Gibson and Grey and I do pro bono work and I'm still a Big Sister. I work over sixty hours a week at the firm and on a good week I keep it under eighty. I'm trying to impress the partners so I can become one myself."

"Wow, I can't imagine that. Never finding time for love." Chace truly did look perplexed. "Love is so important. How can you have a truly happy life without it? I mean, even the crappy parts like fights and breakups—they're worth it."

"There'll be time after I make partner to find a husband and have kids and all that."

"You didn't mention falling in love."

"That's implied, isn't it?" She said without looking directly at him.

Chace shrugged and gave her a smile before picking up his wrap again. "Just throw it in with the rest of your purchases, huh?"

Whitney laughed. "Something like that."

Chace took a bite of his wrap and swallowed. Then he said, "Enough of the heavy talk. Let's talk about something less depressing and serious."

"Like what?"

"Anything as long as it's about you. I just want to know more about you."

His words sent a thrill through her that she wasn't expecting, but it was nice. A little too nice.

Whitney told him about life at the firm, about D.C. and her friends, and everything else she could think of. They spent the rest of the afternoon in the coffeehouse. Whitney called her mom, telling her she'd be home late that night. Her mom had said she would see her in the morning. Jo was still worn out from Christmas and was probably going to bed early.

"I'm starving," Whitney said after they'd been in the booth for hours. Five solid hours of talking. She had never done that with anyone before.

"You wanna get dinner?" Chace asked.

"Yes." She hoped that hadn't sounded too eager. She'd been worried he'd suggest they part ways for the evening. She wasn't ready to let him go just yet. "I mean, um, what did you have in mind?"

"I was thinking Vito's. I haven't had that in a while."

Whitney closed her eyes, salivating at the very thought of it. "Mm. So good. I haven't had Vito's since I got back here for Christmas. I always have it at least once before I go." Vito's was a family-owned Italian restaurant in town.

"Then I guess we better get to it." Chace pulled himself out of the booth as he spoke.

They went out to Whitney's car since it was already in the parking lot. Chace had walked over since his apartment complex wasn't far away.

"You know, Rob is the only person I've ever met who doesn't like Vito's," Whitney said as she pulled out of the parking lot. She sometimes brought Erika and Rob home with her when she came to visit.

"Oh yeah? Tell me more about this Rob. He seems like a cool guy. All I know is you guys met at a poetry slam?"

"Yeah. He's so much fun. Not the reliable type, but he's so loveable you can't even get mad at him about it. At least he finally moved out of his parents' house."

"Oh?"

"Yeah, he was living in their basement ever since he dropped out of G.W., trying to get his T-shirt business off the ground. The business is really taking off now. He finally decided to move out a few weeks ago." Whitney laughed, thinking of her wild best friend. "He said it was either that or kill them, and his parents had kind of grown on him over the years so he didn't want to have to do that."

Chace laughed. "Probably for the best."

"Yeah. Now he's looking for a roommate," Whitney said as they pulled up in front of Vito's. The parking lot lights were on already, casting a glaring white light over the cars parked there. Even though the days were starting to slowly lengthen again, it was still night-dark out at six in the evening. She swung her car into one of the narrow parking spaces and killed the engine.

Chace turned toward her. "Why don't I move in?"

"Huh?"

"I mean, there's no reason for me to stick around here anyway and there's gotta be more opportunities for me to get my work in front of the right people in D.C."

"You'd pick up and move to D.C. just like that."

He shrugged. "Why not?"

"I mean, you have an apartment here and don't you have a job or something? How can you just move on a whim to a completely new place?"

"Life is all about taking chances and living in the moment. Besides, I don't have family or roots or anything here." Chace shrugged and gave her a teasing grin. "Some of us don't plan out every detail of our lives five years in advance."

"It's good to have a plan in life," she said.

"I was kidding. Really. Are we gonna go get this pizza so we can get back to my place and eat it or what? I'm starving."

"Yep." Whitney climbed out of the car. She was starving, too, but not just for pizza. Her face reddened as the thought crossed her mind. What was this ambitionless stranger who had an aversion to shoes doing to her? Numbing her mind. But maybe her mind needed to be numb for a while.

"So what do you think?"

"Huh?" Whitney asked, looking up. If he'd said something to her, she'd completely missed it while thinking about what he looked like under his sweater and distressed denim.

Chace grinned. "About me moving to D.C."

"Um, well, if you're serious—" She pulled her coat closer to her in attempt to block out the bitter cold of the late December night.

"And I am," he said. It was amazing. Not even the bright lights in the parking lot could wash out his attractiveness.

She swallowed hard and forced herself to focus on their conversation. "I'll ask Rob about it. Tomorrow."

"Good."

Whitney grinned. "Yeah." It could be. She certainly wouldn't mind seeing Chace around. And considering she was at Rob's place all the time, she probably would. With both of her best friends living in the city, she enjoyed being there more than she did at her own lonely condo in the Virginia suburbs of D.C.

They took the pizza back to Chace's and ate in his living room. She thought back to the picture she'd seen the night before, but she didn't mention it. She had to remember that Chace was rebounding and she had to be careful. Besides, she had never had a serious relationship before. Why start thinking about something like that now? She had plenty of guy friends. Chace would just be another one of those.

They sat on the floor in front of his sofa with the pizza box between them and greasy paper plates on their laps. Earlier, Whitney had suggested wine without thinking. When she saw the grimace on Chace's face, she realized that anything with alcohol was probably the last thing he wanted to see or taste. They had water instead.

"This has been the most relaxing day I've had in a long time," Whitney said.

"I hope your mom won't be mad I stole you away." Chace shook his hair out of his eyes.

"Nah. We go shopping basically every day between Christmas and New Year's. She'll be fine missing one. Plus, she sounded exhausted on the phone earlier," Whitney said, polishing off a slice of cheese pizza. They'd gotten half cheese and half mushroom. Neither of them were vegetarians, but neither ate much meat. One of the many things they'd found out they had in common.

"Good. 'Cause I really enjoyed spending the day with you," Chace said.

She looked at him and smiled. He was dangerous with that handsome face. Square jaw. Long nose and a strong chin. And of course those eyes. She'd never seen eyes quite that shade of blue. Well, on a person anyway. His eyes reminded her of those of a Siberian Husky. He could have been the one in front of the camera easily, but he'd told her that he'd rather be the one behind it any day.

"What?" Chace asked, returning her stare.

"I'm just—thinking."

"About what?"

She couldn't tell him that. So instead, she said, "About how crazy the past not even twenty-four hours since I met you have been. How crazy it is that I even met you at all."

"A good kind of crazy, I hope?" He raised his eyebrows.

"I think it can be." She scrunched her lips and fidgeted with her paper plate. "Well, I think it probably is."

He laughed softly. "Good." Tracing circles on the carpet with his finger, he asked, "You have any plans for New Year's?"

"I'm planning to go back to D.C. that day. To hang out with my friends for New Year's. Why?"

"Could I tag along? Maybe be your date?"

Whitney had never had a date for New Year's. She'd never really thought about it because she went out with her friends every year in a big group. But why not? Chace was coming to D.C. anyway. He wouldn't know anyone.

They already had their tickets, but Rob knew the promoter for the club they were going to, and Whitney was sure getting Chace in wouldn't be a problem. She couldn't leave him alone on New Year's. And if he would be with the group anyway, sure, he might as well be her date. She tried not to think of it in any terms different from that. Any interest he had in her was probably rebound interest. And she wasn't looking for anything serious anyway. But there was no harm in making new friends. And if those friends were fun to look at, all the better.

She smiled. "Sure."

"Great. Well, thanks." Chace flashed those white, even teeth at her again. He had to know the power of that smile.

"For?"

"For turning the worst Christmas of my life around."

She laughed. "You're welcome." No one deserved to get dumped on Christmas Eve. Surely not someone as sweet, funny, and gorgeous as Chace. What was wrong with this Kelly? Or was the better question what was wrong with Chace? She'd only known him barely a day, after all.

Chace put his plate on top of the pizza box and turned toward her. "I know you must think some crazy things about me after last night, but I want to make a good impression on you."

"You have. That's what you did all day today. I think we'll be good friends," Whitney said quickly before Chace could say something more damaging. She felt it coming. Could see it in the serious look in his eyes.

Chace grinned. "I look forward to it, too." He moved the pizza box from between them after she set her plate on top of his. She turned toward him and with them both sitting cross-legged, he moved closer until their knees were touching. Her temperature rose through the roof and she was no longer capable of swallowing. For a moment, it seemed as if he were going to reach for her, and then he clasped his hands together and put them in his lap.

"So what do you do anyway? I never asked you that." She realized that most of the talking they'd done had been about her.

"Well, to pay the bills, I've been doing a little of everything. Most recently, work on a cleaning crew that cleans offices at night in Richmond. But what keeps me going? Photography."

"Yeah." Whitney looked around the room, surprised she hadn't made the connection before between the photos and the little comments he'd made throughout the day about taking pictures. The room was full of stunning photographs. Mostly landscapes and people she'd never met before. But Kelly was conspicuously absent.

There were also pictures of random things. Like hands. Feet. An overflowing garbage pail that somehow didn't look disgusting. A close-up of a cluster of leaves.

"You're good," Whitney said.

"Eh. I can't seem to really find the spark in anything. I haven't had inspiration for any of it in ages. But I've had a few paying gigs. Mostly high school girls who want me to do their senior portraits."

Whitney grinned. "Yeah. I bet they are girls."

Chace laughed, his face reddening. "Yeah, whatever. My high school groupies."

"Ah, dreamy, dreamy Chace."

"Like you don't have a line of admirers waiting for you every time you step out of your door. Just because you ignore them doesn't mean they don't drool."

He reached over and brushed a lock of hair away from her face. "Well, there are the admirers." He moved closer so that his lips were inches from her ear. "And then there are those who are admired." His hands moved up her arms and stopped at her shoulders. "Guess which one you are."

No. This was wrong. No distractions allowed. She was coming up for partner in a few months. Nothing was going to derail that. She cleared her throat and leaned away from him a little. "I should get going."

He nodded. "I guess it's getting kind of late."

Chace walked her to her car and before she could slip inside, he surprised her by wrapping her up in a tight hug. Taken off guard, all she could do was hug back. She was almost certain he could feel her heart thundering through both of their jackets.

It was both weird and wonderful to her that she'd had kisses before that didn't have intensity and intimacy equaling what she felt just wrapped in Chace's arms. A lot of kisses. She wondered what it would be like to kiss Chace. That was when she knew she had to pull back from him even if she didn't want to. She definitely didn't want to.

Chapter 8: Lunch Snack

The next morning, Whitney sat in her room with the door locked after sneaking away from her mother while she was on the phone with Aunt Brenda. It was driving her crazy not checking her email. And every time her mom caught her with her laptop or her BlackBerry, Whitney felt the guilt full-force. So she found it easier to sneak away throughout the day.

There'd been nothing important the day before, but that day Whitney opened her email to find a message from Kim with a copy to the leader of the practice group, Andersen. She rolled her eyes, opened it, and found an inter-office memo attached. Apparently they had a new case coming in, and Kim wanted a memo concerning the legal issues presented and the areas of law that were probably applicable by New Year's Day. It was a big case and they had to move quickly. Yeah. Kim always said that.

Kim was handing off the preliminary memo to a couple of first-year associates and she just wanted Whitney to look over their work and report to her. Whitney deleted the email and buried her head in her hands. She wasn't looking forward to dealing with Kim when she got back. Her supposed mentor was the bane of her existence. Unfortunately, Kim was going to be instrumental in deciding whether Whitney would make partner or not.

She sat back from her computer and decided to call Rob, since none of her other emails looked urgent. After grabbing her cell phone, she went over to her bed, buried herself in the mound of pillows there, and dialed Rob's number.

Rob picked up on the first ring. "Yo, Whit. What up, what up?"

She laughed. "Hi, Rob."

"Merry Christmas, I miss you, you didn't call me for Christmas. Did you like my present? I loved yours. You know me too well. Did I cover everything?"

She'd had a Brandon Lee *The Crow* collage T-shirt made for him since *The Crow* was his favorite movie, and he had an obsession with graphic tees. Which probably explained his vocation.

Whitney grinned as she answered him. "I loved yours, too. Thanks. And yes, you did." He'd gotten her a couple of audio books he'd recommended to her, but that she hadn't gotten around to picking up for herself, and he'd made her a shirt with finger paints that said "Politics Are Sexy" since she was a political news junkie.

He owned a T-shirt design company that made screen tees, usually with clever phrases on them. Her favorite was still "Have You Hugged A Socially Awkward Person Today?" He'd had it framed for her birthday one year, and it currently hung in her spare bedroom, which she used as a study. Whenever she got too stressed, she could look at it and break the tension.

"How was your Christmas?" She turned on her side and looked at the posters from her high school and college days that were still on the wall.

"You know, the usual. The folks ragging on me for dropping out of 'G dub' even though it was a million years ago, the girl throwing a fit about me not going to her house for Christmas. I should have since Mom was all about throwing bro's degree in my face. You know he graduates this May." Rob's company was really successful so far, especially with the high school and college kids around town. That didn't make his parents like it any better, though. They hadn't liked much of anything he'd done since he dropped out of George Washington University. He was still working out of his trunk and online only, but his sales numbers were growing every quarter. His dream was to open a physical store, and he was trying his hardest to make it happen. He was almost there. "Anyways, glad that's over. How was yours?" he said.

"Another Jones family Christmas."

"Your aunt behave herself?"

"Of course not."

Rob laughed.

"So, I have what might be the weirdest question in the world for you."

"Shoot."

"What if I said I found a roommate for you, but I only just met him Christmas night? He seems like a normal guy, not an ax murderer or anything."

"What?" Rob stretched out the word longer than Whitney had ever heard anybody do it.

"It's a long story, but I met this guy, he wants to move to D.C., and I told him you're looking for a roommate—"

"Wait a minute, wait a minute. Let's go back to you met a guy. Whitney Jones met a guy? We know this does not happen every day."

"What? I meet guys."

"Correction. You scare guys off. And you haven't even done that for about a year now."

"Anyway, what do you think?"

"Give me his number. I'll give him a call. We'll chat. He can't be worse than Scary Feet Sam. And this rent is a biotch for one person. I need somebody, and Craigslist is failing me. I keep getting these sketchy people who ask me things like if I've ever narked on anybody or if the cops come by my place a lot. This one guy asked me if I think our government's conspiring against us via Twitter. I ended the convo not too long after that."

Whitney laughed. "Okay, I'll give you his number and we'll see what happens."

"I still want the full story."

"And you'll get it. When I get back to D.C."

"Not fair."

"It's a long one, and I have to get out of here soon for after-Christmas shopping fun."

"Ugh. The nightmares. I think I still have PTSD from Thanksgiving. I'm not ready."

"Has Delaney dragged you out for any of it yet?"

"We're supposed to go to Potomac Mills today. I've spent the morning hiding from her, but I think she's coming over to the apartment soon, so I won't be able to get out of it."

"You know you love it." Whitney grinned, waiting for his reaction.

"Yeah, whatevs. Gimme that number if you're not going to let me in on your I-met-a-man story."

"Okay." Whitney gave him Chace's number. Then she said, "Oh, and he's probably coming out with us for New Year's."

"You can't tell me things like this and then leave me hanging. What makes you think you can do that?"

"It's seriously not a big deal. I couldn't just leave him alone in the city on New Year's. He won't know anyone. He's just going to be part of our group."

"Is he?"

"Well, I kind of said he could be my date. But it doesn't mean anything. You know it'll be a whole group of us like it always is."

"Yeah, well, most everyone's going to be paired up this year. Erika won't, though."

"What?"

"She didn't tell you?"

"No."

"Really? This is big news. I'm surprised."

"Well, maybe I forgot to call her back or something. Spill. Now."

"See, it doesn't feel good, does it?"

"Rob!"

"Okay, okay. A.J. says he's not going."

"You're kidding."

"He's getting worse by the day. Did she tell you he didn't even get her a present this year?"

"What? Really?" Whitney couldn't believe what she was hearing.

"Yeah. He basically tried to make it look like her fault that she didn't get one. You know how he is."

"Unfortunately, I do." He was being a jerk, like always. And Erika just kept putting up with it.

They talked for a little while longer about Erika and her questionable taste in men and then Rob had to go because Delaney was there.

Whitney, her mom, and the others left for the mall a little after Whitney got off the phone with Rob.

Whitney put on the warmest coat and gloves she'd brought to River Run—her black leather ones—because it was freezing out there. Aunt Brenda had gone home the day after Christmas. They were meeting her at the mall since she lived closer to it than she did to River Run. The closest mall was an hour's drive away, and, surprisingly, Alicia was the one pushing them out of the door. She'd gotten up early. She couldn't wait to spend all her Christmas money, so she wanted as much time in Fredericksburg as possible.

Melinda sat in the backseat with Whitney. She started up her one-person interrogation squad as soon as they got in the car and Jo and Alicia immediately began squabbling over the station and volume of the radio.

Melinda leaned in close. "So you were gone all day yesterday."

"Yeah." She fiddled with her gloves.

"You were with him, weren't you?"

"Who?"

Melinda's eyes sparkled with the anticipation of learning juicy gossip. "Don't play dumb. That guy. The drunk one we helped home."

She couldn't stop the smile from playing at the edges of her lips. "Maybe."

Melinda shook her head. "You backed out of after-Christmas shopping. Which you love. You were gone all day, and there ain't that much to do in this town.

You were with him. Now, dish before I tell your mama what you been up to."

"I haven't been up to anything. We were just talking."

"So tell me what you talked about." Melinda grabbed Whitney's knee. "You know I don't let you keep these kind of things from me."

Warmth spread from her heart out over her entire body as she remembered her day with Chace. "Everything, Melinda. Just…everything and nothing. Our families. Our lives. What we've done and what we want to do. Places we've been and places we want to go. Big things. Small things. We just talked about… life."

Melinda shook her head. "Look at you. You can't be gone over him already. You barely know this guy." Melinda's mouth dropped open, and she covered it with one hand and pointed at her with the other. Then she whispered so that Jo and Alicia wouldn't hear. "But you are. Look at you."

"I'm not anything. He's just fun to hang out with, that's all." She hoped her expression didn't betray too much to her cousin.

"Yeah. Well, you better get in all the 'hanging' you can now. You're leaving for D.C. in a few days."

"Actually, he's moving to D.C., I think. He's talking to Rob about being his roommate today."

"He what?" Melinda exclaimed.

"Shh," Whitney hissed.

Alicia turned to look into the backseat, and Jo eyed them from the rearview mirror.

"What's going on back there?" Jo asked.

"Oh, nothing, Aunt Jo. We're just talking about a... guy we know from high school," Melinda said.

"Mmm-hmm," Jo said in a tone connoting she didn't believe it for one minute. She never pressured Whitney about where she went or what she did. She always let it be known that she knew there was something to know, and then she waited for the guilt of not telling to cripple Whitney until she had to tell. Most of the time, it worked. Whitney hoped it wouldn't this time. Besides, there was hardly anything to tell.

"C'mon. Let us in on it. This have something to do with where you were all day yesterday?" Alicia said.

"Regardless of where I was all day yesterday, I was home last night," she said, giving her sneaking-out sister a pointed look. Alicia narrowed her eyes at her and then turned back to the front of the car.

When they stepped out of the car and into the mall parking lot, it was freezing. Her gloves did little to protect against the cold as the wind seemed to slice right through them, turning her fingers into ice. Wind whipped all around them, and it seemed to be trying to cut right through them. They hurried toward the mall, not paying much attention to the wreaths and garlands adorning the light poles in the parking lot.

Whitney had a great life and she needed to remember that. A wonderful—for the most part—family, a great job, and the best friends a person could ask for. Absolutely nothing was missing. Not one thing. Not even a gorgeous brown-haired man with ice blue eyes holding her close the way he had when they'd shared that blazing goodbye hug the night before. Especially not him.

She stepped into the mall and felt her body thawing all over as a sudden rush of heat embraced her. She looked around at the store windows still filled with red, green, and gold holiday cheer. Shoppers bustled up and down the main aisle, packed almost shoulder-to-shoulder, all on missions to get the best after-Christmas deals. Teens walked around in giggling groups, many of them with ear buds in their ears. Even with all the chaos, she loved the mall at the holiday season. Or maybe she loved it because of the chaos.

They split off into groups. Jo and Aunt Brenda went to hit the housewares and discount Christmas decorations for next year's celebrations. Not even she could think that far in advance. Alicia, Melinda, and Whitney went for the clothing stores. Alicia soon saw some friends of hers in a music store and she branched off to hang out with them, telling Whitney to tell their mom she'd get a ride home with her friends.

Whitney and Melinda wandered in and out of clothing stores, trying a few things on, but not buying anything. Melinda complained about having spent all her money at a giant sale at Barney's in New York. She just couldn't concentrate on the clothes enough to look for something she might actually be interested in buying. She flipped through racks of dresses and ran her hands over sweaters and blouses set up on tables in the middle of store floors, but her mind was with Chace.

She kept seeing those eyes—fire and ice. Feeling his knees against hers. That simple touch the day before had nearly caused her to burst into flames. It was still burning up her mind. She imagined that she hadn't just sat there last night. That instead, she'd moved her hands over his thighs, up to his hips, hooked them into the waist of his jeans. And—

"Whitney." Melinda was snapping her fingers in front of Whitney's face. She realized that Melinda must have been trying to get her attention for a while.

"Oh, um, I'm sorry. What did you say?"

"I asked what you think of this?" Melinda held a multi-colored scarf up to her neck.

"Looks nice," she said, still trying to bring herself back to that store.

Melinda made a face, running her fingers over the fabric. "I dunno. It's kind of scratchy. Ah, well. I don't have the money for it. I told you not to let me buy anything anyway."

She sighed exaggeratedly, but then grinned. "Fine. It's the most horrible scarf I've ever seen."

They laughed.

"Let's go get coffee."

They left the store and headed for the food court.

∾⤳∾

Whitney and her mom didn't want to go see the movie that Aunt Brenda and Melinda were so interested in at the theater across from the mall, so they stayed behind and to hang out until they were picked up afterwards.

Whitney tried to think of things they could do to kill the time since neither of them seemed too excited about going in the stores any longer.

Whitney said, "We could go get something to eat now if you want."

Her mother looked at Whitney for a moment without answering. After a long pause, she said, "Didn't you eat?

"I had coffee earlier."

Her mom shuffled her bags around in her hands. "Oh."

"Why? Did you eat?"

"I had a snack," Jo said in a guilt-tinged tone.

Perplexed, and with her lawyer's brain constantly alert, Whitney asked, "What kind of snack?"

"I had a lunch snack."

"A what?"

"Well, I went to Ruby Tuesday and had a burger and fries. And then I had dessert."

Whitney laughed. "That's not a snack. And it's not lunch. That's dinner!"

Her mom shook her head emphatically. "No, it was a lunch snack. It's lunch food. But it's not lunch time. And it's not enough food to be dinner. So it's a lunch snack."

Whitney couldn't stop laughing. She wrapped her arm around her mom's shoulders and walked her toward a nearby nail shop, having decided to treat her mother to a manicure while they waited.

∽✕∽

Whitney tip-toed into the kitchen a little after midnight. She hadn't eaten much for dinner, and she'd awakened in the middle of the night with her stomach rumbling.

"Couldn't sleep either, huh?" her brother said.

She gasped and put a hand over her heart. "Devon, you scared the crap out of me." She went over to the wall and switched on the overhead light. He sat at the kitchen table wearing a ratty navy blue robe. "What are you doing sitting here in the dark?" She grabbed the tea kettle from the stove and filled it with water.

"Thinking." He stayed seated, but he watched her move around the kitchen.

"About?" She set one mug in front of him and another across from him.

"Trina."

She sat in the chair across from him. Maybe he was finally going to tell her why he'd been playing the Grinch for the past few days. "What about her?"

He slid his mug back and forth between his hands. "I don't think things are too good between us right now."

"Is that why you've been acting more like Aunt Cheryl than any of us would like lately?" she asked.

He grinned sheepishly and nodded. "I'm sorry I was a butthole all morning, but I've been in a really bad mood." He put his hand over hers. "I'm glad you came down here tonight, though. You're the only one I feel like I can talk to about this kind of stuff."

"And you definitely need to talk to somebody about this. I can tell it's eating you up inside."

"Yeah." He sighed. "I do."

"So tell me."

"It's her parents. I told you they never really liked me much. I could always tell. They'd get along great with your grandparents." He gave a humorless laugh.

"What about her parents?"

"Not long after we got engaged, I overheard them talking. I didn't mean to listen in on their conversation, but I heard my name and I got curious. They started saying stuff about our family. How we're poor and we're trash and you're the anomaly out all of us Joneses." He folded his arms over his chest and pushed his chair back from the table. "They said I wasn't good enough for their daughter and I wasn't ever going to make anything of myself. And they couldn't stand the thought of me marrying Trina."

She didn't understand. "I thought you told me you asked for their blessing before you asked Trina to marry you."

He nodded. "Yeah. But I guess they don't want Trina to know they hate me. They're afraid that'll only make her more determined to be with me. I heard them saying something about that, too."

"So what does Trina think about all of this?"

"She doesn't know."

"You haven't said anything to her about what you heard?"

Devon shook his head. " I guess I've been kind of picking little fights with her a lot because I'm mad about it, but she probably doesn't know why."

"How very passive aggressive and not grown-up of you, Devon."

He shrugged.

She ran a hand over her face. "I'm sorry, Devon. I know, that wasn't helpful." She tapped her fingers on the table. "What they said was wrong. Clearly. But you need to tell Trina about it. You two need to talk about this. Don't let them eat away at your relationship." She went over to him and put a hand on his shoulder.

He looked up at her. "So that's your best advice? I thought you'd be full of tips for dealing with snobs."

He never missed an opportunity to take a cheap shot at her paternal grandparents. Of course, they weren't much better when it came to the Joneses. Still, they were her grandparents and she loved them. If she refused to love people because of their flaws, she wouldn't have had very many people left in her life.

She said, "The most important thing is Trina. Anyone can see you two are the real thing. Don't let her parents or anyone else steal that away from you."

Devon shrugged and mumbled something she couldn't discern.

"Promise, Devon?"

"Yeah. I'll call her in the morning."

The tea kettle began to whistle and she ran to grab it before the sound woke up everybody in the house. She poured water into both mugs. Devon put tea bags in the water while she set the kettle back on the stove.

While they waited for the tea to steep, he said, "Thanks, big sis. You're really all right. I know I give you a hard time, but you're always there for me when I need you. I want you to know I appreciate it."

She smiled. "I know."

She could fix her brother's love life, but she didn't even have one of her own. Not that she wanted one of her own. Not really, anyway.

Chapter 9: Just Can't Wait

Chace talked to Rob, and it seemed they would get along great. They were almost the same person. Neither one was as organized and together as Whitney and they were both crazy about her, although Chace knew better than to admit he was already.

It was all set. Chace would leave for D.C. when Whitney did, and he'd move in with Rob that day. After the call Chace had a long day of nothing to do ahead of him. Whitney was out shopping with her family.

Alone again, with no Whitney to distract him, Chace was feeling pretty low. He was happy he was moving to D.C., but being alone in that apartment with memories of Kelly for several more days was going to be harsh. He'd gone to the store and gotten boxes and he'd pulled out his suitcases and a few crates, but he was too bummed to get moving when it actually came to packing up his things and leaving the apartment that had been home for the past two years.

Even with all of Kelly's stuff gone, she was still in that apartment with him. Yes, moving to D.C. would be the best thing for him.

It was weird. He didn't even miss her as much as he thought he would. He just missed the idea of her being around. And having someone to cuddle up with and be close to. He missed her massaging his feet even though she teased him about his stinky toes and gross socks. He missed cooking for her. But he didn't know that he actually missed Kelly.

Ethan had told him he fell in love too easily because he picked out a pretty girl and fell in love with the idea of being in love more than he fell for the actual girl. Well, wait until Ethan heard about Whitney. He would definitely rip into him for this one. But he couldn't help it. If there was such thing as love at first sight, he'd fallen into it for Whitney. It hadn't even been that quick with Kelly. With any other woman. Something about her made him just…know. What he felt didn't have anything to do with rebounding.

Still, two years was a long time to invest in a person, and Chace couldn't help moping around the apartment where he and Kelly had spent so many happy times together. They'd laughed, cried, fought, made up—the making up being best of all—so many times right there in that apartment.

"Well, the smartest thing would be to get rid of all the Kelly stuff first, I guess," Chace said. He dragged his feet over to the bedroom closet to take down boxes of photos. They were the hardest Kelly things to get rid of. The two things he'd thought he'd loved the most in the world—his camera and his girl.

He didn't even look at them. He just emptied boxes of photos—black and whites and colors both—into a black garbage bag and set it aside. He ran his hands through his hair and blew a harsh breath through his nose. He bit his lower lip and looked at Kelly's empty side of the closet, once again feeling the pang he'd felt for the past few mornings—she really was gone. And she wasn't coming back.

He then grabbed the neck of the plastic bag and dragged it around the apartment with him, dumping in framed photos, clothes and other stuff Kelly had bought for him, any kitchen stuff they'd bought together—anything that reeked too much of Kelly, in other words. He kept the towels, though. They were really nice and the only ones left because she had thrown out all the old, threadbare ones he'd had when they moved in together.

She'd tried to call him more and sent some texts. She'd even gotten Amy to try to call him, but he didn't want to hear about being friends. Seeing her, talking to her would be too hard. The only way to do it was to have a clean break. He couldn't do it any other way without making a mess.

When he was done, he set the garbage bag by the front door and sat down next to it, drawing his knees up to his chest after grabbing the remote for the stereo.

He flipped it on and the opening bars of Brian McKnight's "One Last Cry" filled the room. He barked a short, bitter laugh and dropped his head onto his knees.

✤

Chace opened his eyes and yawned, realizing he must have fallen asleep. He looked at his watch and realized he'd been out for quite a while. After taking the bags of memories down to the dumpster in the apartment complex parking lot, he came back up to his apartment. He was ready to start packing. Enough of that. Time to move on.

He decided to check his Skype before getting started and he saw that Ethan was on. He grinned, sat down at his computer, and connected with Ethan via video chat. His best friend in the whole world since they'd met through their frat in college popped up on the computer screen. Ethan's black hair was tousled and didn't look recently combed, he wore a light blue T-shirt, and he was tanned a dark golden brown as if he'd spent every minute outside since arriving in New Zealand. Knowing Ethan, he had.

"Chace, what is up? Merry belated Christmas, bud. How ya been?"

"Merry Christmas to you, too, man. I've been— good. How are things? How's life with the Kiwis?"

"Oh, great, man. I've been hiking every day. It's beautiful here. I love it that I'm in summer right now and you are freezing your butt off," Ethan said before going into a detailed account of his most recent hiking adventures, which had involved a pretty nasty spill when Ethan leaned too far over a ledge. Ethan held up his leg and showed Chace a nasty gash.

"Nice. So you haven't gotten eaten up by anything yet, I see?"

"Man, all the animals are tame here. Nothing dangerous. They don't even have snakes or big cats or anything. Well, there are rumors of some big cats running around, but I haven't seen anything." Ethan made a face. Ethan didn't seem to be happy unless he was putting his life at risk.

Chace was all about adventure, but Ethan gave the word new meaning. There was the time that Ethan had convinced him to wander away from their guide when they were on safari in Africa. They'd almost made themselves targets of a very big and angry rhino. Apparently he'd chosen to miss out on the tamest of Ethan's trips so far. "Well, are there sharks, at least? Maybe you can go swimming with them or something."

"Man, you've known me too long. I'm going shark diving tomorrow."

They laughed.

"So, how's Kelly Kellz? She around there some-where? I don't hear her nagging you."

Chace looked down at his keyboard, running his fingers over the keys. "We broke up."

"What? Really? When?"

"She moved out on Christmas Eve. Said she was leaving me for Hank."

"Christmas Eve? That's just cruel. And what, Hank? That's that old guy she works for, right? And isn't he married? Has kids older than us? Gross."

Chace nodded. "Apparently they'd been having an affair since before Kelly and I even got together. At least they were broken up when we met. Or so she tells me, anyway."

"Dude, that's just nasty. And I mean it in every pos-sible way. But really, you're better off. I always knew that girl was shady," Ethan said.

"Yeah," Chace said, staring down at his bare feet.

"Yeah, uh, you probably don't wanna hear that right now."

"Nope."

"So…now that you've killed the conversation…"

He laughed. "You're the one who brought up Kel-ly."

"Yeah, not knowing she'd gone straight up—well—Kelly on you. Hey, the good news is you can leave Nowheresville now. You should come back to Rich-mond."

"Actually…I'm moving to D.C."

"Oh yeah? When?"

"Uh—in a few days."

"Uhm, so I leave the country for the holidays and you just go and completely rearrange your life, huh? Were you gonna even tell me? Send me a postcard? Something?" Ethan scratched his head in mock confusion.

"Dude, it's all been very spur of the moment. It's kinda hard to get in touch with you with this ginormous time difference, you know."

"Ha, it is pretty big. The jet lag is gonna be ridiculous when I get home. Man, but this has been one amazing Christmas. You really shoulda come with me."

"Yeah," Chace said, but not regretting his decision to stay for one moment. Even though he'd wanted to go earlier, and he'd been really pissed at Kelly for making him stay—especially after she tried to wreck his Christmas anyway. If he'd gone to New Zealand, he would have probably never met Whitney. And not meeting Whitney would have been a true tragedy.

Chace debated for a moment over whether or not to tell Ethan about Whitney. In the end, his desire to not hear a lecture from Ethan about how he shouldn't be dating again so soon won. No, it was best to keep quiet about Whitney. He waited for Ethan to finish bashing Kelly for making Chace stay in Virginia. And then he bashed Chace for listening to Kelly.

When Ethan was finished, he said, "What are you gonna do with your apartment?"

"I guess break the lease if she doesn't want it. I need to do something with my furniture, I guess." Most of the furniture in the place was Chace's. And movers were coming in the morning to take what was Kelly's and put it in storage. Or so the voicemail she'd left him had said.

"You know, I could use some furniture."

"You certainly could," Chace said. Ethan's apartment had little more than floor cushions, bean bags, and an air mattress in the way of furniture. He'd been a nomad for most of his life, although he'd been in Richmond for quite a while by Ethan standards. "You know what, man? You can have it. You have a spare key to the place. Come get it when you get back to the States. I'll pay the January rent, so you shouldn't have any problems getting in or anything."

"Thanks. You're always helping me out, bro. I really appreciate it."

"No problem."

After his conversation with Ethan, Chace started packing. He was ready to get out of that place forever.

Chapter 10: Let It Snow, Let It Snow, Let It Snow

Whitney knocked on Chace's door. It was a few days before New Year's Eve. She'd seen him almost every day since they'd first had lunch together.

He opened the door and pulled her into a hug, dragging her into the apartment.

She laughed, trying to back away from him. "Hey. I brought you something. You're crushing it."

"Oh, sorry. What is it?" He loosened his hold on her, but didn't let go.

She held the box up between them. "Cookies."

"You made me cookies?" He took the box from her.

"My sister made 'em. I helped. Trust me, that's the way you want it."

He laughed and set the box of cookies on the coffee table.

"It looks so empty in here." The walls were bare. Little was left in the apartment besides the furniture and the huge television in the living room.

"Yeah, well, we're leaving tomorrow, right? Had to pack up my crap sometime." He shrugged on his jacket.

"Where are you going?"

"*We* are going for a walk."

"It's freezing out."

"Nah. It's not that bad."

She gave him a wary look, but let him take her hand and lead her toward the door. He liked being outside a little too much.

It was pretty cold out, but not unbearable. Whitney's cheeks were frozen, but, other than that, she was snug inside of her hat, scarf, winter coat, and Uggs. Chace wore a lighter jacket than the weather called for, but he promised he had a hat tucked away somewhere. He said that he would put it on if he felt like he needed it. At least he had foregone the flip-flops that day. He wore dark brown loafers instead. Whitney turned her face up to the sky, which was lit by a weak, watery yellow sun.

As they were walking around near the empty basketball court near the back of his apartment complex, large, feathery snowflakes started to fall from the white-gray sky. She loved snow. It was so rare and wonderful in both Virginia and D.C. The forecasters had promised flurries, but she rarely believed them as they were often wrong about such things. She usually waited to see for herself instead of hoping and being disappointed. As she did with a lot of things.

"Look, Chace, it's snowing," Whitney said as a large white flake landed in Chace's hair and melted.

He pulled a black knit cap out of his pocket and tugged it onto his head. "Yeah. I guess it is."

"It's been so long since I've seen snow falling out where I can really enjoy it. Back in the city it turns into grimy slush almost as soon as it falls. But here, it's so beautiful. Peaceful."

"It probably won't even stick, so you better enjoy it while it lasts," Chace said.

"I know, but isn't it pretty?"

He made a face. "I'm not a fan of snow. I've seen way too much of it. I grew up in Pennsylvania, remember?"

"I'm a firm believer that you can never have too much snow."

"You wouldn't be saying that if it was your family winter chore to shovel the sidewalk every time it snowed," Chace said in a sing-song voice.

"Family winter chore?" Whitney raised her eyebrows.

Chace grinned. She could barely keep herself from turning into Jell-o when she saw that grin. He said, "I have weird parents. Don't ask."

"What was your brother's winter family chore?"

"Chopping wood. We had the old-school kind of fireplace that actually took logs."

"My parents have one of those, too."

"I like it. Another thing we have in common." He squeezed her hand. "Dad wouldn't hear of buying firewood." Chace's voice became gruffer, and she assumed he was imitating his father. " 'We have five good acres of land out there. Why on earth would I buy firewood? Waste of good money, that's what it would be.' "

Whitney laughed. "I guess that makes sense."

"Of course it does. My father was nothing if not practical," Chace said. "He's lightened up a lot since he retired, though."

"You said they travel a lot," Whitney said. "Your parents."

He looked up. "Yeah. They love it."

She watched snowflakes melt into her gloves. "Must be nice." She couldn't imagine waking up and going where she wanted to go in the morning instead of going where she had to go.

He put an arm around her. "You okay?"

She nodded. "Fine."

"You sure?" He put his hands on her shoulders.

She thought about moving for a moment, very aware of his body behind hers. However, she quickly decided against moving away. She liked the warmth of him and the movement of his chest between her shoulder blades as she leaned against it. She turned in his arms and pressed her cheek to his shoulder.

"Whitney," he said.

"Hm?"

"I'm glad we met."

She wrapped her arms around him. "Me, too."

"About me moving to D.C. I'm not doing it because I expect—"

She put a finger over his lips. "That's enough."

Chace kissed her finger. He then moved closer so that her finger and his lips were only inches from her lips. Snowflakes melted on their jackets and hats and in their hair, but she barely noticed them.

The late December air didn't affect her at all in that moment. There was only Chace. She didn't resist when he removed her glove and pressed her finger back to his lips.

He moved closer until the only thing separating their lips was her finger. His pale blue eyes burned into hers. Their lips and noses lined up on either side of her finger, desire palpable in the air. Everything inside of her wanted her to move her finger aside and let their lips meet. He kissed her naked finger, just a light touch of lips to flesh.

She tore herself away from him and took a few steps backwards. Hugging herself, she watched his face fall.

"So, I guess we should get back to your place," Whitney said. "It's getting colder."

"Yeah. It definitely is. Uh, we should. Start. Loading up the cars, I mean," Chace said. "With…my stuff." They were heading to D.C. in a couple of days.

Walking back to his apartment, they pretended it never happened. That was what she wanted, but something about that fact still made her feel restless.

With every step she took toward his apartment, she wanted more. She wanted to know what it felt like to have his lips under hers. To taste his tongue against hers—feel the warmth of his mouth. His breath on her skin. That was why he was dangerous. All other guys, she'd been able to take or leave. She had the feeling that wouldn't be the same with Chace if she made the mistake of letting him get too close.

❧

After Whitney and Chace were finished packing his SUV with boxes and bags, they took a break for dinner before packing the rest of his stuff into her car.

Chace baked fish for them and they took it and a bottle of wine into the living room. The stereo was one of the few things he hadn't packed yet. He turned it on low volume and dimmed the lights.

Whitney sipped her wine. "You're going to try to make a career out of photography when you move to the city. Right?"

He nodded. "Yeah. Finally."

"That's nice." Not very practical, but it wasn't like his choices affected her life.

125

"I'm really looking forward to it. There's nothing like doing something you really want to do. It just gives you this strong feeling of purpose. You know?"

"Sure." Ambition was a much stronger motivator, and she had plenty of that. Dreams didn't pay the bills. They didn't bring you power or prestige, either. Some things were more important than floating around, dreaming, chasing after wants instead of leading a disciplined life.

He gave her a crooked smile that wiped away all thought.

"What?" she said. She took another sip of wine. The pleasant warmth she felt could've come from the wine, but maybe it hadn't.

"I'm gonna take your picture." He stood and set his plate on the coffee table. "I'll be right back."

He returned with a camera. He flipped on an overhead light, and she squinted until her eyes adjusted to the sudden brightness in the room.

"Here, sit on the sofa for a minute." He offered his hand to help her up, and she took it. Warmth surged through her body.

She sat on the sofa and he leaned in close, putting his hand under her chin.

"Turn your head a little this way," he said, pressing his fingers gently into her skin and tilting her head. She jumped a little, startled in a pleasant way by the warmth of his touch.

126

"Like this?"

He leaned closer. "Exactly like that."

"What should I do with my hands?"

He set his camera down and took her hands in his. He ran his thumbs over the backs of them. Then, he positioned them in her lap. He was in no hurry to move his hands away from hers. When he did, he brushed his palms along the length of her thighs.

"Is this good?" She hoped not. Hopefully he would reposition some other part of her body.

"Yeah," he said, giving her a hungry look. But instead of coming back to the sofa, he picked up his camera and backed away from her a few feet.

While he adjusted the lens, she tried to focus on the camera and not on what she wanted to do to the photographer.

The shutter clicked a few times. He then set the camera aside, turned off the overhead light, and came over to the sofa. He sat next to her.

"You're very photogenic," he said, trailing a finger across her collar bone, which was covered by her sweater. She had the sudden urge to rip it off.

"Thank you," she whispered.

"Should we finish dinner?" he said. His hand migrated to her shoulder and down her arm.

Dinner wasn't what she wanted to finish. "I'm really tired." She bit her lip and grabbed her purse so she would have something safe to do with her hands. "Really tired."

"Oh?" he said, slipping his hand inside the collar of her sweater.

She jumped up from the couch. "Yep. Extremely—tired."

He stood. "Okay. I'll see you tomorrow then." He put his arms around her and squeezed her low around the waist, giving her a hug that made her want to show him just how "tired" she was.

"Goodnight." She pulled away from the hug and hurried to the door before she could change her mind.

∽∾

For Whitney's last dinner at home, Jo made a huge feast. Devon brought Trina over, as they were in the process of making up.

Jo made all of Whitney's favorites. Fried chicken, roast potatoes, corn, homemade yeast rolls, and Jo's famous sweet tea to go with it. Shorty called it liquid diabetes, which always earned him a love tap across the head.

Aunt Cheryl had decided to come over for dinner and to see Whitney off as well. There was still plenty of tension between Aunt Cheryl and Jo, but Jo was being her usual, gracious self. It was hard to tell how angry she was at her sister. Aunt Cheryl, on the other hand, was not afraid to let those feelings float on the surface.

"How've you been, Trina?" Whitney asked once they were all seated and passing platters around the table.

"Great," Trina said. She grabbed Devon's hand and smiled at him. "Guess what Devon and I did on the way over here?"

"What?"

"We set a date. Next October."

"Congratulations," she said.

Jo went over to them, shouting about how happy she was, and hugged them both. Aunt Cheryl muttered her congratulations, but seemed to be chewing on her resentment of losing the spotlight. Devon smiled at Whitney and mouthed a thank you to her.

"Fall weddings are so beautiful," Whitney said.

"Know a lot about weddings, do you?" Aunt Cheryl snorted.

"Not tonight," Jo said, turning to face her sister.

"Jo, I don't know what I did to you for you to be treating me like this," Aunt Cheryl said as she piled her plate up with food. "You never want to listen. Even when it's for your own good. Especially when it is."

"Don't start that again, either. I don't need you to lecture me. Quinton is not your business. Nothing to do with me and him is," Jo said.

"Shorty, what do you think about this?" Aunt Cheryl said.

129

"Same as Jo does," Shorty said quietly before turning to Whitney. "Baby, would you pass me the greens?"

"Sure, here you go." Whitney passed the white ceramic dish containing the leafy boiled greens across the table.

"Nobody in this family has good sense," Aunt Cheryl muttered, poking her chicken with her fork.

"Why don't you get out of here then?" Devon said.

"What did you say to me, boy?"

Jo held up a hand to Devon. "That's enough." She said to Aunt Cheryl, "Yes, if you're going to keep this up, you should probably leave. I don't know what's wrong with you lately, but I'm tired of you taking whatever it is out on me."

"Lately?" Devon snorted. "How 'bout all her life?"

"That's enough," Jo said.

Cheryl fired a string of choice words at Devon.

"You're going to stop that right now," Jo said. "And you're going to get out. Now."

Cheryl jumped up from the table. "I can't believe you're kicking me out of your house."

"Believe it."

"Well. I hope nobody here never needs anything from me. I'm done with all of you. Fools." Cheryl left the dining room and Jo followed her. They argued all the way to the front door. Then the door slammed. Shortly after that, Jo ran past the doorway and down the hall.

Whitney went after her. She found Jo in her bedroom. She sat next to her mother on the bed.

"I'm so sorry your dinner got ruined, baby," Jo said.

"Don't you worry about that." She rubbed a hand over her mother's back.

"I just can't—that woman gets under my skin so bad sometimes."

"I know."

"She keeps at me. I know how she is, and I try not to let her get to me, but there's only so much I can stand. Especially right now. It seems she's on the warpath every day, always trying to pick a fight with me about something else 'cause things aren't going right in her life."

Whitney nodded, patting her mother's shoulder. "She can certainly work a nerve."

"That's like saying Warren Buffet has a little money."

They laughed and Whitney hugged her mother close, feeling guilty about the fact that she had to leave soon. She never seemed to have enough time with the people closest to her and, ironically, that was because she was working so hard to make them proud and help them.

Chapter 11: Leaving Town

Chace came back from the Goodwill juggling a bag of takeout Chinese food, the pile of mail he'd retrieved from the post office before closing his P.O. box, and a couple of DVDs he'd bought for him and Whitney to watch later. He'd picked up a couple of movies that she said she'd never seen and he couldn't believe that anyone in the world hadn't. He would make her watch them some time after they got to D.C. There'd be plenty of time since he planned on spending a lot of time with her up there.

He was so busy trying not to drop any of the stuff in his arms that he didn't notice Amy until he almost ran into her. On top of him being distracted, she was a small and sneaky one.

"Ah!" he cried, startled. "Didn't see you. What are you doing here, anyway? Kelly got all her stuff, didn't she?"

Amy sighed, running a hand through her short blonde hair. "That's why I'm here. I want to talk to you about her."

"What?" Chace was going to drop something if he didn't set everything down soon. "Hold on." He managed to get the door to his apartment unlocked and open without dropping anything. He then walked into the apartment. Amy followed him.

"She really misses you."

He set everything on the dining room table and then turned to face Amy. "What?"

"It's really immature, the way you're ignoring her calls. What if she had something important to tell you?" Amy said, crossing her arms over her chest and tapping a foot against the floor.

"She can leave me a voicemail. Which she's been doing. I check my messages."

"Still, she really wants to talk to you. Why won't you just pick up the phone? Just once?"

"She left me. Not the other way around. And weren't you the one who told me I was better off? You were right. So why are you trying to get me to talk to her?"

"What if she has something really important to tell you?" She avoided his eyes as she spoke.

"Are you trying to tell me something right now?"

Amy looked around the apartment. She ran her hand over the empty bar counter. "Where's all your stuff?"

"In my car." He flipped through his mail. "I'm getting out of this place. You know I was only ever here for Kelly, so I don't see how you can be surprised."

"But you just—and your lease—when are you leaving?"

"Later today," he said. He crossed the room and sat down on the edge of the sofa. "Ethan is coming to get my furniture for his place when he gets back into town. My new roommate's place is fully furnished. January's rent is paid here, and I'm breaking the lease after that unless Kelly wants the place. If she does, tell her to call the landlord. I told him she might be calling."

"Okay, not commenting on how messed up that is that you would leave town without even saying anything to her," she said.

He shrugged.

"If I hadn't caught you today, how were you planning on letting Kelly know that?"

Chace snorted. It wasn't like he had to tell her anything. "I was going to send her an email after I got to D.C."

"Why not before?"

"To prevent a scene like this with Kelly instead of you." He sighed. "Or maybe even both of you. But looks like I didn't really do that anyway."

"You really want to talk to her. Trust me."

"I don't want anything to do with her, Amy."

"You're making a huge mistake right now. You don't even know how—disastrously huge."

"Are you kidding me? She's the one who left me for that old lawyer dude. Why should I talk to her if I have nothing to say to her? Why shouldn't I cut her out of my life after what she did to me?"

Amy folded her hands into the sleeves of her sweater and stared up at him. "Don't do this. Believe me, you really don't want to."

"Why don't you come out and tell me what you're trying so hard not to tell me?"

Amy sighed. "It should come from her. Please just call her. Or answer when she calls you."

"Amy, you're cool, and I have nothing against you. Your husband's a great guy and I'm gonna miss playing ball with him. Tell him I said bye. But I'm done with Kelly's games. My time with all of that ended on Christmas Eve."

Amy started to say something else and then she just smiled.

Chace ran a hand through his hair, temporarily lifting it from his forehead. "What?"

"She's a real idiot. I love her, but she is. If I weren't married…I'd show her what you do when you find a good looking man with a good heart. How could you ask for more?"

Chace grinned. "Thanks, Amy."

She walked over and hugged him. "Goodbye, Chace. And good luck. You'll do a lot better with your photography up there, I'm sure."

Chace laughed off her compliment. "I'll see you around."

"That's right. You don't like to say goodbye. Well, later, bud."

He walked her to the door and then slumped against it after closing it behind her.

ᕦᕤ

When Whitney arrived that afternoon, Chace leaned against his white SUV in the parking lot, hands shoved into his pockets, waiting for her. He had the engine running, warming it up.

"Aren't you cold?" was her greeting to him, her eyebrows raised.

"A little. More than that, I'm just excited to go. Get out of this place," Chace said. He breathed in the scent of her perfume, which he could smell over the exhaust fumes from their vehicles.

"Yeah," Whitney said with a sigh. That sigh contained more than just a little exasperation. Worry was written all across her pretty face.

"Hey. What's wrong?" He rubbed her shoulder briefly. He made himself move his hand even though he wanted to let it linger there longer than what would probably be appropriate.

She shook her head. "Just family stuff. My aunt's stressing my mom out."

"I'm sorry. Wanna talk about it?"

She bounced up and down and hugged her arms to her chest. "Man, it's freezing out here."

"Yeah." He knew what would warm her up.

"We should get going. We're going out tonight, remember? Let's get you there and unpacked."

He couldn't argue with that, although he would have liked to replace "unpacked" with "undressed." He pushed that thought aside, though. He didn't want Whitney to think he was some rebounding creep only out for one thing. There were already signs that was what she thought. And why wouldn't she think that? But it wasn't true. Yeah, he wanted that one thing, but he wanted the rest of her to go with it.

"Chace?"

He slapped his driver's side door a couple times. "What are we waiting for? Lead the way to the big city."

Laughing, they got into their cars.

Chace followed Whitney north for over two hours out of Virginia and into D.C. She took them through the city to a part of town near the Shaw neighborhood, not far from U Street. They parked on the street. Whitney called him and told him to take the space that happened to be in front of Rob's building since he had most of his stuff in his car. She parked around the block a bit and came back to meet him.

"Well, let's go meet your new roomie," Whitney said, taking his hand and heading to the building.

He squeezed her hand.

"I can't wait for you to meet Rob. It's eerie, but you're actually kind of perfect for each other. It's like you two were separated at birth." She rang a bell and Rob buzzed them up.

Chace saw what she meant immediately. The door flew open and a Korean-American man grabbed Whitney, pulled her into the apartment, and swung her around. "Whit!" He then turned back to Chace. "Brother from another mother. What up?" Rob held out his hand and Chace shook it.

"Rob. Hey," Chace said as Rob pulled him into a half hug, still grasping his hand.

"This is the beginning of a beautiful friendship." Rob dragged out the word "beautiful."

Chace grinned. That reminded him of the night of Beautiful Whitney. "You know it." He looked around the apartment. High ceilings and hardwood floors. Spacious. The place had originally been built as a factory in the past century.

"So let's go get your crap so Whit can go home and purdy herself up for the night. Otherwise, we'll never get her to come out with us." Rob bounded out of the apartment and was already halfway down the stairs before Chace and Whitney made it to the door.

"I like that guy," Chace said.

"I thought you probably would," Whitney said.

"I didn't think you'd know anybody so…chill." She laughed.

"What's so funny?"

"Oh, nothing. Just…he said the same thing about you."

"Doesn't surprise me. After all, you're the girl who plans her planning." Chace laughed as she pretended to strangle him, savoring the feel of her gloveless hands against his skin. He barely noticed that they were cold.

Chapter 12: If I'm Going to Fall in Love with Someone, Please Don't Let It Be Him

It was good to be home, back in her condo, surrounded by all her favorite things. The sleek, black television with all the latest gadgets attached. One of her iMacs sat on her desk in the corner. The other one was in her office. She kicked off her shoes and sank her toes into her plush, custom-designed beige carpet. The carpet was a unique feature available only from the developer from whom she'd purchased her condo.

They were just things, objects. It was nice to have them, but that was all. Might as well enjoy what made the golden handcuffs golden.

She sank into her suede couch and placed her hands over her eyes, resting them for a moment. She'd spent almost every moment of her life over the past few days either with Chace or on the phone with him. It was taking its toll. She was feeling all sorts of things she couldn't afford to feel. She hadn't thought about work much at all in the past few days, and the fact that she hadn't scared the crap out of her.

She hadn't meant to fall asleep, but she realized she had when Erika's knock at the door woke her up.

Erika had come over so that they could get ready for the night together. They hadn't seen each other in over a week. So when Whitney opened the door and Erika hopped into the apartment, there was a lot of squealing and hugging involved.

"Is that your dress?" Whitney grabbed a garment bag from Erika.

"How was your trip? Yeah, that's it."

Whitney slid a slinky maroon dress out of the garment bag. "Fine. Oh, this dress is gorgeous. A.J.'s really not coming?"

Erika looked down and shook her head. "He doesn't feel like going out."

"Erika…"

"Hey. Show me your dress. You've been talking about this dress for weeks. I haven't seen it since it came back from the tailor's." Erika grabbed her hand and pulled her toward the bedroom.

Erika could do so much better, but she wouldn't listen to Whitney or Rob or anybody. She said that she was in love with A.J. and no matter what anyone said, they were made for each other. If that was love, Whitney wanted none of it.

But if Chace was love, she wanted all of it.

She couldn't let herself start thinking that way. The next thing she knew, she would be distracted from what was important in life, Chace would be over his rebound slump, and everything would be wrecked.

∽◌∾

Whitney and Erika went to Rob's place after they were done getting ready for their night out. Voices echoed around the vast, high-ceilinged apartment. Ulrich and Abbott stood on one side of the living room, laughing about something. Delaney was trying to get Rob to stand still so that she could straighten his bow-tie.

Erika wore her maroon dress, and Whitney wore a slinky black dress that hit perfectly at her ankles. It fit as if it'd been made for every curve of her body. She couldn't stop herself from hoping Chace liked it.

Erika walked over to Ulrich and Abbott. Whitney started to follow her, but then Chace walked into the living room. If she thought he'd looked good before, then she didn't know what to say about him that night. Where had he found a tux so quickly?

For a moment they just stood there staring at each other. She wanted to run her hands over his broad, black clad shoulders. The crisp white at his throat contrasted sharply with the black bowtie. He looked a lot different from the way he had in his fuzzy sweaters and threadbare T-shirts. Not that he hadn't looked good in those. Especially the T-shirts, leaving so little to the imagination, so closely molded to his pecks.

"You look amazing," Chace said, breaking her out of her lecherous reverie.

A grin spread across her face. "Thanks. You, too. Where'd you find a tux?" She moved her shawl from her shoulders to her elbows.

"Apparently, Delaney's brother and I are just about the same size. He doesn't like to rent them, so he had this one lying around." His gaze dropped from her face to the plunging neckline of her dress.

Whitney nodded, her eyes once again roaming over the fabric of the tux. Suddenly she was aware that there was no talking going on in the room. And she felt eyes all over her. She turned away from Chace and turned to her friends. They were all watching her and Chace with intent stares.

"What?" Whitney said.

They all mumbled responses and pretended they'd been looking in different directions. Whitney stepped away from Chace, very much aware of his eyes still on her back. She went over to Rob and Delaney. Apparently, Delaney had finally gotten the bowtie to do what she wanted it to do because she'd stopped readjusting it.

Rob put his arm around Whitney. "So. Did you convince our friend to come to her senses while you two were taking forever to get dressed and do whatever else it is you do that takes you so long to get ready to go anywhere?"

"You know the answer to that," Whitney said.

"Ah. Unfortunately, I do," he said. They laughed.

A tight smile twisted Delaney's thin lips. She slipped a skinny arm around Rob's waist. Delaney was jealous of Whitney for some reason. Rob had told her so. But he'd also told Delaney that friends came first and there was no way he'd stop being friends with Whitney for anyone. So Delaney tried to get over herself. Most of the time.

Delaney really had nothing to worry about, though. Whitney had known Rob long before Delaney had, and there'd been plenty of time for something to develop if it was going to. But it wasn't going to. Rob was the best guy friend she'd ever had and the idea of him being something else was just unfathomable—whether that be not in her life at all or in it as a boyfriend.

"Yeah. Mine was great until Delaney here dragged me through two states and the district, looking for what, I couldn't tell you," Rob said. "I was just counting down to the end of the horror." They all laughed except for Delaney, whose ears turned pink. Whitney would have never put her with Rob, but apparently they had something going she just couldn't see. They'd only been together a few months, but Rob was crazy about her.

"Well, I didn't mean to bore you," Delaney said, looking put out.

He squeezed her shoulders. "I was kidding. You really can't take a joke, huh?"

"Speaking of countdowns, shouldn't we get going soon?" Abbott, who'd wandered over to them, looked down at her watch. Ulrich followed her.

"Yeah. I didn't get all dressed up just to waste it on you people," Ulrich said, grinning.

"Okay, people, let's hustle," Rob said. "Since loser Chace there doesn't have a ticket, we have to get there early so we can be sure to get him in." He laughed and ducked as Chace took a lazy swipe at his head. The two of them walked out of the apartment together behind Whitney and Delaney, talking about decorating the apartment. From hearing them talk, it was hard to think they'd only met a few hours ago. And that they'd only been roommates for that length of time as well.

～⌘～

When they arrived Rob went to the front of the line to ask to speak to the promoter. Whitney pulled her shawl tight around her. Her black heels clicked against the sidewalk as she paced back and forth for warmth. The muffled sound of the bass from the music inside the club mixed with the chatter of people waiting in line. She made sure to keep at least one person between herself and Chace at all times. She didn't trust herself any closer to him than that.

Ulrich pulled Whitney aside. "What's the deal with you and this Chace?"

"Nothing. Why?" Whitney shrugged and tried to laugh off his words.

"No reason. Besides the fact that he moved to D.C. today from your town, right?" Ulrich glanced over his shoulder. He lowered his voice. "And you stare a hole into his head any time you think no one's looking."

"No, I don't." Did she?

"Whitney, you've never been the impulsive type. It seems a little suspect to me is all." Ulrich's brown eyes swept over her. "I'm just trying to look out for you." His handsome dark face clouded with suspicion.

"Okay." She looked at her hands, which were still wrapped in the ends of her shawl.

"Is he the reason you didn't check in with the office while you were gone?"

"I was on vacation. That's the reason. I don't have to check in with Kim every minute of my life. Gibson and Grey does not own me." Whitney suddenly felt defensive because Chace had been part of the reason. When she was with him, she just lost track of time. She lost track of—everything.

Ulrich laughed. "Oh, yes they do. They own both of us, at least until we make partner. You know Kim is looking for reasons to throw you under the bus. Don't make it easy for her."

Ulrich knew about Kim's animosity toward Whitney. She was surprised that no one else had picked up on it. She said, "I guess that means that you're checking in. Did she say anything about me?"

Ulrich shrugged and frowned—his trademark evasive move. "She grumbled a little. She's always grumbling, though. I think she's really antsy about this new case. Apparently it's the kind of thing that could make her look really good to the senior partners. I think she's going to be worse than usual on this one."

"Worse than usual? Is that even possible?"

He grinned. "I guess we'll find out Wednesday."

Whitney groaned. She didn't want to think about Wednesday.

He laughed. "It won't be so bad. We'll get through it together."

"We always have." She bumped her shoulder against his arm. "I don't know what I'd do if you weren't in my class."

"The *Kim face* would have probably killed you by now."

Whitney laughed. The *Kim face* was the look Kim gave them whenever she was pissed. The face was usually sighted several times a day by various people in the IP, or intellectual property, group. "Probably."

"So you're not going to tell me anything, huh?"

"About?"

"Your new friend over there." He nodded in Chace's direction.

"He's just a guy I know. Like you're a guy I know. And Rob. And many of our co-workers. Should I go on?"

"All I know is…those clowns you go out on a few dates with before you give up on them. I've never seen you act around any of them like I've seen you act tonight." Ulrich thoughtfully tapped his chin near the cleft in it. "I find that suspect. That's all."

Whitney shrugged. She didn't want to get into all of that with him. In fact, she didn't even want to think about it herself. She already felt like she was getting in too far too fast without Ulrich pointing out the painfully obvious.

∽◊∾

She caught Chace's eye across the room and gave him a shy half smile. He flashed her a dangerously sexy grin in return. The poor girl trying to keep his attention finally gave up and moved away to her next victim. Walking across the room, he held her gaze prisoner with his.

When he reached her, he put his hand low on her waist and whispered to her. "I'm going to ask this again. And I want a better answer this time. Will you dance with me?"

She could only nod and then allowed him to lead her out onto the dance floor. He pressed his body in close. The intimacy and the lack of space between them caused heat to rise in rolling waves inside of her. His hand on her bare shoulder, skin to skin, made her want to do more than dance with him.

"I've had my eyes on you all night. You know that?" His low, sexy voice was enough to seduce all on its own.

"Kind of hard not to notice." She swallowed hard against her mostly dry throat.

"I can't get enough of you. Is that going to be a problem for you?"

Whitney could only stare at him, her tongue working against a dry mouth. Her palms, pressed against his back, began to sweat.

He said, "So. You and Ulrich…"

"We're friends and co-workers. That's it."

"Good."

He leaned in close, so close that his hair brushed the side of her face as he spoke. "I think about you all the time. Can't get you out of my head. Not a problem for me, though. I want you there."

She still couldn't speak. She was trying to wrap her mind around what his words really meant. He shouldn't have been saying those things. They'd known each other for a week. He'd only been single for a week. Most importantly, she shouldn't have been feeling those same things he was talking about.

"You're so beautiful, but you've known I think that since the first time I met you."

She laughed a loud, nervous laugh as she remembered "Beautiful Whitney."

"But you're also sexy. So smart and together. That makes you even sexier. I'm so glad you're in my life now. The only thing I'd like to change is making you more in it." His fingers found the nape of her neck, and she felt a guilty pleasure from his touch.

"Chace, I…" She forgot what she was going to say with him so close. His hands rested low on her hips. His nose grazed the tender skin under her earlobe.

"What would you say if I told you I want more of you?" His ice blue eyes scanned her face. "If I don't want to just be your friend?"

She finally found her voice. Just in time. "That you just got out of a two-year relationship a week ago."

He chuckled softly and pressed his cheek to hers. "I thought you'd probably say something like that. That's why I was trying to keep it to myself. I held out pretty good until tonight. You and that dress caused me to come all undone."

Held out pretty good? Meaning he'd had those feelings for how long? If he kept the conversation going in that direction, she was leaving him alone on the dance floor.

Instead, he changed the subject completely. "Hey, I'm good at that, huh? Killing the convo between us? Let's talk about something that doesn't make you cringe."

She didn't know how to follow that statement, so she said nothing.

"I've told you about my friend Ethan, right?" Chace said.

She nodded. "The daredevil, right?"

He laughed. "Something like that. He's in New Zealand right now. He told me last night that he almost got himself killed yet again."

She grinned. "What did he do?"

Good. She could handle talking about Ethan. She could handle almost anything except for what he'd almost done.

Chapter 13: Midnight Kiss

Whitney went to the table her friends had staked out and sat across from Erika. Erika drummed each of the manicured nails of her left hand on the table, one after the other, slowly and repeatedly. Her right hand was in a fist under her chin.

"Heard from him tonight?" Whitney asked.

Erika shook her head.

"Big surprise."

"He's just stressed because he can't find a job."

She snorted. "That would make sense if he were actually looking for one."

Erika stopped drumming her fingers. "I know what you guys think about him."

"That he mooches off you and treats you like crap even though you would do anything in the world for him?" She put her hand over Erika's. "You know what I want to know?"

"Probably not."

"I want to know why you put up with it. Don't you think you deserve better?" She moved her chair closer to her friend's. "I know that you do."

Erika pushed her red clutch back and forth between her hands on the table. "He loves me. I know it. He's just—we're going through a rough spot. When he finds a job, things'll get better."

"He's been living there two years and hasn't helped you with rent once. Hasn't even helped you with so much as groceries." It would be a miracle if things did improve. The two of them seemed to always be going through a "rough spot." It was always "when" and "if" and "maybe" with those two.

"I just don't want to believe I'm wrong about him," Erika said.

"It's okay if you are," Whitney said. "Sometimes these things are just beyond our control." She put a hand on Erika's back. Erika hated to admit defeat. Especially when it came to men. And for some reason, she really seemed to love foolish A.J., no matter how outrageously he acted.

Erika waved away Whitney's words. "Enough about me. What about you and this Chace? You can keep denying it all you want, but I can just feel the attraction between you two." Erika grabbed Whitney's hands and leaned in for a conspiratorial whisper. "I've never seen you look at a guy like you look at him."

It was her turn to be dismissive. "It's nothing. If I feel anything for him, it's infatuation. He's fun to look at." She glanced across the room as if she had to confirm that fact. He waved. She waved back and fought the urge to wave him over to their table.

"No. I've seen you with some pretty boys before, but he's more than a pretty boy. More importantly,

153

he's more than a pretty boy to you. You and I both know it," Erika said.

"Yeah, yeah." She laughed off her friend's words, but she was secretly afraid that Erika was right.

◦◦◦

Chace and Whitney stood near the edge of the dance floor as midnight approached. They were taking a break from dancing and waiting for the countdown to begin. Erika had gone outside to call A.J.—argue with him was more like it. The others were scattered around the club.

Someone cut the music. Heads turned toward the large projector screen near the D.J. booth that displayed the ball in Times Square.

"I've never been kissed on New Year's," she said as the countdown began, voices chanting numbers all around them. The dark room packed with people holding up plastic champagne flutes filled with amber liquid.

Chace was about to reply when the entire space around them erupted in a din of cheering.

"Happy New Year!" The shout went out around the room.

He leaned in and pressed his hand to her cheek. His lips rested against hers for a moment, soft and warm. He then opened her lips with his just enough so that she could taste the tip of his tongue. After brushing soft kisses along her bottom lip, he pulled back. She leaned slightly toward him when he did, wanting more.

"Now you have. Happy New Year," he said.

She stood there, just staring, full of desire. So full of it that she couldn't even wrap her mind around wishing him a Happy New Year back. That was it? That couldn't be it. No matter what waited on the other side of that kiss—the kiss she'd expected to get—she had to have it. She wouldn't be cheated.

"I'm sorry. That was out of line. I should have never—"

"Shh." She locked her fingers behind his neck.

He raised his eyebrows, perplexity shadowing his angled, handsome face.

"Kiss me again. I want to touch and taste every corner of your mouth."

He wrapped his arms around her, pulling her close. His lips moved over hers with a painful slowness. He seemed to want to move faster, but he took his time and gave her what she'd asked for. He acted as if he was trying to control himself the way she was.

She buried her hands in his hair, kneading her fingers into his scalp. This won a small groan from him, and he pressed his lips tighter to hers. She wanted to press him against the wall and wrap her legs around him, but she was still aware enough that they were in a roomful of people not to do that. It was a good thing they were in that room of people because she wanted their kiss to lead to more so badly that her whole body ached.

When they had to come up for air, Chace pressed her tightly to his body.

She knew it was stupid to do that with a man who'd just confessed he wanted more from her. And maybe he really was confused and didn't know any better. She guessed a broken heart could do something like that to a person. In any case, she knew he was rebounding even if he didn't. She wouldn't allow herself to get carried away.

Now she would have to explain what'd just happened to the friends she knew had seen. They'd been keeping curious eyes on Chace and Whitney all night.

But could she say that kiss hadn't been worth it? Not a chance. She buried her face in his chest, closed her eyes, and smiled. For the moment, she was just going to live in the fantasy. For as long as she could get away with it.

Chapter 14: Gotta Have a Day Job

Wednesday morning Chace sat on the couch in his new apartment, browsing through websites, looking for new cameras. Whitney and being in D.C. had inspired him to get serious about his photography. He also had a webpage open with job listings on it, telling himself he was looking for a day job. Rob had left early that morning, off to do whatever small business owners did, Chace guessed. Apparently Rob was trying to open a physical store soon, so he was really busy with things related to that. He'd gotten his loan from the bank a while ago, and he was overseeing renovations on the space he'd leased for his store. The place was supposed to open in less than two months.

He smiled, feeling his whole body warm when he saw that Whitney had emailed him back. They'd been emailing back and forth ever since she'd gotten on the metro that morning for her first day back to work since her vacation. He already missed her. They'd spent all of New Year's Day together. They hadn't talked about the kiss, but he hadn't been able to stop thinking about it. Or about what he'd wanted that kiss to lead to. Whether he was allowed to say it or not, he was falling for her. Hard.

The way she held her head when she laughed. How she put her hand on the side of her neck, right in the delicate, delicious curve of it when she was thinking. The way she scrunched up her lips when she was disgusted by something. All these small things and more he'd noticed and adored over the past few days.

After holding her in his arms a few moments, he wanted more. He wanted to hold her in them forever. But Kelly was screwing things up for him even though she was supposedly out of the picture. Because of Kelly, Whitney didn't think he was serious. Because of Kelly, Whitney thought he just wanted to use her as a way to get over the girl who'd broken his heart and moved on.

Truthfully, he'd moved on from Kelly pretty quickly after she'd left. He'd just been so disgusted with her, it hadn't taken much. Once her stuff was gone, he'd been able to exorcise the rest of her, too. He'd cared about her, sure, but he didn't have any patience at all for what she'd done to him.

Now Whitney. There was someone he could trust. Someone real and beautiful and so full of life when he could get her to loosen up enough so that he could pry it out of her. He admired her drive in life, but he was worried that maybe she'd let that drive take over her life. Crowd everything out but work.

Chace was about to email Whitney back when he saw that he had an email flagged "urgent" from Kelly.

On the chance that it was, he opened it. He nearly dropped his computer when he did. A few sentences had the potential to change everything. It read:

I'm pregnant. I don't know if it's yours or Hank's. Haven't said anything to him yet. I'm scared, Chace. Call me.

He just wanted to be done with Kelly. Kelly preggers? No good, no good, no good. He'd always wanted kids, but not like this. If anyone was going to have his kids now, he wanted it to be Whitney. Not lying, cheating, scheming Kelly.

At that moment, his cell rang. He picked it up and looked at the caller ID. Ethan. And from Ethan's cell phone. He'd forgotten Ethan got back in the country that day. He put the phone to his ear.

"Hello," Chace mumbled while reading Kelly's short, horrifying email over and over again.

"Hey, bud. I'm back in the R.I.C., good ole Richmond. How goes it? Haven't heard from you in a while. I tried to Skype you a few times."

"Yeah. Sorry about that."

"What's wrong, Chace? You sound weird."

Chace's stomach clenched up on him and he pushed his laptop aside. He didn't know how to tell Ethan, or if he should. He'd just found out himself and hadn't had a chance to digest the information. He couldn't be with her again, no matter what. He'd take care of the kid if it was his, but he was done with Kelly even if she wanted him back. Done. Forever. He'd moved on to a woman who didn't realize he had yet.

"Chace? You still there?"

"Uh, yeah, bud. I'm fine. How was your flight? How many movies did you watch? Anything good?"

"Chace. I've known you too long to buy these lies. What's up, man? What is up?"

He felt like he was going to die, but that didn't feel appropriate to say.

"Is this about Kelly? Whatever it is man, she's not worth it. You're free. Please don't go back into the darkness."

"She's pregnant," Chace blurted out.

This time, the silence on the line was on Ethan's end.

"Ethan, man, why do these things happen to me?" Chace clasped his hand to his forehead. He then read the email to Ethan verbatim.

"That's crazy, man."

"It gets worse. I think I'm in love."

"With Kelly?"

"No." Chace took a deep breath and told Ethan everything about Whitney.

When he was done, Ethan said, "Man, I don't know what to say."

"Don't say I don't know what I'm talking about or I'm crazy. I heard that already from Whitney."

"Smart lady."

"The smartest, most wonderful, most gorgeous creature in the world. That's what makes this even more screwed up than it would be in the first place. But anyway, I don't wanna hear that mess. I know how I feel. I've dated a lot of girls. I've rebounded before. I know me well enough to know this is real. This is love."

"Well, I don't know what to say to you then, man."

"Just say something that doesn't make me want to jump out of a window right now."

"I went to Australia to spend a day or two before I flew out. I almost got bit by one of the deadliest snakes in the world. Twice. I woulda made Erwin proud, man." That was why Chace was glad to have Ethan for a friend. His best friend.

Chace laughed. He laughed so hard he almost dropped the phone. He'd needed that worse than anything else in the world. "You're an idiot."

"Hey, you act like this is news to you."

"True."

"You should have been there, man. The most amazing experience of my life. I swear."

"You say that after every trip."

"That's because it's always true."

They talked for a while longer, and by the time Chace got off the phone, he felt a little better. Until he realized he couldn't put off talking to Kelly any longer. Even though he had no idea what to say to her.

With a heavy sigh, he picked up the phone and dialed Kelly's number.

"Finally. All it took was me getting knocked up to get you on the phone," Kelly said.

Chace didn't laugh at her attempt at a joke because it wasn't funny. "What is this, Kelly? You were on the pill." Chace shuddered, thinking that he wished he'd used a condom, too, but he'd stopped doing that after a few months of what he'd thought was a monogamous relationship. How was he supposed to know his girlfriend was sleeping around?

"You act like I did it on purpose."

"All I know is I want this to be over. How long until you can find out whose kid it is?"

"Why are you being so mean?"

"What are you talking about? I'm just asking questions."

"You could sound a little less angry."

He laughed mirthlessly. "What do you want me to say? You're having my baby? What a beautiful way to say you love me?"

"Fine. Be an ass. I can't get tested until the second trimester. I asked the doctor."

"How pregnant are you?"

"Six weeks. I was late and I kept putting off taking the test, hoping I'd get my period. Finally, I took one—actually three—and the doctor confirmed it this morning."

Chace put his forehead in his free hand. "This is unbelievable."

"So it'll be at least another two months before we'll know."

"Will you start showing before that?"

"There's a good chance, I guess. But it'll probably just look like I need to lay off the cookies or something. I dunno. I haven't known many pregnant women. But, well, there is this other procedure they can do. It makes me kinda squeamish to think about, but they can do it at ten weeks. So in a month from now. But I really don't want to do that one."

Chace groaned. This had to be the worst conversation of his life.

"Chace?"

Chace cleared his mind of the memory of his father and focused on the crisis at hand. "Well, what do you want to do if it *is* mine?"

"I don't want anything to mess up things with Hank," she said. Of course her mind went to herself first. That was just the way Kelly operated.

"And I don't want to mess up things with—never mind." Chace hesitated to tell her about Whitney.

"What? Chace, are you seeing somebody?"

"That's none of your business, and I don't even see why you would care." He tapped his fingers against his knee.

"Chace, I still care about you and I don't want to see you jumping into anything. You know you're kind of impulsive and you don't think things through all the time. Are you sure you should be getting into a new relationship already?"

"If I am in a relationship, I'm grown, Kelly. Even though you rarely treated me that way. I can make my own decisions and I know what's best for me. And were you thinking of how much you care about me while you were screwing around with that old man who's abandoning his family for you? Were you thinking of his family when you did it, huh? What about them? Who's going to care about them?"

"That's not fair."

"What is? You drop this bomb on me that you're pregnant and it might be mine, and then you want to talk about fair?"

"It's pretty obvious you don't want anything to do with me and I want to start a family with Hank. Maybe we should just pretend it's Hank's either way. I just wanted you to know. I wanted you to have the option. But if you want to just—we could just—pretend."

If the baby was his, he wouldn't let the three of them live that lie—the child not even aware of living it. "I couldn't do that to my kid. If it's mine, I would want to be in its life. I understand you're with Hank, and more power to you guys. I don't want to be in your life. Just the baby's."

"So what's the next step?"

"I guess we have to wait until you can get this paternity test," Chace said, wishing he could just disappear into the couch cushions and never come back out.

"I guess."

"You gonna tell Hank about any of this?"

Kelly was silent for a moment before saying, "If the test comes out—wrong. I mean. Well. There might not even be anything to tell him."

"Well, I gotta go. I have a lot to do today," he said, not wanting to be on the phone with her any longer.

"Okay. Um, Chace?"

"Yeah?"

"Can I call you sometime? Will you answer the phone?"

"If it's about the baby, yes. If you keep calling for things other than that, no. I know you want to be friends or whatever, but I don't. Please respect that I'm moving on with my life."

"Being friends doesn't mean we can't move on."

"It does to me."

She sighed heavily on the other end. "Bye, Chace."

"Bye." He tossed his phone on the coffee table, curled up into a ball on the couch, and pulled a nearby throw pillow over his head.

Chapter 15: Gibson and Grey

Whitney walked down the sidewalk, headed to her building. The cold wind actually felt good cutting against her face. She was still warm from the over-crowded rush hour train she'd taken to Farragut West and from the brisk pace of her walk after getting off the metro two stops too early. She'd needed the exercise since she'd skipped the gym for a few days, and the train had gotten oppressively full. Besides, she needed at least some distraction from emailing Chace back every two seconds. She didn't want him to think she was constantly waiting for the next email from him. Whether or not it was true, she didn't want him to think that.

She pressed her fingers lightly to her lips, almost unaware she was doing it. The kiss had felt so good. Too good. His had been more than a hurried, lustful, just-wanting-to-get-to-other-more-interesting-things kind of kiss. Tongue moving slowly, lips thoughtful. Mouth promising what she'd never have believed from words.

It was going to be hard not to get attached. Very hard. Chace could probably make a rock fall in love with him. Even if he hadn't been turning on the charm—which maybe he didn't even know how not to—she doubted she would have been able to get him out of her mind.

Not only was he gorgeous, he was sweet, funny, kind. Nothing like the jerks it'd always been easy for her to turn down before. She'd never come across someone real before. Not that she'd been looking. But, looking or not, Chace had literally come out of nowhere, and she had the feeling he wasn't going anywhere.

Suddenly, she had a strong desire for it to be just them again. The way it had been in the club. Her arms wrapped around him. Just kissing the way they had on New Year's. Always. Feeling his skin—his warmth beneath her fingers. Pulling back only to look into the endless depths of those ice blue eyes. Fire and ice in a very non-Frost way. Or maybe that was exactly what Frost had meant.

Whitney brought herself back to the present as she opened the ornate glass door with the gold handle and walked into her office building. After saying hello to the security guards, she walked over to the elevator bank and pushed the number for her floor. Her firm had the top ten floors of the building. No longer able to resist, she pulled out her phone and responded to Chace's most recent email.

It wasn't anything important. And neither was her reply. Mostly, she thought it was just that they liked the idea of being able to communicate even though they were unable to see each other for the first time since a couple days after Christmas. She tried not to keep track of such things, but she couldn't help it.

She wanted to kiss him again. Catch his bottom lip gently with her teeth and hold it there. Just hold it gently. Feel connected to him in a very intimate way. See, she shouldn't have even been thinking that way. He just did something to her. Something unnatural. That same thing also made her think about laying on a blanket in a park with him that spring, her head on his chest, their fingers intertwined, just tangled up in each other with no desire to go anywhere outside of that moment—that sphere of intensity. It was odd. She'd never had thoughts about a guy like that. Not even any of her crazy crushes in high school. Yeah, she'd had dreams of lust. But never intimacy.

Again, Whitney had to bring herself back to the here and now as she walked out of the elevators and onto her floor.

She said hello to people she passed and asked them how their Christmases had been, while heading to her office. When she got to her office area, she greeted her assistant, Bettina, who handed her a stack of folders.

"Hi, Whitney. There's more on your desk. And Kim is on the war path. She wants to see you right away," Bettina said, pushing her black hair away from her face. Bettina was just over five feet tall. Other than the height thing, she could have probably been a model. She had slight, fine bone structure, thin eyebrows, high cheekbones, and bright green eyes.

Whitney took the stack of folders from her. She thought for just a moment about trying to fix Bettina up with Chace to take away the temptation, but quickly realized that she'd never be able to do something like that. Regardless of what she said or wanted to think, she didn't want to imagine Chace being with anybody but her.

"You have a ton of messages, there are some inter-office memos you should probably read, there are a couple of articles highlighted in the most recent copy of that one IP journal we subscribe to that you always read, there's a meeting at two about the case. You know the one. Bevyx. Everybody's talking about it. Oh, and you have a lunch meeting with the team. Apparently, it's a strategy planning session for the case."

"Okay, let me sort through some of this stuff and then I'm going to see Kim."

"So hold your calls?"

"Please."

Bettina smiled. "Welcome back, Whitney."

"Thanks," Whitney muttered.

Bettina laughed and closed the door after her.

Whitney rifled through the folders on her desk and scanned her work email. At least she didn't have anything urgent waiting for her. Not wanting to put Kim off any longer, she took a deep breath and walked to the woman's office.

Kim's assistant let her right in, telling her Kim had been expecting her. Kim was a junior partner and supposedly Whitney's mentor on the partnership track. She thought that mentors were supposed to help. Kim seemed like an adversary most of the time. Maybe as the only black female junior partner in the D.C. office, Kim had a chip on her shoulder. Well, that didn't mean she should expect Whitney to help bear it.

Kim looked up at her briefly with beady black eyes set in a dark brown face. Her black hair was pulled tightly away from her face in the bun she always wore. She was writing something on a legal pad, and she gestured with her free hand for Whitney to take a seat.

When she was done writing, Kim capped her pen and set it on the desk. She sat up straighter in her chair and folded her hands beneath her chin. "Whitney, I've never known you to have trouble following directions before. Is there a problem?"

She was jolted by the abruptness. Kim was being even more...Kim than usual. No small talk, how was your Christmas, anything.

"I'm sorry?" She had no idea what the woman was talking about.

"When I ask for a task to be completed, I expect it to be done. The associates who wrote the memo I asked you to review sent it to you on New Year's Day.

That was two days ago. I haven't heard one word from you about it."

All of the blood drained out of Whitney's face. She'd forgotten all about that memo. She hadn't looked through her many emails thoroughly yet. She'd been too busy playing cutesy with Chace.

"I—I'm sorry. I'll take care of it right now. I'll go back to my office and—"

Kim held up her hand. "No need. I've already given it to Cynthia. She has drive. She really wants to make partner. I'm beginning to question whether you do or not."

"Of course I do. It's the most important thing—"

"Do you even know the facts of the case, Whitney? Do you even know the parties' names? How about just the name of our client, Whitney? Do you know that?"

Even though she knew, she didn't answer. She was trying to keep her temper from flaring. Plus, Kim probably wouldn't have let her finish her sentence anyway.

"Vacations are no time to play around unless you're happy where you are. Now, if you're happy being a senior associate, fine. Enjoy your cookie making and caroling or whatever it is you do down there in Virginia. But this is a huge case." Kim's nostrils flared, and she tapped her pen against her legal pad. "Andersen says this is the sort of thing that could be in casebooks, law students reading it for decades to come. This could bring the firm back from the slump we've been fighting since that little embezzling scandal last year. New York is watching us on this one." Kim sat back in her chair, tapping her pen on her desk.

The firm was headquartered in New York. The big guys were there. The sons of Gibson and Grey themselves, even.

Whitney knew that she'd really screwed up this time. She'd never given Kim a real reason to berate and belittle her before so she'd always been able to brush off Kim's words in the past. But this time was different. Whitney was dependable. More than that, she'd always gone beyond the extra mile. So, she'd messed up once. It was demeaning. Kim was acting like she hadn't always given every part of her heart, mind, and soul to that job. She worked at least sixty hours a week. She rarely took any vacation time except at the holidays, leaving well over half her vacation time untouched every year. Kim didn't have the right to treat her like this. Tears pricked the backs of her eyes.

"I'm sorry, Kim. It won't happen again." She bit back her emotion.

"It better not," Kim said. The hard set of her jaw matched the tone of her voice. She straightened a stack of paper on her desk with a slow deliberateness that was meant to be a sign that she was dismissing Whitney.

"I'm going to go get caught up on everything right now. Is there anything else I should be doing for the case before our lunch meeting?"

"Making sure you know what it is. That's all. You're capable of reading a file, aren't you? I mean, I never had any doubts before, but now…"

"I'm on top of it. Don't worry," Whitney said, managing to keep her voice from cracking.

She didn't talk to Chace for the rest of the day. She was too worried about work to think about sending him any more emails or even to notice that he'd stopped sending emails to her.

Chapter 16: Dinner in French

Whitney decided to take the firm's car service home. She was tired, cranky, and didn't feel like putting up with the metro that day. When the car pulled up in front of her building, she was startled to find Chace sitting on the steps outside of it.

The air was sharp, cold, crisp. The sky was clear—completely cloudless. The stars weren't completely drowned out by the city lights that night.

"How long have you been here?" Whitney looked down at her watch. It was past nine.

Chace shrugged. "A little while."

She shivered and pulled her overcoat tighter. "I usually work late. I would have told you that if you'd called so you wouldn't have to just sit out here."

"I know. Rob told me that. I was just wandering around the city. And I ended up on the metro. Then I ended up here."

"Okay," she said. Chace seemed different and to have had just as bad a day as she had. Maybe the reality of the breakup was settling in on him.

"Yeah. I know you're probably tired and everything. I just wanted to see you. I can go if you want," Chace said, standing and shoving his hands into the pockets of his fleece jacket. For the first time, Whitney noticed a camera on the steps near where he'd been sitting. He stooped to pick it up.

"You were taking pictures today?"

"Yeah." He turned his camera over a few times in his hands.

She smiled. "Come on up for a while." She took out her keys and headed for the door to her building.

Finally, her favorite grin came out and spread across his face. "Okay." He jogged up the steps behind her.

They went up to her condo and the first thing Chace did was take off his shoes and socks—shockingly, he must have thought it too cold for flip-flops. Which was good. She didn't want him getting frostbite. He sank his toes into the carpet.

"Man, I really love this carpet."

"It's okay." She stifled a yawn. The effects of her long day were catching up with her quickly. "Listen, I was gonna order some dinner. You want something?"

"Why don't we go out to eat? That is, if you're not too tired?"

She looked at him and smiled. She was tired and aching and she'd really just wanted to stuff down some dinner, take another look at some cases she'd had the paralegals pull for her, and crash. At least that was what she wanted until she saw Chace. Looking at his bright, eager face, so different from the dark look he'd worn when she'd first walked up to him in front of her building, she really did want to go out with him.

"Sure. Let me just change out of this suit," Whitney said.

"Great," Chace said, sitting down on her couch. She handed him the remote to the television, which she'd left on the bar that morning, and then went to her room to change.

Once Whitney was dressed and ready, she drove them out to her favorite restaurant in Georgetown. The place was a cozy little café she loved. And it was reasonably priced enough so that she wouldn't feel too badly if Chace wouldn't let her pay for him.

Once they were seated, the server brought them plates of bread and olive oil.

"This place is nice. Very…Frenchy," Chace said as he looked around the small European-style café.

She dipped her bread into the oil. "I love this place. You will, too. Just wait until you have the soup." She hummed along with the Edith Piaf song that was playing.

"Which one?"

"Any. It doesn't matter. They'll all make you beg for more."

"I'll bet."

The way he said it was probably innocent enough. Her lecherous mind was most likely responsible for making her hear it in a way that was not. When she looked up, Chace was looking down at his menu. Yes, just her imagination.

"How's the job hunt going?" Whitney put her menu aside. She already knew she wanted the quiche of the day and a salad. She wanted to keep it light that late at night.

"Um, okay, I guess. I'm going to go by some places tomorrow. Drop off some résumés, applications. I just sent a few emails and made a few calls today. I figure in-person would be a better bet."

Whitney nodded. It probably was. Who wouldn't hire Chace on the spot? Attractive. Friendly. Charming.

"How was your day at work?"

"The first few days back after vacation playing catch-up are never fun." She didn't want to get into the Kim drama. She wanted to forget it herself. "You settling into the apartment okay?"

"Yeah. Living with Rob is the ultimate," he said. "It's like there are two of me. We're going to get some stuff for the apartment this weekend."

"That should be a disaster." She laughed, picturing the sight.

"Funny you should say that. 'Cause I'm planning on trapping you into going with us."

"You are?"

"Sure. You can't trust two guys with these things. You just said so yourself. That is…if you don't have to work?"

"I can probably squeeze you in for a few hours." A smile played across her lips as her eyes connected with his light blue ones. He dipped his bread into the oil. Then, he reached across the table and teased it across her lower lip.

"Any time I can be squeezed in with you? Is a good time," Chace said. There was no denying the heat in his words that time. He slid the bread between her teeth.

When Whitney realized she'd picked the menu up and was fanning herself with it, she put it down immediately and started looking out over the tables, muttering about wondering where their server was. She felt Chace's stare, but refused to look at him.

After dinner they drifted in and out of bars for hours, mostly just talking. She had a drink or two. They stayed out too late, but she barely noticed the time passing. When the bars closed, they headed back to her condo. She had so much fun with him, she didn't even know how it'd gotten to be nearly three in the morning while they were talking on her couch.

"You could stay the night on the couch," Whitney offered. "The Metro isn't running any longer and sometimes cabbies get cranky about going into the District from here."

"I'll be okay. I really don't think it'd be a good idea for me to spend the night here. Too much temptation." The way he said the word "temptation" sent shivers all over her body. Her mind went back to their New Year's Eve kiss and suddenly, with every part of her hot for him, she didn't think it was a good idea, either.

"At least let me call a cab before you go downstairs."

"Sure thing. Thanks."

"I had a really great time tonight, Chace. Thanks for coming over. I'm glad you did." She picked up her phone.

"I'm glad you're glad." Chace brushed a kiss against her cheek.

She looked at him, having to hold herself back from jumping all over him. She tightened her grip on the phone to keep from dropping it.

"The best," he said, brushing his hand against her cheek.

"Well, I, uh, better call that cab. It's getting late." The words were awkward, clumsy. Because they weren't what she wanted to say. She wanted him to stay. With her. And not on the couch. And that wasn't the kind of thought she should have been having. He was rebounding.

She was already messing up at work and didn't need any further distractions. All she'd wanted in life was to get with a huge law firm and be successful. So close to partner, she couldn't screw up now. She owed it to herself, her mom, and even her grandparents. She had to be everything her father hadn't been. That was the only way to make his mistakes less hard for all of them. She had a lot of broken hearts to mend. She didn't need Chace interfering, messing with hers. Clouding her mission.

"Yeah." Chace nodded, looking down at the phone in her hand before repeating himself. "Yeah."

When the uncomfortable silence had gone on for too long, Whitney said, "I'm going to get a glass of water after I make this call. You want anything?" He looked at her with greedy eyes, and her face roasted for what felt like the millionth time that night. "From the kitchen, I mean?"

He shook his head.

She went to the refrigerator, arranging for the cab as she did. She put down the phone and grabbed the water pitcher with a shaking hand, nerves and hormones raging inside of her.

"Whitney?" he called into the kitchen.

"Yeah?" Her voice quavered despite her efforts to make it not do that.

"Would it have been different? If there was no Kelly? Would there still be this—uh—distance between us? Making us not able to get to the thing I think we both want?"

Whitney pretended not to hear his question, but she did let out a soft curse when she realized she'd overfilled her water glass and water was spilling onto her black, sable, and gray marble countertop.

☙❧

The next morning Whitney refused to believe that her alarm clock said ten o'clock when she rolled over and looked at it. She was sure she'd set her alarm the night before. She must have turned it off and gone back to sleep without realizing she'd ever done it. She hadn't done that in ages.

"Crap," Whitney muttered, jumping out of bed. "Kim already hates me. This is not going to go over well."

She'd meant to get up early that morning and read over some stuff she'd put off reading the night before when she'd gone to bed. Instead, she'd done the exact opposite. Even if she drove into the city instead of taking the train, she was still going to be really late. Still, she'd save a little bit of time. Maybe Kim would give her a chance to explain instead of killing her on the spot.

Whitney undressed while talking to her assistant on speakerphone, telling her she'd be in as soon as she could be. She then took a shower and got ready faster than she ever had in her life, almost leaving her condo without tossing her work shoes—a pair of black pumps—into her bag, she was so distracted.

She got into her car, juggling her coffee thermos, laptop bag, a briefcase full of papers, and her purse. And made it to the office in record time.

Still, when she got to her desk, she could tell it was going to be bad. Even before Bettina gave her the message from Kim written on a memo pad sheet in red ink: *Come to my office as soon as you get in. Urgent.*

∽༚∽

Chace opened the package at the post office, too excited to wait until he got home. His grin widened as he turned the camera over and over in his hands. Again, Ebay hadn't failed him. This was the third camera he'd ordered in a week, and he hoped his credit card would keep supporting him for the next few weeks.

The Nikon F6 was a beauty. He hadn't been able to resist at least one film camera even though the digitals he'd ordered would probably give him better shots. Film cameras were his weakness. There was nothing like developing a black and white photo in a darkroom. It was almost a spiritual experience.

He loved everything about photography. From the feel of the camera in his hands to looking through the viewfinder to the silent solace of the dark room. Finding the perfect subject. Light and perspective. The way those two things could come together in a breathtaking instant without any warning and you'd better have a camera ready when they did. Because it wouldn't last for long and there was a certain thrill in that.

He still needed to get some lenses, and he was about to bid on a couple he was watching online. He didn't like to start bidding too many days before the end of the bid period. Still, he'd decided to stop by a nearby camera store he'd noticed and have a look. He liked holding them in his hands, getting a visceral feel for them.

Entering the small camera store near the post office, he noticed he was one of only two customers at the moment. He walked right over to the Single Lens Reflex, or S.L.R., and Digital Single-Lens Reflex, or D.S.L.R., lenses since the digital camera he'd gotten the other day would work with the D.S.L.R.'s. He gave a low whistle when he saw the price and was once again thankful for online auctioning.

He knew he was spending way too much and hoped he wouldn't go through his savings and credit before he got his first paycheck from his new job, but he couldn't help it. He'd just gotten hired at a small catering business. It'd been started by a woman who used to work at the Hawk and Dove.

He was obsessed with photography, especially now that he was someplace where his dream could actually come true. And he had someone in his life who inspired him so much. Whitney was his muse without even knowing it. She just made him see the world in ways he could have never imagined without her.

"Can I help you with anything, sir?" A balding, fortyish man walked up to him. His stomach protruded over the waist of his pants and he waddled a little when he walked.

"I was just looking at lenses. Just got some new cameras." Chace patted the box he carried under his arm that contained his camera.

"Have anything in particular in mind?"

"I like this Nikon wide angle, but I'm trying to decide if I should get the rectilinear or the full-frame or the four-thirds. I mean, I want them both eventually, but there's the money thing to consider, you know? Then, there's length to consider." Chace frowned. "I'm probably going to need a better computer, too. This is getting really expensive really quickly."

"You a photographer?" he asked.

"I'm trying to be," Chace said. "I'm Chace, by the way."

"Archie," the man said, his moustache moving up with his smile.

"Well, Archie, I've been thinking of going professional for a while, and I'm ready to give it a real try now," he said. "I was thinking of trying to put together something to show a gallery maybe."

"So you say you have a camera," Archie said.

He grinned. "I've bought three in the last two weeks." Chace told the man about his online buying spree and his new equipment.

"You seem pretty serious about this, to put down all this money into high-end equipment. Good choices, though."

"Thanks."

"I belong to a local photography club. They're pretty good. I can give you their information." Archie began rifling through his wallet. "We maintain a pretty good blog if you want to have a look-see at some of our work. We meet on Wednesday nights." Archie handed him a business card.

"That sounds great," he said, getting excited at the prospect of talking craft with people. Being isolated in River Run for the past two years, he hadn't come across many people who used cameras for much more than memorializing birthdays and baptisms. He definitely wanted to know more about the club.

Chace walked out of the store with a list of lenses Archie recommended. He saw a bistro that Whitney had pointed out as one of her favorites in the city when she'd given him a tour the other night. He pulled his small digital camera out of his pocket—a simple one he kept with him just in case a perfect shot crept up on him when he wasn't expecting it—and took a few shots of the place. Looking back through the shots on the screen on the back of the camera, an idea started to form in his mind. Pleased with himself, he put the camera back in his pocket, hurrying toward the metro. He had to get home and bid on some of those lenses and look up the ones Archie had recommended.

He wanted to do something nice for Whitney because, for one thing, she was everything to him, whether she wanted to believe it or not. But another part of the problem was the guilt he felt.

He couldn't tell her about the baby. That would just scare her off all the way. She was already acting iffy and kept hinting and poking, trying to see if he still had feelings for Kelly. If he told her about the baby, what little progress he'd made with her would be done for. Just over. She would tell him that meant for sure he and Kelly were getting back together. She'd probably never even hear that it might not be his. And that even if it was, he still wanted to be with her. That he never wanted to be with Kelly again.

So for now, he was just going to do as much as he could to prove himself to her until he could figure out a way to tell her about Kelly being pregnant that wouldn't send her running in the opposite direction. Maybe if he did that, she wouldn't be able to run away from him. He didn't know what he would do if she did run. Didn't want to think about it.

Instead, he would think about Whitney's collage. And his cameras. And all of the good things happening or about to happen.

Chapter 17: Not Gonna

Erika gave boxing lessons at a local gym that she owned. Whitney often got free workout sessions as a result. With the way work had been going lately, she really needed to work out some aggression. She'd been grateful when she'd called and Erika had said she had an open slot.

"Dang, girl. You trying to break my hand?" Erika joked after one of Whitney's jabbing sessions. "Something's got you more keyed up than usual. What is it? Work? Chace?"

"Why would you say Chace? Why would you automatically assume that?" Whitney said, aware that her response probably gave her away.

"Just that you spend every moment of free time with him these days. Not that you have all that much of it. If he's not with you when I see you, you're talking about him. And that's not even mentioning your hot New Year's kiss. That was something. I'm surprised you didn't burn down the whole club with the fire from that kiss." Erika put her punch mitts aside, and they went over to the punching bags.

"I do not want to talk about that kiss." Whitney punctuated every word with a blow to the punching bag that Erika held for her.

"So you keep telling me."

"And what do you mean, every moment? He's only been in town a couple weeks and he doesn't know anyone. What am I supposed to do, just abandon him?"

"Don't get so defensive. I was just making an observation."

Whitney stopped punching and pulled off her gloves with a heavy sigh. "I'm sorry. It's just—work is stressing me out. And Aunt Cheryl's stressing Mom out, like always, so she's stressing me out. And this Chace situation. It's more complicated than I even want to think about."

Erika sat down on a weight bench and patted the space next to her. "So come tell me about it."

Whitney plunked down next to her and buried her head in her hands.

"Kim is on the warpath with this case. The absolute warpath. Any time something goes wrong or looks like it might go wrong, she's ready with a finger to point at me," she said. "She has Andersen, the practice group leader, thinking I'm the devil. I'm always exhausted. I'm staying out way too late with Chace way too many nights of the week I don't get nearly as much work done on the weekends as I used to. The weekends used to be my time to get ahead on things." She shook her head. "What's wrong with me?" she moaned, pressing her hands tighter to her face.

"Oh, my goodness. I think I know," Erika said. Whitney looked up to see Erika with her hand over her heart, an exaggerated look of shock on her face. "A life. She finally has a life."

Whitney laughed. "Shut up. You're useless."

"Seriously. This is the most I've heard you talk about anything outside of that job. And the most I've heard of you doing things outside of that job. Chace is good for you. Maybe he's what it's gonna take to make you realize there's more to the world than Gibson and Grey and climbing the ladder to the top."

"Whatever. I don't need a man."

"No, not financially, but you don't feel like something's missing? What's the point of partner and all that other stuff if it's all you have? I'm worried you'll end up with this great life and no one to share it with. And if you don't have anyone to share it with, what's the point?"

"I have people. My family. You, Rob, Abbott, and everybody."

"You know that's not what I mean. There's an intimacy—a bond that comes from what Chace can give you that friends can't. I think everyone can see that he wants to." She leaned her shoulder into Whitney's. "Even you no matter how much you try to deny it."

"If I were interested, he's still not over his ex. He can't be."

"Whitney, you mention that woman more than he does. I can't even remember her name. That's how rarely she comes up. Now you? He talks about you all the time."

"It's just a bad idea."

"Can you give me a reason why? A real reason, not some lame excuse."

Whitney shrugged.

"Just think about it, Whit. Think about it. Because that boy is gone over you. And I think you may be gone over him, too."

"I'm not gone over anybody or anything. But I may be gone for good from Gibson and Grey if I don't get my act together on this Bevyx case."

Erika raised her eyebrows. "Not buying it."

Whitney jumped up from the bench and started jogging in place. "C'mon. How about a mile or two around the indoor track?"

Erika snorted. "Do I look crazy to you?"

"I don't understand how you can be a boxing coach and not like to run."

"We ran a mile when you first got here. Besides, just because I know how to box doesn't mean I'm in boxing shape," Erika said. Her dad had owned a box-ing gym and had been a trainer for semi-pro boxers for years before he retired. Erika didn't train semi-pros—she taught boxing for fitness.

Whitney shrugged, draping a towel around her neck.

Erika scrunched her lips in a way that meant she wasn't buying what Whitney was selling. "You usually complain about running yourself. Something is definitely up with you whether you want to admit it or not. And I think it's more than your job, no matter what you say."

"I just have some excess energy to work off."

Erika gave her a knowing look. "I'll bet you do. It's been how long? You dropped Barry at least a year ago."

Erika was right, more or less. It had been fourteen months, actually. "Mind your business."

They laughed.

Erika said, "I'll let that go. I know it's gotta get lonely with just you and your C-battery-powered friend."

"Okay. I'm gone now. Gonna get this mile in," Whitney said after playfully swatting Erika with her towel. She jogged over to the track that encircled the weight area on one side of the gym's main floor and the cardio equipment on the other side. Starting her first lap, she tried to shut out the true, even if annoying, words Erika had just spoken.

Every time she saw Chace, it was more and more frustrating not to touch him. And that kiss and what she'd wanted to follow it had dominated her dreams for weeks. But she wasn't going to get in deeper. She was already distracted enough by him, just barely keeping pace at work. By normal standards, she was still going above and beyond, but by Whitney standards, she was flagging.

Still, she couldn't help thinking he was a worthy distraction. Any other guy, she would've blown off while she was in the midst of a huge case at work and a brewing family drama. But Chace was one of the few things she looked forward to through it all. Suddenly her life didn't seem the drab, make it from one day to the next kind of thing it had on a daily basis before him. She was seeing her friends more, she was experiencing life outside of Gibson and Grey more, and most importantly, she was experiencing Chace more.

She just had to remember that work came first. Chace, the too-welcome distraction, wasn't worth destroying her dreams of making partner. Nothing was worth losing what she'd fought so hard for.

A lot of things rested on that dream. Her mother's ability to live through her and experience all she'd been denied in life, her ability to show her grandparents that neither she nor her family were inferior, and a chance to finally fix her father's mistakes.

Chapter 18: This Life

Whitney had to get out of the office for a little while. When she saw that Abbott had responded to her text asking if she wanted to meet for a drink at happy hour, she was grateful the answer was yes. After telling Bettina she was running out for a moment and that she'd be back in about an hour, she hurried out of the office. Normally she would've invited Bettina, but that day she just wanted to get away from everything that had anything to do with Gibson and Grey for at least an hour.

She opened the door to the small, dingy bar and warm air rushed over her. She welcomed the feel of it after walking several blocks in the numbing cold. She slowed her walk, no longer having to hurry now that she was indoors.

The place smelled of stale beer and fried food. It was her favorite bar because it was cozy, the happy hour bartenders loved her, and it was close enough to walk to from the office, but far away enough that she didn't see any of her co-workers outside of the select few she'd shared her secret discovery with—Ulrich, Bettina, and a third woman who sometimes came out with them.

Abbott wore a long, dark-colored dress. Her plaid overcoat was thrown over the back of her chair. She never wore any makeup and she didn't need any. Abbott had a natural beauty. A glow, almost. She flipped her long red hair over her shoulders and looked up at Whitney with smiling light blue eyes. Abbott's eyes were the palest blue Whitney had seen until she'd met Chace. Chace Murphy. Why did he keep popping up in her every thought?

Whitney gave Abbott a quick hug and then sat in the chair across from her at their small table near the bar. "Oh, Abbott, they're trying to kill me. I have to get back right after this to finish up a few things, but I had to have a break from that place. Thanks so much for meeting me."

"Well, I'm glad you called me for a quick escape. I feel like I haven't seen you in forever," Abbott said.

"I think this quick escape is saving my sanity." Whitney then gave Abbott a quick recap of her crazy day. "Sometimes, I wonder if it's even worth it. Kim hates me, the partners are frowning on me because of her, and I've always worked twice as hard as anyone there. Just because I haven't been dedicating my whole life to the firm recently, she jumps down my throat? It's like she's waiting for me to mess up. Some mentor."

"Well, Whitney, you know what I'm going to say. I don't see why you should torture yourself. Why don't you just do what makes you happy? Remember when we were in law school and you used to say you wanted to do civil rights law and change the world?" Abbott sat back and spread her long fingers out on the table. She buffed her fingernails and sometimes used nail strengthener, but she never polished them.

"Yeah, that was a long time ago. Civil rights law doesn't pay. And what was I going to do to change the world anyway? I mean, realistically? I was just dreaming and not being practical back then."

"So I'm not practical?"

"No, Abbott, I'm not saying that. It's just—always been different for you."

"How so?"

"You didn't—" She stopped herself before she said something she didn't want Abbott to know. Abbott didn't know what it was like to come up with nothing. Abbott's parents were both doctors. She couldn't possibly know about overhearing her mom cry, not knowing how she would pay the bills. About fathers and stepfathers running out and doing their families wrong. Abbott didn't know about all the weight she carried on her shoulders, never had. Nobody knew the whole story, not even Erika, and she told Erika almost everything. She didn't want anybody to know. Didn't want to show them the scars. She kept those well-concealed from everyone because she didn't want people to look at her differently, whether that look was one of pity or disdain. It didn't matter.

"What is it, Whitney?"

Whitney slumped down in her chair with a sigh. "Nothing. You ready to order?"

Abbott nodded and signaled a bartender who happened to be standing nearby, a pretty woman who was probably a local college student. There was a lot of gel in her short dark hair, and a silver lip ring hung over the left corner of her lower lip.

"You guys ready?" The woman tapped her order pad against her open palm. Each of her fingernails was painted a different color.

"I'll have a gin 'n' tonic," Abbott said.

"Vodka on the rocks, please. Double," Whitney said, leaning back in her chair.

"That bad, huh?" Abbott murmured when the server walked away. "That's what you always ordered in school when you thought you'd bombed an exam. Which you never really had, you Order of the Coif overachiever, you," Abbott said. She smiled briefly. "It must be not so pretty for you to order that."

Whitney gave a mirthless laugh and raked her hands over her face. "You have no idea."

❧

Thursday evening, Chace went over to Whitney's as soon as she got home from work. He'd jumped on the metro as soon as she texted him that she was leaving the building for the day. He got there almost as soon as she did even though her office building was a closer metro ride to where she lived in Virginia than Chace's apartment was.

"How was your day?" Chace asked, knowing the answer would be none too positive.

"Awful. They filed the complaint. That means we have a motion to dismiss coming up. Preparing an argument for this thing is going to be nearly impossible. We've been trying to come up with something for weeks, anticipating their arguments, and it's just not going well." She kicked her shoes off and gave a small grimace.

"You want me to order some food?" He kicked off his flip-flops and dropped them near the front door.

"You can get something. I nuked a frozen dinner and ate it at my desk a few hours ago," Whitney said, stifling a yawn.

Chace nodded, looking around the apartment before settling his eyes once again on her. She looked like she could barely still stand on her feet. "I'm actually not that hungry." He walked over to the doors leading out to the balcony. "I love this place. The lighting is fantastic. From what I remember, the few times I've been here during the day."

"Oh?"

"Yeah. You have all these huge windows. And those double glass doors leading out to your balcony? And it's all west-facing and you have this amazing angle so that you don't get too much glare at the time of day when you get your best light. It's like a photographer built your building or something. And if that weren't enough, you have this incredible view of the skyline from your balcony."

"You really love this photography stuff, huh?"

"Yeah. I guess I kind of do," Chace said, looking around her place again and feeling like he could create bigger and better things than he ever had. He didn't dare tell her that. He had an idea her reaction to something like that wouldn't be positive considering how wary she was of talking about anything involving relationships. Considering what he still had to tell her, he didn't bother pushing the issue. No telling how she would go off when she heard that he was potentially a father.

"That's good. It's good to have something you're really passionate about."

"Yeah." Chace was thinking that being near her was better than having all the cameras in the world. Since he couldn't say that, he asked her a question instead. "Well, that's the way you feel about what you do, right?" She sure devoted enough of her life to it. Devoting that much time to anything had to require a ton of passion.

She smiled wearily and shrugged out of her overcoat and suit jacket in one move. The sudden sight of her bare shoulders, exposed by her dark-colored, silk sleeveless top, drained every thought out of his head, along with all of the blood. He was glad he never wore his shirts tucked in and that he liked his jeans a little on the loose side. He didn't think she'd approve of where all his blood had gone.

"You know why I wanted to become a lawyer?" she asked.

"Why?" He moved closer to her.

"I wanted to help people." She laughed. "I wanted to be like Thurgood Marshall."

"Well, isn't that what you do? Advocate for your clients and all that?"

Whitney laughed bitterly and stretched out her calf muscles, complaining about her muscles feeling tight all over. Was she doing this on purpose? It wasn't fair if she was. "I help the rich get richer. I don't think that counts."

"Are you happy?"

She looked up at him, stopping in mid-stretch, giving him a startled look. "What do you mean?"

"If you're not happy, why do you give your life over to your job?" He stepped behind her and began kneading his fingers into the tight, tense muscles in her shoulders.

She started to move away from him, but he took the massage deeper, pushing his fingers harder against her muscles, and she stayed where she was. "Now you sound like Abbott. You two act like it's so simple."

"Because it is. It should be, anyway."

Her head fell to one side. "You don't understand. People like you never do. Life isn't all happy and fun and doing what you want. Unless you want to be—"

"What?" He stopped pushing his fingers against her overworked muscles.

"Nothing. Never mind."

"What were you going to say?"

"It's not important." She shook her head and put her hand over his. His heart lurched a little bit. "Please. Don't stop."

"I'm not just playing around with a camera, you know." He went back to massaging her shoulders, neck, and upper back. "I tried the corporate path. I graduated top of my class from Dartmouth. Even got a job with a huge investment management firm in Manhattan."

"Really?" She rolled her head back and looked up at him.

He nodded.

"What happened?"

"It wasn't for me. I hated it, so I quit." He moved his hands lower on her back.

"Just like that?"

"Sure. I realized some things are more important than money and what people think of you based on what you drive and how nice your suit is. Things like going your own way instead of simply doing what people expect you to do."

She let her head drop forward and he felt her muscles begin to tense under his fingers again. He moved his hands up to the gentle curve of her neck. He leaned in close so that his mouth hovered over her neck.

"You know what I was just thinking about?" The part he could tell her anyway.

"What?"

"Remember that Saturday I was actually able to steal you away from your legal pads and your Black-Berry for the day and I took you rock climbing? I couldn't believe it was your first time. You were so good. We were out there for hours. You looked happy. Free." He brushed her ear with his lips. "I liked it. A lot. You were so beautiful that day. I mean, you always are, but it really shone through that day."

Whitney didn't say anything to that.

That thought sparked another in his mind. "I'd love to shoot you sometime."

"Huh?"

"You know, with my camera. In this apartment. Especially with your great lighting, if I could actually catch you here during the day."

"Oh."

He grazed his teeth over her earlobe. "Whit, would that be okay with you? I think you could be some of my best work. I don't usually choose people as subjects, but you're special. I know it."

"You shot Kelly."

He stepped away from her a little. "Those photos in my place back in River Run were just me fooling around with the camera. She happened to be around a lot, we dated for two years, so yeah. I happened to take a lot of pictures of her. She was never a serious subject of mine, though."

"I just meant—"

"You don't have to explain. Just stop bringing her up all the time. She seems to matter more to you than she does to me."

She locked her hands together and looked down at them.

He scribbled his website address on the top of a page of newspaper, tore off the slip of paper, and handed it to her. "My work's there if you want to see it."

"You never told me about this before." She looked down at paper he'd handed her and then up at him.

He shrugged. "It never came up."

She pressed the slip of paper between her hands. "I don't ask you a lot about how things are going for you, huh? I'm always whining about work. I'm so sorry. I—"

"Shh. It's fine," Chace said.

Whitney wrapped her arms around him. "You're so good to me. Thank you."

Chace moved his hands slowly across her back, savoring the moment of returning that hug. He wished it would never have to end. Even though he knew it couldn't last forever.

"No problem." He held her close. He breathed in the scent of her shampoo before settling his cheek against hers.

"Yes, you can shoot me. I'm so sorry. After this motion is done, I'll make a point of being here during the day." She locked her fingers behind his neck. "I tell you what, why don't you take my spare key? You could come in and check the light out for yourself, maybe get some ideas or whatever it is you photographer types do."

"Really?"

Whitney searched his face with her soft brown eyes for a moment before nodding. "I'll be right back."

He watched her walk to her bedroom. She came back a moment later with the key. When she placed it in his hand, he curled his fingers around hers. He looked into her eyes, and she looked away. He wanted to hold her close again, but he had the idea going for a second hug wouldn't go over well. He was lucky he'd gotten the first one. And so freely. It made him think that maybe, hopefully, he was making some progress in getting her to open up to him.

"You want me to go?" he asked.

"No, but I do have a lot of work to do," she said with a wistful sigh.

"What if I just sat here really quietly with my laptop and browsed through some photography blogs while you work?"

She gave him a huge smile. "I'd like that. A lot."

"Good."

She grinned. "Good."

"Listen, I have to work tomorrow evening, and Saturday during the day, but how do you feel about dinner Saturday?" he said. He resisted the urge to run his fingers up and down her bare arms when she sat next to him on the couch.

She moved closer to him. "I have to work, but I should be able to get home by seven or so."

That was a major improvement over her usual "I don't know." He said, "Rob and Delaney will probably want to come along. And maybe Erika will, too." He didn't mention A.J. as he still hadn't met the man yet. It didn't seem A.J. went much of anywhere with Erika.

"Yeah, I'll ask my friend Abbott, too. I hadn't realized how much I missed her until the other day." She yawned. "You remember her? From New Year's Eve."

"Yeah. Abbott…isn't that something to do with the priesthood or some monk type or something?"

Whitney grinned. "Yeah. You should meet her parents. They're definitely two of a kind."

No longer able to resist, he traced his fingers lightly over the skin of her shoulders until he raised goose bumps on them. He kissed the corner of her mouth.

"Um, work. I have a lot of work to do." She pulled away from him. "I should really get to it. I'm gonna go get my laptop." She rushed her words. She seemed to want to say something else, but she didn't. Instead, she went across the room to grab her laptop.

Chapter 19: Grapes

Whitney was starting to resent giving Chace the key already. He'd only had it a little over a week—she'd given it to him the past Thursday and it was now Friday—and he'd been there almost every night when she got home from work. Only when he had to work did she have the place to herself anymore.

It wasn't that she didn't like having him there. That was the problem. She liked having him there too much. Even though he came over with his laptop ostensibly to work, sometimes bringing his pocket camera, as he called it, and his cables so he could upload pictures and sometimes just doing research online, they always did more talking than working.

She used to get twice the amount of work done at home before he'd started coming over all the time. Every time she thought of staying later at the office than her usual eight or nine, she wasn't able to do it because she thought too much about how nice it would be to sit next to Chace on the couch while she worked. And she promised herself each time that she wouldn't get distracted that night. Of course, that was always just a lie she told herself so that she would let herself slip home and spend time with him.

But that night she was going to have to tell Chace she needed her place to herself more. She'd screwed up big with Kim again. That morning at the motion hearing, she'd done everything right, but they'd still lost. Their argument was terrible. It was hard to make a good one when the plaintiff had such a strong case. Their client was still being too stubborn to talk about settling, though.

Kim had reamed her as soon as they'd gotten back to the office. It had taken a whole lot of discipline for Whitney not to shout back. She hadn't been in the best of moods. She was going on only a few hours of sleep every night, staying up extra late to finish her work after Chace left at night.

Chace didn't understand that she didn't have the luxury of dabbling in dreams. He was lovable, but clueless. She couldn't let herself get wrapped up in that. She was a pragmatist, and that had always worked well for her.

She'd also had trouble finding the passion for her work that usually came naturally to her. Normally she loved the strategizing and arguing that went into her job, but lately she spent too much time questioning why she was defending these people who probably really should have just paid the people they'd wronged and been decent human beings. That was the problem. You couldn't think too much about the human side of these things. You just had to go with it.

With all of that weighing down on her, she needed some more space from him. She had to make him understand that there were boundaries he couldn't cross. Because when he crossed them, everything just ended up out of whack for her in scarily pleasant ways—ways that she couldn't afford for them to be.

The worst part was she started to imagine more and more with every moment she spent with him a life in which they could be together all the time. And in which she didn't think about work or Kim or anything. She could just be free like him. And they could be happy. And broke. And unsuccessful at everything but love. No. She couldn't afford to even think about that life. She had to make him back off.

When she threw open her apartment door, having steeled herself to tell Chace that he just couldn't drop by all the time, she was hit by the aroma of the most heavenly jerk chicken she'd ever smelled outside of a Caribbean restaurant.

"You cook?" Whitney dropped her briefcase to the floor and kicked off her shoes. Leaving her laptop bag on the coffee table, she followed her nose into the kitchen where he stood, looking like a Hollister model posing as a cook. He wore deconstructed denim and a black T-shirt beneath an apron. She was surprised he'd found one. She didn't do much cooking. Well, that was an understatement. She rarely used her stove for more than boiling water for tea.

"Yeah. Don't look so shocked." Of course he gave her the grin that made her want to dissolve into a puddle at his feet. She hated that grin because it made her so weak for him. Especially when he'd cooked for her. "I used to be a short order cook. I really liked it, so I took a few culinary courses at a community college back when I lived in Richmond. Cooking is kind of therapeutic. Besides, I like making people happy. What makes people happier than food?"

"Mm. Dirty rice. And plantains, too. Why do you know me so well?" Whitney hovered over the pots on the stove, her stomach growling.

"I pay attention," Chace said, coming up behind her and resting his hands lightly on her arms.

She sank against him. It would be so easy to give in. She'd had such a tiring day at work. He'd cooked for her. A serious meal. Something she would've never been able to do in a million years. His chest felt so solid and warm and reassuring.

"Chace," she whispered as he ran his fingers up and down her arms.

"I have something else for you, too. I made you something. A present. I'll give it to you after dinner."

"Why are you doing all of this?" She looked up at him, and he looked down, giving her a crooked grin.

"Because I like you," he said simply. "And you've been more stressed than usual this week. And your motion was this morning, right? It's over. We need to celebrate."

"We lost."

"We still need to celebrate it being over," Chace said matter-of-factly.

She grinned. "I love—"

The silence between them was heavy as she scrambled for a way to end that sentence that wouldn't incriminate her.

"Being around you." Whew. She'd almost slipped in a huge way.

He chuckled. "I love being around you, too. You should go change out of that suit. Dinner will be ready in a few minutes."

Whitney smiled all the way to her bedroom. She changed into a pair of sweatpants and worn light blue T-shirt. She put her hair up in a ponytail. She didn't want anything to give the idea that she was trying to impress him at all. Because with the way that night was going, she was already going to have to fight the impulse to give Chace the wrong impression. She really wanted him to have it. She decided not to make it easy to give him that dangerous wrong impression.

She came back out and dinner was already on the table. They sat down to a savory, well-spiced meal. She made an absolute pig out of herself. She had hardly eaten all day, and the food was almost too good to be true.

After dinner Chace told her it was time for her present. He pulled a giant board filled with pictures out from behind the sofa and brought it over to her.

"What is this?" she breathed, taking the board from him. At the top was the heading *Whitney's Favorite Places*.

"It's all your favorite places in the city. There's the bistro you like, that place near H Street, the National Portrait Gallery, the bird house at the zoo, and more. They're all there."

Whitney grinned. They really were. He'd made a collage with digital prints and had them printed onto the white background of the board he'd given her. She ran her hand lovingly over the whiteboard—sturdier than poster board and thicker as well—and then propped it against a leg of the table.

She felt so bad for being angry at him even though he hadn't known she was before she walked through that door. Sitting there, eating food he'd made for her, she couldn't believe she'd almost snapped at him.

She stood up and hugged him close. "Thanks."

"For?"

"Being you. Just being you," she murmured into his shirt. "How can it just be like—you're everything I need sometimes?"

"Only sometimes?"

She laughed. "You know I don't like to have this conversation."

He pressed his nose to hers and his hands into the small of her back. "Yeah, but you could change your mind about that. Or maybe I could change your mind about that."

"We can't start talking this way."

"Why?" He kissed her lower lip and her knees nearly buckled.

"Because…" She couldn't finish her sentence. It just didn't feel right to tell him that she couldn't let herself fall in love with him.

He pressed his forehead to hers. "How about dessert?"

"Huh?" She was in a trance as he nuzzled his face against her neck. In that moment, he could have had anything he wanted from her—anything at all. It was a good thing he couldn't read minds.

"I'll be right back."

She bit her lip to keep from telling him not to pull away as he pulled back and walked to her kitchen. She stared at his back hungrily, as if she could stare away his T-shirt.

Chace came back to the living room with a bowl of grapes. They sat on the couch and put the bowl between them. He turned on the television, but neither of them watched it. They were too busy watching each other. She couldn't concentrate on their conversation because he kept feeding her grapes. The words weren't important. The grapes were.

Chace took the last grape from the bowl as she reached for it.

"Hey!" she cried. Then she laughed. "You can't do that."

"Why not?" He held the grape between his index finger and thumb, giving her a playful grin.

"Because I wanted that grape."

"If you want it, come get it," Chace said, putting the grape between his teeth.

Whitney swallowed hard and moved closer to him on the couch. She put her mouth close to his, looking up into his pale eyes. Her heart beat faster as she ran her fingers along his chin. Emboldened by the fact that he almost dropped the grape, she moved closer until their lips were almost touching. He put his hand behind her neck, gently resting his fingers there.

Her tongue slid past his teeth and around the grape. For a moment, they sat still, teeth, tongues, and grape becoming the focus of their worlds.

When she thought the anticipation of the moment would kill her, she pulled the grape into her mouth. His lips closed over hers in a kiss. She kissed back, deep and hard. She straddled his lap without ever separating their lips. He pulled her close and she closed her eyes, gratefully sinking into the escape he provided.

She grabbed him by the front of his shirt. She leaned in close, running her nose from the underside of his chin, down his throat, across his collarbone. He groaned, a small encouragement, but all she needed. She traced kisses over every place that her nose had touched. He

213

rested his hands loosely at her hips. She reached up, planting kisses behind his ear.

"We need..." She murmured the words into his skin before caressing it with her tongue. To her disappointment, he pulled back.

"I should go," Chace whispered over her lips.

"I know," she said, but she still moaned in disappointment when he pulled back from her. She didn't want him to, but he was right.

"Whitney." His fingers made their way slowly through her hair and down to her neck, then her shoulders. "I really want you. But I have to go. It wouldn't be right. Not tonight. Not yet."

"I've told you—"

"Shh." He was dangerously close to her lips when he shushed her. "I know." He stood and reached for her hands. She gave them, and he helped her to her feet.

She wanted another kiss so badly she could almost taste his tongue on hers, but she didn't go in for it and neither did he.

"I'm gonna go. Right now," Chace said, but he didn't move from the spot where he was standing.

"Okay," Whitney said, but hoping all the while that he wouldn't.

Eventually Chace stood and Whitney walked him downstairs. She looked through the window of the door that led out of her building. Flurries of snow danced through their air, but nothing stuck to the ground. He reached for the door, and she stopped him. She wrapped her arms around him and pressed her head into his shoulder.

"I'm sorry," she murmured into his shirt before breathing him in.

"Hey. You don't have anything to be sorry for," he said, rubbing small circles on her back.

"I've never tried to do this before and I don't know how it works. And I just feel like everything in my life is going crazy right now and—"

"Sweetheart. I've never asked for more than you can give, have I?"

She shook her head.

"And I never will."

"I hope you don't give up on me."

"I'll never do that, either."

She gave his cheek a soft kiss. "Good night."

He kissed the top of her head. "Good night, Beautiful Whitney."

She hugged herself as she watched him walk away, wondering if it was possible to really have something more with Chace. Could he possibly be over Kelly so quickly? Regardless of whether he was or not, she was too close to making partner to screw up now. Everything could fall apart if she lost focus. Things were already starting to crumble around the edges.

Chapter 20: The Accidental Chef

Whitney was going through the argument for an upcoming hearing in the Bevyx case for what felt like the thousandth time and it still didn't make sense to her. She was surrounded by a paper sea, made mostly of cases she'd printed out. Other cases were up on various windows on her computer. She was chewing the pen cap in the corner of her mouth into oblivion. Worse than seeming illogical, the argument seemed just plain wrong.

The thing seemed impossible to win. Any way she looked at the facts, their client was liable, although Whitney wasn't allowed to say the l-word out loud, of course.

There was another l-word she wouldn't let herself say as well. But the situation was different there. She didn't have to worry about saying it anyway because it wasn't true. She couldn't afford for it to be true. She was drowning in the middle of the biggest case of her life, Kim kept dropping hints that she wasn't partner material, and even Andersen was starting to look at her differently. Andersen had never taken Kim's warnings about Whitney too seriously before, but ever since she'd lost that motion argument in the Bevyx case—which had been impossible to win—things had been different with him. Colder. She couldn't afford to lose out on making partner. And that meant she couldn't afford to feel anything for Chace.

She sighed and flipped a page. Her eyes were nearly crossing after reading pages and pages of technical crap. They had a patent guy on their team since the case involved both patent and copyright issues. Still, she had to wade through some of the patent stuff to get to the heart of her part of the case. And it wasn't fun. She'd never been the technical, science-oriented type.

Kim wanted her to fail. That wasn't paranoia. She was certain of it. That was why Kim had her working on the most technical angle of the copyright argument. Of course Kim had phrased it as knowing Whitney was capable. With a mocking smile on her face that only Whitney could see as Kim's back had been turned to the other associates in the room at the time.

Whitney jumped when her phone rang. She'd been so intent on the section of the Copyright Act she'd been reading that the ringing sound startled her. She punched the button for speaker phone.

"Yeah?" she snapped.

"Wow. You don't sound like a happy girl right now," Chace said with a grin in his voice. So carefree. Not a worry in the world. They were worlds apart. What had she been thinking, inviting all of that chaos into her life?

She grunted a response, still poring over the statute in front of her.

"Sounds like this would be a bad time for me to come over."

"Come over? Why?"

"Well, it's just—you said I could start shooting you tonight." His voice changed.

"Oh." She winced. She'd forgotten all about that. She'd forgotten all about everything when Kim had dropped the news about the upcoming injunction hearing. The plaintiff was still busy throwing rocks at them and their client still refused to talk about a settlement conference. They had very little time to prepare a defense. Then there was the counter-claim the junior associates were working on, and she was supervising them on that. And a new case had just come through and Kim wanted Whitney to take the lead on it, take a couple of associates, and get a memo to her by Monday.

Did Kim do these things on purpose? It was like she'd hidden the news about the injunction until the last moment. The only thing that made Whitney realize that couldn't be true was that Kim might have been petty, but she wouldn't have risked her own legal career by doing something that would have made her look bad as well. Still, it hardly seemed fair that she'd ended up with the most assignments and the least amount of time to do them more often than not.

"Whit? You still there?"

"I'm sorry. Tonight is bad. Really, really bad. Kim dumped a ton of work on me today."

"Oh. Wanna talk about it?"

"Actually, I have to go. I have lot of work to do."

"Okay."

"And Chace. I—I think you should come over a lot less, actually. A whole lot less."

"Really?"

Her career was at stake. Nothing could come before that. Not only for her—not even most importantly for her. But because of what it meant to those she held close to her heart. "I can't do this."

"Can't do what?" His tone grew colder.

"This. You. It's just—you're distracting me. You're screwing everything up."

"Oh. Really."

"Could you just respect me needing space, please?"

"What? Are you serious?"

"Yes. Just—I have to go. I don't want you around all the time."

"Fine." He hung up.

Whitney picked her phone up and flung it across the couch. Everything hit her at once—job, Chace, being mean to Chace, the stress that came from mediating her mom and her aunt's fights.

Her gaze fell on Chace's extra tripod—the one he kept at her place. She dropped her legal pad, pushed her laptop aside, and burst into tears.

∿

Whitney felt like crap after what she'd said to Chace. Especially since he'd followed her wishes so well. Not one phone call, email, or text message, zip. And this made her realize what a huge part of her life he'd become without her even noticing. She'd been more sad and lonely that week than usual. She'd stayed at the firm until nearly midnight every night that week, and she'd never hated her job—a job her life had once revolved around—more.

On the day after the injunction hearing, she decided to try to make up with Chace. But she was afraid to contact him directly. She knew she'd been wrong. Really, really wrong. Besides, she wanted to surprise him. So she called Rob.

"Hey," she said to Rob. "How are you? How are things going with the store?" Rob was supposed to have a grand opening for his T-shirt store's brick and mortar location soon—Valentine's Day weekend—which was only a couple of weeks away.

"I'm good. And don't forget how well I know you, Whit. That's not the reason you called."

"What? I'm just being a good friend, checking in to see how things are going."

"We were texting back and forth a little while ago. You wouldn't have called just to ask that. You're calling about Chace."

There was no point in trying to deny it. "How mad is he?"

"Pretty mad," Rob said, seeming to know exactly who she was talking about.

"I need him to come over. I want him to know how sorry I am for the way I acted."

"Whit, you know I love you, but you can't just go jerking people around. Especially this guy. I really like him. He's nothing like the stray losers you usually find."

She told Rob what she'd done. She was sure he'd gotten a version from Chace, too. "What did he say to you?"

"Not much. He spends a lot of his time either on his laptop looking all sullen and emo or else out taking pictures."

Whitney's heart hurt. Taking pictures. She remembered her collage. The collage that had taken so much thought to put together and time in taking pictures and designing the layout, which was unlike any she'd ever seen. He must have known quite a lot about graphic design in addition to photography. She smiled. Chace was amazing. She'd been so oblivious.

"How are things coming along for the grand opening?" she asked.

"Pretty good, but don't try to butter me up."

She laughed. "No, really. I'm so happy for you. And proud. That's big, finally getting something you worked so long and hard for." Like Chace was trying to do. Her heart sank.

"Stop it. I'm gonna start blushing over here or something."

She tapped her fingers on the arm of her sofa. "Do you think you could get him over here? I feel like I've been such a crab to him."

"You have been. And I don't know…"

"Try. Please? Trick him. Lie. Do something. I feel really horrible and I have to apologize."

"I'll try. I'm not making any promises. He's really pissed. What you said to him really ticked him off. And he's not easy to tick off. That guy's really laid back. More than me. What did you do to him?"

"You know how I am when I'm stressed."

"Yeah. Barely human."

"Quit it."

"Okay, okay. Don't take my head off now. I'll do my best, Whit."

"Good. Bring him over at eight, okay?"

"I'll call you if I'm not able to talk him into it."

"Sounds good."

Whitney hung up the phone, biting her lower lip. It was time to get started.

To make up for what she'd done, Whitney decided to do something she'd never done. Which, in retrospect, probably wasn't a good thing to do for the first time for a person she was trying to make something up to. She decided to cook.

How hard could it be? She could read a cookbook. She could follow instructions. Why hadn't someone warned her that it took more than those two basic skills?

Before calling Rob, Whitney had gotten out a cookbook she'd been given for Christmas one year, looked up a recipe that sounded good, made a grocery list, and then she went to the store. Now she stood in her kitchen, surrounded by ingredients, pots, and pans, and with only a cookbook to guide her through the wilderness.

She was attempting to make chicken pot pie. She remembered Chace mentioning that he liked it once, and so she'd gotten it in her head to make it. And knowing she was a rookie, for some reason she'd still decided it would be a good idea to make the pie crust from scratch. Weren't lawyers supposed to have logic skills? What had happened to hers?

She spent almost an hour on the crust before she gave up on it. Next, she decided to just bake the chicken instead of attempting to make a pot pie. So she put chicken, vegetables, and oil into a baking pan and stuck it in the oven. She set the oven temperature at five hundred degrees since she didn't have much time left before Chace was supposed to show up. If he showed up.

She realized that her mother had been right when she'd said that a higher temperature doesn't cook it faster. Yes, right at the moment that her smoke alarm went off and her beautiful, Italian marble filled kitchen was hidden by a fog of black smoke, she realized it. Coughing, she ran over to her balcony doors, opening them despite the freezing February night air. She then turned on her ceiling fan, exhaust fan—any fan she could reach.

Whitney looked around her kitchen before burying her head in her hands. For all her efforts, all she'd really made was a mess. Blackened chicken—and not the Cajun kind—on the counter. A gooey flour mixture that had never become a pie crust. It never would, either. Other kitchen casualties that all added up to make one giant hot mess.

Of course, just then her front door opened and in walked Rob and Chace. She wanted to crawl into one of her kitchen cabinets. Chace looked around the condo, coughing subtly into his fist. He looked so delectable in even the simplest outfits. The fact that she could still notice despite her state of distress proved that he could make anything sexy. He wore khakis and a brown long-sleeve T-shirt. He made them look runway good. He'd already removed his jacket and thrown it over the back of her leather recliner the way he always did.

Rob ran over to her. "You tried to cook? Whitney, no! Why? You had to know no good could come of this."

She looked up plaintively at Chace. "I wanted to cook for you. I wanted to make it up to you for being so horrible to you the other day."

Rob said, "Yeah, but did you have to risk burning down your house to do it? You should have just gotten him a card or something. Or 'I'm sorry' works, too."

"So I'm not a great cook," Whitney said, glowering at Rob.

"Understatement. Of the year," he said.

"I tried to make your favorite," Whitney said to Chace, trying hard not to laugh at her own ridiculousness.

"It's the thought that counts," Chace said, the corners of his mouth twitching with the laugh he was obviously trying to hold back.

"Yeah, you know, you would think that's always true, but this time, I don't think it is. This is one of those rare exceptions," Rob said, scrutinizing the kitchen with his eyebrows raised.

"Rob, you're not funny."

Chace burst out laughing. It seemed he couldn't stop once he got started.

"Is it that funny, Chace? Really?" Whitney sighed, rubbing a flour-specked hand across her forehead without thinking about it, leaving a trace of flour behind.

"You're just adorable, that's all. Too adorable." Chace walked over and wiped the smudge of flour from her forehead. He then furrowed his brow for a moment, and Whitney could almost see the light bulb going off. He turned to Rob. "In fact, hold on. Rob, let me see your keys. I need to get something out of your car."

Rob handed over the keys. Chace left the apartment and returned a few moments later with his camera bag.

"Oh, no," Whitney groaned.

"Oh, yes," Chace said with a grin, unzipping the bag.

"Chace, please?"

"You promised I could shoot you and I haven't gotten a good shot yet. This is too good to pass up. I promise, if you really hate them when I show you later, I'll delete them all."

Whitney rolled her eyes, but it was too late. Chace was already snapping away. He continued to do so as Rob helped her clean the kitchen, which involved lots of mocking and laughing, and slaps to the side of Rob's head with a dish towel. Chace sometimes laughed too hard to even snap the shots and eventually he gave up and went back downstairs for his tripod.

It was the most fun Whitney had had since she kicked Chace out of her life. Even if she had almost destroyed her kitchen and several thousand dollars worth of remodeling. So much fun she realized she should never kick Chace to the curb again. No matter what. With work, she would deal. She always had before. Just another new adjustment to make. Chace's company was more than enough in the way of compensation.

After the kitchen was cleaned up, Rob picked up Delaney, and the four of them went to a Thai restaurant near Rob and Chace's neighborhood. Rob gave an animated re-telling of the cooking incident, complete with acted out scenes in true Rob fashion. They were all laughing so hard that the other people in the restaurant probably thought something was wrong with them.

Chace sat next to Whitney and they sat across the table from Rob and Delaney. He draped his arm casually over the back of her chair. She enjoyed the intimacy that came from having him so close even if they weren't touching. The scent of his cologne was clean and sharp and she breathed in deeply every time he shifted position in the chair, loving the smell of him again. She'd missed it so much over the past few days. She'd been an idiot.

❧

Chace realized once they were across the Potomac and almost back home that he'd left his camera at Whitney's. He had Rob let him out at a metro station and he took the train back to Whitney's place. Once he was back in the building, knowing her code now, he went up to her floor and knocked on the door. It would have been awkward to use his key when she was there. It wasn't like he lived there or anything.

She opened the door a crack and poked her head out, stifling a yawn. She'd already gotten ready for bed by the look of it. She'd had a rough week—well, rough weeks. He knew. He'd experienced her frustration first-hand. She probably just wanted to turn in now that she had the chance to before the wee hours of the morning.

"Oh. I thought you guys were long gone by now." Whitney opened the door wider.

Chace didn't know how to react when she stood in the open doorway wearing only tiny shorts that looked like cut-off sweats and a threadbare T-shirt with no bra. He could clearly see the outlines of the rounded mounds of her breasts beneath the white shirt, the circles in the center of them darker. He had a sudden desire to caress those circles until her nipples showed through the shirt. He shook away the thought, forcing his eyes back to hers.

He worked hard to focus enough to speak. "I. Camera. Forgot. Um, I forgot my camera."

"Oh. I should have known you wouldn't go far without that thing." Whitney walked back into the apartment. He followed. Those shorts were teasing him to death. He willed them to be just a half inch higher so he could see the gentle curve of her buttocks, which was currently hidden by a scrap of fabric.

Her hand closed over the strap of his camera bag. He pressed his body to hers, wrapping his arms around her waist.

She froze for a moment and then relaxed into his arms, making him bolder. He caressed her sides, letting his fingers play into her flesh with only the thin material of her T-shirt separating skin from skin.

"I don't want to leave," he whispered the words against her ear. "But I will if you want me to."

She turned to face him, pressing her cheek to his shoulder. "I don't want you to," she murmured into the skin of his throat. "Stay."

He picked her up and carried her to her room without another word. They lay on her bed just staring at each other, his hand loosely at her hip, his thumb stroking the bare bit of flesh exposed by her shirt having ridden up above her shorts a few inches.

She sat up and rolled over so that she was sitting just above his hips. She took his hands and laced their fingers together.

"I've never felt the things you make me feel. And I want to feel them. It's scary, but it's also wonderful."

Chace smiled at her, but didn't speak. He reflected on her words, back when she'd told him that she'd never been in love before. He put his hands on her waist, slipping them under her shirt. She closed her eyes and arched her back, responding completely to his touch. She seemed to melt into him. He could almost feel the tension leaving her body.

"I never thought I could like living life without a safety net," she murmured.

"I am your safety net," he said, his voice barely audible as he stared at her with hungry eyes.

She smiled down at him, but said nothing. She shifted against him, her short shorts riding up enough for him to see that she didn't have on any panties and that she waxed. Bikini. He slid his hand up her inner thigh and let it rest against her hip. He was intensely aware that the only thing separating skin from skin was the scrap of cloth that her shorts were made out of. At that thought, all others fled from his brain.

∽⚬∾

The next morning, Chace woke up with a smile to Whitney's kisses on his cheeks and chin.

"Hey." He grinned and nuzzled her nose with his.

"Hi." She kissed him just below his lower lip.

"You're friendly this morning."

She grinned. "You're in my bed. How can I not be?"

He kissed her neck.

"Sorry about last night."

"Nothing to be sorry for." He took her hands in his and kissed her fingers.

"We didn't even—"

"Shh. Like I said, you don't have to apologize to me for anything."

"Do you know how perfect you are?" She gave him a quick kiss on the lips.

They weren't ready for that next step yet. She was still too hesitant about her feelings for him. And he hadn't been completely honest with her yet. He hadn't mentioned a word to her about the Kelly situation. He didn't know how he had stopped things from getting out of control, though, when all he had been able to think of was making love to her. He'd wanted her for a long time, and he hadn't done anything with anyone in months.

Self-control wasn't easy.

She curled up against his side and he stroked the area between her shoulder blades.

"The past few weeks since Christmas and New Year's have been unbelievable." She smiled and curled her fingers against the sides of his face. "I guess I'm lucky."

"Hm?" He moved his hands up and down her arms, raising goose bumps on them.

She said with an exaggerated drawl, "You don't scare off easy."

"Not when it comes to you. I refuse."

She kissed him, let her lips linger on his before pulling away. "I could get used to this. You sleeping over."

He could, too. He just hoped he wouldn't explode. He buried his face in her hair, ignoring the impulse to think about how much he wanted her or his Kelly problems.

She turned onto her stomach and he stayed on his side, propping his head up with his hand. He traced his fingers over her bare back, raising goose bumps on her warm brown skin. He moved his fingers under her left shoulder blade.

"Tattoo, huh?" Chace moved the pad of his index finger over the intricate lines of the tribal pattern inked into her skin before kissing it. She laughed, her body moving under his touch when she did.

"That was college. Erika has one, too. Different tattoo, but we went to get them done together."

"Looks good on you."

"Thanks." She sighed. They lay there like that for a while in silence, the only movement being Chace's hand on her back.

She turned her head to the side and looked up at him. "I want you around. I'm sorry I told you not to come over as much. I missed you so much."

Chace rubbed her back. "It's okay."

"You should come over whenever. I mean it. Whenever you want."

"Don't tell me things like that. You might never get rid of me."

"What makes you think I would want to?"

He smiled. "We should do something for Valentine's Day." He spread his fingers out across her back. "You know, nothing big, but just so that we're not single people with nothing to do on the big day." He slid down on the bed so that he was lying next to her.

"We should." She moved closer to him.

He wrapped his arms around her and pressed his face into her neck. He couldn't tell her about Kelly now. Not when he was finally making the progress he'd been trying to make for weeks.

"Do you have to get to work or something? Should I go?" he said. He hoped for the answer he was almost sure he wouldn't get.

She shook her head. "I don't think I'm going to work today."

"Really?"

"Yeah. The injunction hearing's done. And besides, I really don't want to," she said, running a hand through her hair. "I haven't had a Saturday to myself away from work in forever. I was thinking we could spend the day together." She pressed her forehead to his.

"I would love that." He kissed her cheek and hugged her to him.

"Me, too."

"As soon as I throw these clothes in the wash and take a shower." He tore himself away from her, finished undressing himself—picking up where she'd left off the night before—and headed to the door. He turned around, grinning, his hand on the doorknob. "Are you staring?"

She smiled. "You have a problem with that?"

"Can't say I do."

Her smile broadened. "Maybe you should leave some clothes here. You know, just in case."

The pre-work, pre-stress Whitney he'd met back in River Run was coming back. Good. "Yeah, okay. I'll bring some stuff the next time I come over."

"I'll clean out a drawer." She stood and stretched and he watched with naked desire. "I'll go get our shower ready."

"I'll be right back." Chace bolted for her laundry room, anxious to make it back to the master bath. All the teasing was driving him insane, but he would rather have that than nothing.

Chapter 21: Valentine's Day

For Valentine's Day, Chace and Whitney went out with Rob and Delaney. They went to a restaurant Rob's friend owned. So they were able to slip another couple of people—Whitney and Chace—into their party even though Rob's reservation was for two.

Whitney wore a low-cut violet sweater and a black knee-length skirt. Chace made simple sexy, as usual. He wore a black blazer over a crisp white shirt open at the throat, exposing a delicious bit of his smooth olive skin. He'd paired the blazer and shirt with dark designer jeans that completed the outfit well. He turned heads, as usual, but didn't seem to notice. He held her hand all night and seemed to see only her.

Could she be falling in love for the first time in her life? He was all she thought about. She didn't want to be anywhere without him. Whenever someone asked her what she was doing later or if she wanted to grab a drink or dinner, Chace always sprang to mind. Inviting him along had become second nature. Even thinking about seeing him made her heart beat faster and brought out the most foolish grin imaginable.

Rob had asked what was happening between her and Chace, and so had Erika. She didn't have a good answer. She didn't know what they were to each other. But she knew she didn't feel right when he wasn't close. And so her friends had labeled it for her. And she neither confirmed nor denied.

"What are you getting?" Chace asked. His arm encircled her waist. He was finding ways to be close to her and touch her, not that she minded.

"Um, I think I'm getting the 'What's It Like' Salmon," she said. The restaurant was having a Jagged Edge-themed Valentine's Day evening. The menu had items named after the group's songs and the music they were playing was the equivalent of a Jagged Edge Pandora station. But the salmon wasn't what she was hungry for.

"Hm. Really," Chace said.

Even though she knew he couldn't read her mind, she blushed, nodded, and put her menu down. "What about you?"

"Hm…I'm thinking of the 'I Gotta Be' Vegetarian Platter."

"Are you?"

He nodded. "I am." He took her hand and kissed every finger individually.

Her sweater was suddenly constricting and hot.

"Um, guys, there are two other people at this table," Rob said in a loud whisper.

Whitney pulled her hand away from Chace and turned back to face her friends. "What? We were just deciding what to order."

"From the menu? Or?..." Rob raised his eyebrows.

"Yes, Rob. You're such a comedian," she said, reaching across the table to bop him lightly on the head with her menu. "See me laughing right now?"

Chace chuckled, tightening his arm around her waist. She leaned into him.

Later, Whitney went to the restroom and Delaney followed.

They were standing at the sink, checking their makeup, when Delaney said, "I have to admit. I'm a little jealous."

"Oh yeah?"

"It just seems so natural between you two. Like you don't even have to try. I've never seen anything like it."

"Thanks."

"There's just so much…fire between you two. I can't believe you're not official yet."

"Yet. Ha." She rolled a tube of lip gloss back and forth across her palm, thinking about Delaney's words. She had her reasons. Certainly, they were good ones. She didn't have time for a relationship. Then there was Erika and that fool she insisted on dating even though he made her miserable. Whitney had to do a lot of damage control there.

Aunt Cheryl had a new boyfriend and was laying off Jo for the moment. But then there was work. There was always work. That meant there was always Kim.

"I know we're not close or anything, and I wish we were closer. But even I can see how you two not getting together is a real shame."

"Yeah?" Whitney leaned against the edge of the sink and studied her reflection in the mirror. She didn't look as tired and rundown as she should have, and she knew that was due in large part to Chace.

"Every woman in here has to be jealous tonight. And with good reason."

Whitney smiled. "He *is* pretty wonderful."

"Are you kidding me? He's gorgeous, funny, nice, and so into you, it's like he breathes in the air you breathe out. If it weren't for Rob, I would take him. That is, if I had a chance. That man can only see you."

"Hm." She kept looking through her bag even though she was already finished touching up her makeup.

"You're one of Rob's best friends. You mean a lot to him. And with good reason." She fidgeted with her handbag. "I'm sorry about how I acted toward you before. It's just…I've never met anyone like Rob. I'm so afraid of losing him."

"It's okay. And don't be. That guy's not going anywhere."

"You really think that?"

"Trust me. I've known him a long time. He can't stop talking about you."

"Okay." Delaney flushed and a huge grin broke out over her face.

"We're going to have to do this more often."

"Meet in restaurant restrooms?"

They laughed. Maybe Delaney had a sense of humor after all. They walked backed to the table, talking and laughing about Chace and Rob.

Once they were all done eating and poring through the dessert menu, Whitney's mind was already on the only dessert she really wanted. Chace's hand had spent most of the night on her thigh, and if she moved any closer to him, she'd be in his lap. She wasn't even really reading the words on the menu in front of her. She couldn't concentrate with Chace's hand now starting to creep under her skirt. Already thinking through excuses to leave, she didn't think they would make it through dessert.

Unfortunately, the excuse to leave was one she wasn't expecting and one that threw off the course of her evening. Hearing her phone vibrate in her purse, she slipped it out and saw that Erika was calling.

She put the phone to her ear. "Hey, Erika." She knew Valentine's Day was always a depressing holiday for Erika anyway because A.J. never did much for it. He said he didn't see the point of one day for love when you were supposed to show a person love year-round. That would have been okay maybe if he'd done anything at all to show he loved Erika.

Whitney could barely understand what Erika was saying. She was sobbing into the phone. "We. Broke up. Can't even—he had a girlfriend. Whole time!"

"Slow down. Tell me what happened."

Erika took a deep breath and continued in a somewhat calmer tone. "Supposedly he had to work today. That was this year's reason we couldn't go out for dinner or something. I called him to wish him a happy Valentine's Day. He was trying to rush me off the phone the whole time. I got a bad feeling about it." Erika paused and a sniffling sound came through the phone. "We fought and he hung up on me." Another pause. "Then, I get a call back a few minutes later from this number I didn't know. This girl gets on the phone and cusses me out for calling her man and don't I know it's Valentine's Day? He was out. On a date. With his girlfriend. For Valentine's Day!"

Oh, this was bad. Very, very bad. "I'm coming over right now, okay?"

Erika managed something that sounded like "okay" through her sobs.

Whitney closed her phone and stuck it back into her bag. She looked around at their curious faces. "That was Erika."

"Bad?" Rob asked.

"Really bad. She and A.J. broke up. She's in shambles."

"Damn."

"Exactly." Whitney nodded. "I have to go. I'm sorry," she said to all of them. Then she turned to Chace and patted his knee. "Really, really sorry."

Rob said, "Call me later? Fill me in?"

"Of course I will," Whitney said, standing and throwing a few bills on the table.

Chace handed them back to her, shaking his head. "No. It's Valentine's Day."

She smiled, taking the money back and kissing his cheek. Then she whispered to him, "Why don't you go to my place when you guys finish here? I'll be home as soon as I can."

He grinned before giving her a quick kiss on the lips. "I'll see you there."

❧

Erika came to the door in a black sweat suit, her eyes red-rimmed, looking only half-alive even in the dim light. She only had one lamp on in her living room. There was a tearjerker movie playing on her television and her coffee table was filled with the types of food Erika usually didn't keep in her apartment out of fear of consuming them in out-of-control quantities.

Erika had probably made one trip out of the apartment that day and that would have been to get those containers of ice cream, cookies, packages of candy, and two liters of soda on the table. Whitney knew all the signs. Erika was at the lowest of lows. Even with all the crap A.J. had pulled, Erika had never gotten this bad during their relationship. In fact, the last time she'd seen this species of low had been before Erika and A.J. even got together.

"I'm sorry. I know you were with Chace. I ruined your Valentine's Day. I just—I had to get it out," Erika said as Whitney walked into the apartment.

"No. I'm glad you called. Of course I'd want to be here with you for something like this." Whitney sat down on the couch and patted the space next to her. Erika sat down and leaned against her side, bursting into fresh sobs.

"I thought he was going to be it. I could just see us married. I could see our babies. All I wanted was him. Why couldn't I have it?"

"I don't know. I don't," Whitney said, knowing this wasn't the moment to bash A.J. "But I do know that everything happens for a reason."

Erika crumpled a tissue in her fist. "I know you hated him. But the way I felt about him? Was real. Pure. Strong."

"I know how you felt about him," she said. "I know this is hard for you." She pulled Erika close.

"Why can't the people we love just love us back? And why do people have to lie? Lies hurt so much," Erika said.

Whitney bit her lower lip, thinking of Chace. Kelly had lied to him. Hurt him. Was Whitney hurting him, too? And for what? She couldn't come up with any good reasons. "I wish I knew. I think anybody with the answer to that question would be a rich woman. Or man."

"He could have just said no when I asked him out that first time we met. He could have just never told me he loved me. Never pretended to feel anything. He could have just never moved in here. I really thought things would be different after that. He could have— just never—broke my heart." Erika broke down again.

Whitney rubbed her back and tried to think of something to say to her to make it better. But she couldn't think of one thing. Eamon's king of breakup songs from 2003 was playing in the background. Erika had it on repeat as far as Whitney could tell. It'd been playing ever since she walked into the apartment.

Whitney vaguely wondered what the new breakup songs were. The best ones always seemed to come out in the winter, but she hadn't been listening to the radio lately. Well, the regular radio. She usually just listened to her stations on her favorite internet radio player.

"Whitney? What am I going to do?"

"First of all? You're going to cry. A lot. And throw things if you have to. Then, tomorrow, you're coming to Rob's grand opening. And the party tomorrow night. And you are going to have a fantastic time."

"Oh yeah. That *is* tomorrow. With everything going on, it completely slipped my mind."

"I'm not surprised, considering all you had going on today."

Erika stared at the crumpled tissue in her hand. "Can you do me a favor?"

"Anything."

"Can you call him? Ask him to come get his stuff while I'm gone tomorrow? I…can't."

"What's his number?"

Erika gave her the number, and Whitney made the call. After a short, tense phone conversation, A.J. agreed to come get his stuff the next day.

"Thanks," Erika said after Whitney tossed her phone onto the end table next to the sofa. "I have one more favor to ask. Will you watch the rest of this movie with me? Stay a while?"

"Of course," Whitney said.

"Good. I'll make us milkshakes." Erika got up from the couch and went into the kitchen. Soon Whitney heard the blender whirring. She sent Chace a text to let him know she wouldn't be back until really late.

After a few hours of sad movies, too much sugar, and a lot of man-bashing, Whitney left Erika's after telling her she'd pick her up in the morning to go to Rob's grand opening.

Whitney walked into her apartment and emotionally exhausted, leaned against the door for a moment. She thought about Erika and A.J. and how she hoped Erika would see soon that having that bum out of her life was actually a good thing. Then, she thought of Chace. And how different her situation was. And how ungrateful she'd been for her wonderful situation until lately.

There wasn't a trace of him in the living room or the kitchen. She went to her bedroom, hoping to find him there.

She smiled at the image of Chace curled up in the center of her bed, his bare shoulder and the top of his chest visible above her comforter. She slipped out of her shoes, padded over on her bare feet, and leaned across the bed, kissing him on the cheek. Then, she went to the bathroom to get ready for bed.

When she finally got into the bed, he pulled her close, nestled his head into her neck like he usually did when they slept together. He'd slept over several times since that night she'd tried to cook for him. He murmured her name without opening his eyes.

That was the moment she knew she was permanently, irrevocably, irredeemably in love with Chace Murphy. Even if she didn't know how to deal with that yet, or how to say it to him out loud, it was a nice thing to know and a good feeling to have.

She wrapped her fingers around his and brought them to rest just under her chin. She stared down at the moonlight streaking across their arms, thinking of how perfect that moment was. If she were ever asked to describe love without using words, having a snapshot of that moment would have been handy. Snuggling closer to Chace, she closed her eyes and fell asleep with a smile on her lips.

Chapter 22: T-Shirts for All

When Chace shook her shoulder in the morning and told her it was time to get up, she hid her head under the pillow.

He moved the pillow aside and kissed her ear before saying, "Rob wants us there by eight. It's already past six." He squeezed her shoulder. "We gotta get up."

He was right, but that didn't make her want to get out of the bed. After all, he'd gotten plenty of sleep the night before. Not so for her.

"I hate Rob and his stupid store," she said with a yawn.

"That's not true," Chace said as she sat up in the bed. He kissed her cheek. "Good morning."

"G'morning." She turned and gave him a full, hot-blooded kiss. "I'm sorry I didn't get home until late."

"It's okay. We'll make up for it tonight," he said in a voice husky with desire. "But we have to get going right now or we'll be late."

"True. Especially since I told Erika we'd pick her up on the way." She rolled out of bed, and Chace was close behind her.

He pressed his hands to her sides as they walked toward the bathroom. "This is going to be a long, long day."

She turned to him and jumped on his hips, wrapping her legs around him. "Very long."

He backed her into a wall and kissed her while pushing his hand under her tank top.

"We better get ready separately or we may never get ready," she said reluctantly, breathlessly, between kisses.

"Yeah," Chace said. He gave her backside a squeeze before letting her down. "I guess I'll go make us some breakfast while you get in the shower."

"Love — that idea," Whitney said, kissing his cheek. She'd barely caught herself yet again.

He grinned. "Me, too."

Once they were dressed and had eaten, they went to pick up a very grumpy Erika. She looked less excited about the early hour than they had been. She came out of her building gripping a takeout coffee cup and wearing gray sweats and a black hoodie. She slipped into the backseat of the car, grumbling a greeting to them.

"Good morning, Erika," Whitney said.

"I hate morning." Erika took a long drink of her coffee.

"Looks like it," Chace said with a grin. "You're still pretty, though, sunshine."

Erika laughed. "You are just made of charm, huh?"

He shrugged. Whitney reached for his hand, and he gave it to her.

She wanted to melt for him at that moment. How could she not always want someone like that? On top of being perfect to her, he'd made her friends love him, too.

They got to the storefront on U-Street, just down the street from Ben's Chili Bowl, a little while before the doors opened. Rob was falling over himself with excitement. The store had been his dream as far back as Whitney could remember. He'd finally made enough money from selling T-shirts from the trunk of his car and online to open an actual, physical store.

He would have to work his butt off to make the store turn a profit, but she knew he didn't mind. The business was something that consumed his every waking moment and his dreams, too. Just like Whitney's job, but the key difference was Rob had a true passion for what he was doing. Whitney had drive, but she didn't know if she would call what she felt for her job a passion anymore. Maybe it had never been one.

Rob's brother, Gi, showed up for the opening as well. He had come down from M.I.T. He supported his brother's dreams way more than their parents did. Rob and Gi couldn't have been more different in personality, but they were still close. Kind of like Whitney and her sister.

"It's good to see you, Gi," she said, hugging him.

"How are you?" Gi wore wire-framed glasses. He was taller than Rob even though he was younger. His hair was cut close, almost in a buzz cut. He seemed to always wear khakis. That day, he wore his khakis with a gray sweater under a brown leather jacket.

"Great. This is my friend Chace."

Chace and Gi shook hands and exchanged hellos.

"And Erika. How are you?" Gi's smile seemed to broaden.

"I'm good, Gi. How you've been?"

"Fine. This is my last year of school. I'm really excited about that. I think I'm taking a deferment before starting grad school even though I've already been accepted to a few decent programs." He passed a hand over his short, black hair.

"Really?"

"Yeah. I need a break. I told Rob I might come help him get his business off of the ground. I'm really happy for him."

"Me, too," Erika said. Soon after that, the two of them were deep in conversation about Rob, T-shirts, and school.

Normally, Gi tried to talk IP law with Whitney, but his real interest was in patents, and he didn't seem to realize science and Whitney were not friends. However, that day he seemed to be much more interested in talking to Erika.

"I think he likes her," Chace whispered to Whitney.

"Good, I hope she likes him back," she whispered to him. "She needs a good guy. She always goes after creeps."

"You wouldn't think she's just rebounding if they got together?" He raised an eyebrow. Touché. She'd walked herself right into a trap.

"I guess it would depend." She settled deeper into his embrace.

"On what?" Chace's lips were right at her ear. He was always cheating, distracting her.

"On…whether…she seemed really serious about him or not."

"And how could you tell that?"

"Maybe if she cooked him dinner. Or came to his place almost every night. Or took care of him in every way he'd let her. Or if she came over to his house and fell asleep in his bed waiting for him to come home and she couldn't imagine a more perfect image ever existing. And he wished he were a photographer, too, so that he could capture that image forever."

The look in his eyes caught her heart up. She could almost hear it beating. It thudded in her chest so hard, she could imagine it jumping out. He put his arms around her and pulled her close, putting his gloved index finger and thumb beneath her chin.

He tilted her face up to his, first kissing her lower lip. Then the top. Then, he smothered her with a deep, passionate kiss. She gripped his back to keep from falling over under the weight of the intensity and desire in that kiss.

Wanting the kiss to last forever, she pushed her tongue slowly over his. She savored the taste of his mouth, traces of coffee and toothpaste mixed together. She moved her fingers along his cheeks, over his ears, through his hair. She linked them together there, in back of his head, buried them in the soft warmth of his hair. His arms circled her waist, and he pulled her closer.

A passerby said, "Don't they look precious together? Why don't you ever kiss me like that anymore?"

Whitney smiled against Chace's lips, but never broke their kiss. Instead, she tightened her hold on him. Maybe it didn't even need to be said aloud. Maybe saying it in a kiss was enough.

❧

Rob's after-party was at an old warehouse that had been converted into a club. It had just opened a few weeks prior and was the newest night spot in the U-Street area. Rob's promoter friend had worked out the deal for him, getting him the club for the night at a price he could actually afford.

Whitney moved through the dark club, lit only by flashes from the strobe lights, with Chace's arm around her shoulders. The music was loud, but good. The D.J. was up in his booth, concentrating intently on his laptop screen. A bunch of other equipment surrounded him.

They walked up to Ulrich, who hugged her and shook hands with Chace. He'd made an appearance with his flavor of the week. She was like all the rest of them. He was such a player, but it would catch up with him one day soon—she hoped. He was a good guy, and she wanted to see him settle down with a good woman. But in the meantime, it would be the top-heavy, tiny-waisted, sweet if vapid girls he picked up with his usual "I'm a lawyer" pickup line. When they found out he was one of the few who could actually back up that line, they fell all over themselves for him.

Ulrich said, "You looking good tonight. Real good."

"Thanks." She grinned. "I'm glad you made it here," she said, hugging him.

"Yeah, I dropped in to say hello, congratulate your boy Rob." He hugged back and said in a low voice, "Looks like he's good for you after all. About time you found one who is."

She pulled back from the hug and nodded.

He turned to Chace and slapped him on the back. "What up, Chace?"

"Good to see you again." Chace shook Ulrich's hand.

"You, too."

Chace pulled Whitney close to him in a possessive gesture. It was a little bit of a Neanderthal move. Especially when she'd told him he didn't have to worry about Ulrich. But it was kind of nice in some small way.

Ulrich put his arm around Ms. Flavor of the Week, and introduced her. Whitney didn't even try to remember their names anymore. She doubted she would see the woman again after that night. She was just another one of those women with dollar signs in their eyes Ulrich loved to string along.

"Rob will be glad to see you. Isn't this place crazy?"

"It is. I'm gonna go catch up with him now. We'll see you two later," Ulrich said. He went off with his date in tow.

"So this whole day has turned out to be a success," Whitney said.

It seemed to be turning into a success for Erika as well. Erika and Gi had been inseparable since the opening. Whitney hoped that meant good things. She hadn't heard one mention of A.J. all day. That was definitely a good sign.

"Yeah. I'm happy for Rob," Chace said, hugging her close from behind. He rested his cheek against hers.

"Yeah. Me, too." She smiled, relaxing against him. "Really happy."

Abbott walked up to them. She'd pinned her red hair up that night with a pair of chopsticks that matched the blue and gold kimono she wore.

"So this party is pretty amazing," Abbott said.

"Yeah. He's finally done it. He deserves this night," Whitney said.

"True." Abbott toyed with the thin gold chain that hung around her neck. "Everyone deserves something that makes them happy."

Whitney thought back to her conversation with Abbott at the bar. She knew what Abbott was getting at, but her friend was wrong. Gibson and Grey made Whitney very happy. Success was happiness. There was no better way to prove that than to make partner.

"Erika looks really good tonight, huh?" Whitney nodded in Erika's direction.

For a moment Abbott looked thrown off by the abrupt change in subject. Then, she looked across the room and nodded. "He was definitely dead weight."

"Got that right." Abbott tugged at the collar of her kimono. She obviously didn't want to drop it. She opened her mouth to say something else, but Whitney didn't let her.

"Here they come." She waved to Gi and Erika.

They waved back as they approached the group. Erika was glowing. She'd even changed out of her sweats. Whitney had been worried about that because the club had a dress code and because—well—coming to a party in sweats? No.

Erika wore a simple long-sleeved knee-length dress which flared out a little at the waist with silver jewelry and knee boots. Gi had actually changed out of khakis into dress slacks. Rob must have made him do it. He wore a light blue dress shirt and black shoes.

"Abbott, it's so good to see you," Erika said, throwing her arms around Abbott.

"Hi, Erika," Abbott said, smiling.

"This is Gi."

Introductions were made all around again.

"Great party, huh?" Gi said.

"Yeah. And there are three more levels to the club." Erika nodded emphatically. "We haven't even seen half of it."

The group got into a discussion about the party, the crowd it'd drawn, and Rob's new store. The day seemed to have surpassed even Rob's expectations. It was hard to catch up with him that night. He was all over the place, thanking people, greeting others, and enjoying his well-deserved spotlight.

Whitney slid Erika back from the group a little and murmured to her, "So, you look a lot happier than you did this morning."

Erika shook her head. "Don't start. It's just good to see an old friend."

Whitney shrugged. "I'm just making an observation. And he's spent more time with you today than with his brother. Just another observation."

"Rob's been busy. This is a big day for him. Not even Delaney can keep up with him. I've been keeping Gi company." Erika smiled. "I never realized he was such an interesting guy."

"Well, I'm glad you two had a good day." Whatever the reason, she was just glad Erika was distracted and seeming a lot less close to the ledge than she'd been the night before. Erika had been lost and gone over A.J. for so long. Like no guy ever before, even though he was the biggest loser she'd ever dated. She was very relieved that A.J. was out of their lives forever. At least she hoped he was.

A new song came on and Erika started bobbing her head and grabbed Whitney's shoulder. "C'mon, we have to get out there."

"Oh, no. You know I don't do these choreographed line dance things." She backed away from Erika.

"I love this song. And the dance is so easy. Just get out here with me, Whitney."

Chace showed up on her other side and grabbed her other shoulder. "Yeah, Whit. Let's go."

Laughing and still half-heartedly protesting, she let the two of them pull her out on the dance floor. She watched their feet for most of the first part of the song, not knowing many of the steps. Eventually, she fell into step and had fun laughing at herself since she still wasn't great at the dance even after she figured out the steps.

When it was over, Chace pulled her close for the slow song that came on next. She rested her head against his chest. Everything seemed better—more interesting, exciting, full of life—with him around.

After a couple songs, he whispered to her, "You gonna be ready to leave soon? I want to. I want you. Bad."

Whitney felt just how much when he pressed close to her. Her thoughts turned to the same place his had obviously gone. They had to get out of there. Soon.

"Yeah, uhm, I don't think there's any reason for us to stick around much longer. Rob's busy, and I don't think the others will miss us, either," she said her words quickly, surprised she didn't trip over them.

"Good." His eyes were filled with desire for her. She backed away a little, afraid that if they started kissing and touching each other at that moment, they might give the entire club a free show.

"Let me just find Rob and Erika and tell them we're going." Whitney straightened out the skirt of her dress.

"Hurry." Chace pressed his lower lip between his teeth. "You know, this is all your fault. That dress is very…distracting. It's taking all my concentration to try and keep my hands to myself."

"You haven't been doing such a good job," Whitney said, wetting her lips with an anxious tongue. "Not that I'm complaining."

"I'm good at other things," Chace said.

"Yeah?"

"Let's get out of here so I can show you."

Whitney smiled, nearly backed into a nearby pillar, and then turned around and hurried off to find her friends so she could say goodbye and get Chace back to her place.

Chapter 23: Gravity

The gravity of not having thought about work all weekend hit her full-force when Bettina reminded Whitney Monday morning that her team had a meeting with opposing counsel that afternoon. They were supposed to talk about the possibility of a settlement. Whitney and her team had finally talked their client into at least discussing a settlement with the other side.

Whitney's stomach dropped through the floor. She hadn't done as much prep over the weekend as she should have. She'd spent the weekend actually acting like she had a life. Most of it with Chace and a lot of it in bed. It'd been Valentine's Day weekend, after all. Not that she expected that fact to matter to the partners. Or especially to Kim.

Bettina walked into the office behind Whitney. "She's really on the warpath. I just wanted to warn you. I heard her in there with Andersen this morning and I think I heard the words 'disciplinary action.'"

"Crap," Whitney muttered. That was the last thing she needed.

"She's a dragon, but you know there's nothing you can do to get rid of her. So don't let her get rid of you."

Bettina put a hand on one of her slim hips. "I couldn't stand this place without you."

"I'm trying not to," Whitney said. Her heart sank when she spied a folder lying on top of her keyboard. She clasped her hand to her forehead. "I didn't have you send anything to opposing counsel Friday afternoon did I?"

"No," Bettina said.

"No, no, no," Whitney moaned.

"Don't panic."

"Why should I? Except for the fact that my life is over?"

"I know your schedule back and forth, remember? I knew you probably meant to have me fax those over Friday. You spent most of Friday afternoon working on them, after all. So I faxed everything in that folder over to Todd before I left for the day. Then I put the folder back on your keyboard so you'd be sure to have it for your meeting today."

Whitney sank into her chair, relief flooding over her. "Bettina, I owe you—my life, the world, just everything. Do you know you're the best assistant in the world?"

"Yep."

They laughed.

"I better go pre-conference with Kim." She made a face.

Bettina made a sympathetic face. "She's looking for you. That's what I was trying to tell you earlier."

"Great." She tapped the folder on her desk. "No use putting it off, I guess." She stood and dragged herself to the door. Bettina followed.

Whitney went to see Kim and got the tell-tale cold shoulder, but at least it wasn't the worst it could possibly be. Kim wasn't happy with her for several reasons that had to do with assignments that hadn't even reached their due dates yet. The woman just wanted to rage at her. She accused Whitney of not being a team player. However, Kim left her as lead on the first round of settlement negotiations although Kim would be a close second-in-command. Nobody knew the case as well as Whitney, after all. Plus, Whitney had a knack for negotiating settlements that impressed even the partners. Even Kim begrudgingly acknowledged it.

At ten that morning they walked into the conference room where the negotiation was supposed to be taking place. Whitney felt like she was being walked to her execution even though it was just a negotiation. She'd been involved in several dozen during her time at the firm.

Their client, Skylar, arrived just after opposing counsel even though he was supposed to show up early so that they could have a brief conference before the negotiation started. Everyone expected that from him by that point, though. They would just have to talk after the meeting. Or they would have to ask opposing counsel for a break so they could have a side conference with Skylar if things got dicey. They had to work around this guy and his whims and on his schedule and terms. That was just the way it was with him.

Whitney and her colleagues referred to Skylar as their eccentric child billionaire client. That was what they called him when he wasn't around, anyway. After skipping a couple years of high school and graduating college a year early, he'd started his own software company with a couple of his friends at the age of twenty. He was a tech genius, and he and his two friends had recently incorporated the Bevyx Corporation. They'd named it after a comic character they had created while in college together.

Bevyx was a freakishly tall alien with a bad fake tan who was good at everything he tried, except for school. The comic had apparently been a running gag and a hit in an e-zine they created in college, but had never made it much further than that, yet Bevyx lived on in the name of their giant software company.

It was rumored the Bevyx Corporation was going to grow up to be the biggest thing since Microsoft. And that given a few years, they would dwarf both Google and Apple. That was, if this lawsuit didn't cripple them first.

They'd been accused of using a woman who worked for one of their rivals for the trade secrets she knew and then forcing her out of their fledgling business before incorporating it. Now, the disgruntled former employee was suing Bevyx and attempting to shut it down before it even got off the ground.

Skylar, their client, had dressed for the meeting in his usual jeans and T-shirt even though he knew it was an important business meeting. At least he'd finally taken their advice about not wearing jeans with holes and frayed threads to the firm. He wore suits to court. It was the best they were going to get, probably. Whitney smiled at the flip-flops on his feet. They reminded her of Chace.

Skylar had propped his Aviator sunglasses on top of his head. He wore his hair in a buzz cut and his face was pockmarked with acne scars. He kept twisting his chair from side to side as if sitting still was impossible for him. This guy made more money than her just by sitting in the chair at the table in the conference room.

The opposing counsel sat on the other side of the table with the plaintiff, Natalie. She was slim and wore rectangular-framed glasses. She wore a skirt suit and black tights. Her black hair was pulled back from her face in a ponytail.

Whitney didn't doubt for a moment that a kid like Skylar, feeling entitled to everything he wanted, would sit back and let Natalie do all the work and then take all the credit for it. She knew his type. Brilliant yet oblivious to the real world because he didn't have to live in it. But that didn't matter. She had to be a zeal-ous advocate for her client.

This case was making her feel for the first time in her life that she was doing something wrong by de-fending the supposed rights of the guy with the most money.

The opposing counsel was a two-person team from a plaintiff's law firm. Whitney had spoken with the lead lawyer, Todd, about the settlement over the phone. A short guy with sandy blond hair, dull brown eyes, and a neutral-colored suit, he easily faded into the background and seemed an odd choice for lead lawyer over his taller, flashier counterpoint. Until he started talking. The guy's short man complex came across loud and clear when it came time for business, even if he could be quite pleasant otherwise.

Todd and Whitney shook hands. The rest of her team hung back. She could feel Kim's eyes on her back, though.

"Thanks for coming over to talk with us," Whitney said to Todd.

"Sure. We were happy to get your call. We want this thing to go away as quickly and painlessly as pos-sible for both parties," Todd said.

She nodded. "So do we. How was your weekend?"

People from both sides sat in the leather high-back chairs at the conference table. They opened the fold-ers in front of them and began rifling through them. A few people started scratching out notes on yellow legal pads with ball point pens. Skylar was preoccupied with his smart phone. He didn't seem too concerned about what was about to take place.

Todd smiled. "Oh, it was great, thank you. I spent it with my wife in the Poconos."

"Oh, yeah?" Whitney opened the leather portfolio in front of her, smoothing her hand over the blank page of a fresh legal pad.

"Yeah. It's gorgeous up there this time of year. How was yours?"

Kim cut into the conversation. "Sounds wonderful. But why don't we get down to business? I'm sure everyone here has a busy schedule they need to get back to." Kim sent Whitney daggers with her eyes.

"Yes. Of course." Whitney swallowed hard and fought to keep a smile on her face as she turned to Todd, his co-counsel, and Natalie. "Have you had a chance to look over the documents that my assistant faxed to you?" Whitney could still feel Kim's glare. "I have copies here as well." She patted the stack of copies that the conscientious Bettina had made.

"We have them right here. And yes, we had a chance to take a look," Todd said as he and his co-counsel pulled copies of the papers from their attaché cases.

"I believe you'll find our offer very reasonable," she said. Kim shuffled papers, and she tensed. Everything about the woman had the ability to set her on edge at that moment.

"Yes." Todd nodded. "It's a good starting point."

Skylar snorted and muttered something unflattering about Natalie under his breath. He never did anything helpful for his case. Kim passed Whitney a note written in all caps, telling her to control her client. Sure. All she needed was a muzzle and a cage.

The negotiation went rather smoothly, all things considered. Whitney shook hands with opposing counsel and the plaintiff before they left. Then she told Skylar she wanted to see him after he spoke with Andersen. Kim caught Whitney by the elbow, holding her back from the group leaving the conference room. "That was a close one, Whitney. Too close."

"I'm sorry?" Whitney tried to keep her composure when she really wanted to snap at Kim the way the woman had snapped at her.

"Skylar almost ruined everything. It's your job to make sure he knows how to act in these situations. We can't afford for you to keep having these little slip-ups. Did you meet with him to prepare for today?"

"No," Whitney said. Kim knew how hard it was to catch up with the child billionaire. "I'm sorry." The words grated harshly against her throat because they weren't what she wanted to say. She thought the meeting had gone really well, and Kim hadn't said one word about that fact.

"Even though there's a possibility of settlement on the table, we still need to prepare for a possible counter-claim. I want a decent brief on my desk with a legitimate argument in it by Friday. Not that pathetic excuse for one you delivered last week. Now, I may be mistaken about this, but I thought you actually attended law school, yes?"

"I'll get right on that." Whitney chewed on the inside of her cheek to keep herself from saying what she really wanted to. That Kim was lazy, Whitney did most of her work, Kim was an ingrate, and the only reason Kim cared that Whitney wasn't killing herself for Gibson and Grey anymore was that it was actually starting to show that Kim didn't carry her share of the workload for the group.

"You'd better. You're not doing much to show me you're partner material right now, Whitney. I really expect more of you." Kim snatched her pile of documents from the table. "On top of that, as one black woman to another, you know we have to hold ourselves to a higher standard to be taken seriously, and you're not doing that right now. I can't say I'm not disappointed in you." With that, Kim walked away.

She took a few deep breaths through clenched teeth before she could even walk back to her office without bursting into tears of frustration and anger.

∽

Whitney put her legs on Chace's lap. "My feet are so sore. I was running around all day between our Tyson's Corner office and my office—the one in the city." Ever since the settlement conference a few weeks ago, it seemed that Kim had gotten it in her head to double Whitney's work load.

"I'm sorry," Chace said, slipping her shoes off of her feet. He began massaging them, kneading his fingers into the soles.

She closed her eyes and moaned. "That feels so good."

"Good." He deepened his touch.

"I have the big eval tomorrow. We're going to talk about whether or not I'm eligible for partner this year," Whitney said. She wasn't looking forward to it with the way Kim had been acting lately, but there was little more she could do than just walk in there and see what would happen.

"Yeah? You ready?" Chace's hands moved down from the balls of her feet and then to her Achilles tendons, relieving the tension there. His touch felt so good that she just wanted to melt into him.

"I guess," she murmured, feeling further and further disconnected from her worry with each new touch of Chace's hands. "How are things with your job? And your photography?"

"Good on both fronts. I was talking to someone in my photography club who said there's a local show I should try to get into. Apparently, a lot of local gallery owners and that kind of crowd go to it," Chace said as his hands slowly moved up her calves, working the tension out of her muscles as they went.

"Mmm. That's good. Any of them doing it?" Her eyes were closed and she was drunk with satisfaction. "The people in your club?"

"Nah. They're mostly just hobbyists. Not interested in shows," Chace said. His strong hands kneaded her overworked muscles. They were now at the top of her calves. He'd shifted up the couch so that she was now sitting on his lap. She opened her eyes and put her arms around his neck. His gaze was so intense that she forgot what they'd been talking about.

His hand moved up to her inner thigh. She gasped and then moaned, lying her head against his shoulder. Not much longer after that, her hose hit the floor and Chace's hand rubbed against her naked skin, pushing her skirt up to her hips.

She looked up at him and realized that neither of them were going to be satisfied with what they'd been doing. That night, they would go further. She was going to forget everything but him for one night. She wasn't going to worry about getting too attached to him or anything else.

Her kissed her greedily. When she was able to pull back, she stood and reached down for his hands. He stood and pressed his hands to her lower back after laying his forehead against hers. She bit her lower lip, wondering how she'd held out as long as she had. She knew their relationship was about to change in huge ways. A part of her she'd tried to ignore until that night was excited, wanting those changes to happen.

"It's been a long time for me, Chace. Over a year."

"I'll take good care of you," Chace whispered to her before tugging at her earlobe with his teeth. "I promise."

Whitney's knees nearly buckled at the heat of his touches. He picked her up and carry her to the bedroom. Lying her down on the bed, he traced his fingers over her stomach and down her thighs. She began unbuttoning her blouse, her hands shaking with desire and anticipation. He sat on the side of the bed and moved her hands away from the buttons, kissing them after he did. He ran his fingers down her now exposed cleavage, around the edges of the top of her bra. But he left the last few buttons buttoned.

"I want you now," she said, reaching for his belt.

He took her hands in his. "No. We're not going to rush it."

His words sent a thrill of shock and pleasure through her.

Sex had always been much like a business transaction before, and she hadn't minded it much because she'd told herself she didn't have time for romance in her life. However, she'd been missing more than she could have ever imagined.

He lowered his head, placing kisses in the areas his hands had just touched, slowly unbuttoning her blouse the rest of the way as he did. She eagerly shrugged out of it and tossed it across the room. She felt his teeth, gentle yet insistent, against the skin just above the cup of her bra. She started to unhook her bra, but he grabbed her wrists and shook his head.

He held her wrists with one hand and ran the other down her sides and over to her navel. He trailed kisses down from her breasts to her lower abdomen and she shivered beneath the feverish warmth of his mouth. His hand slid between her back and the mattress to unzip her skirt and she moaned her gratefulness when he yanked it off her and tossed it to the floor. He pressed his hands into her thighs, massaging the creases at the tops of them with his thumbs. She writhed beneath him, her mind numb with pleasure and thoughts of pleasure to come.

"Chace," she whispered, burying her hands in his hair as he planted kisses that brought her nearly unbearable amounts of pleasure on her hip, just above where she really wanted his mouth. She was out of her mind with need for him. He teased the sensitive skin where her thigh and hip joined with his tongue. She cried out and pushed her legs further apart for him.

He responded by moving his kisses lower, pushing the wet folds of skin open with his nose before setting her on fire with his tongue. Her desire for him had been building ever since he'd started her foot massage and it didn't take long for the waves of pleasure to roll over her and for her to feel the sweet release all over her body.

Chace trailed kisses back up to her mouth, kissing her softly as she helped him out of his clothes with a hot eagerness. They threw his pants and shirt across the room. His grunted with pleasure as she nibbled at his ear before kissing his neck, her hands moving up and down the tense muscles of his back.

He tossed her bra to the floor and bit at her nipples, causing her to whimper, weak with pleasure she hadn't known it was possible to feel. His hand slipped between her thighs and found the spot his tongue had found a few moments earlier.

"Make love to me. Now," Whitney whispered to him.

He rubbed his thumb over that very sensitive spot until she came to the brink a second time, stopping just before she went over. She whimpered as he pulled back.

He grabbed a square packet from the nightstand. She heard it rip open. She closed her eyes and arched her back in anticipation, hungry for him to touch her again. She opened them when she felt the welcome pressure of his body on top of hers. He leaned on one elbow and used his free hand to guide himself into her.

She barely noticed the momentary tightness. She reached up for his shoulders he thrust against her slowly at first, but with a growing intensity.

He reached down, surrounding her breast with his palm. The pad of his thumb caressed her nipple. She ached for him. Each touch made her want the next one even more.

"How can you know all the right ways to touch me?" she whispered.

He responded not with words, but by shifting against her so that she felt him in just the right spot with every move of his hips against hers. With every move, in, out, up, down, he took away her ability to utter another word — to even think one.

Just as she began to hit her mind-obliterating apex again, he rolled her over and entered her where she was wet and hot for him from a new angle. She let out a scream of pleasure that she could no longer hold back.

∽⚬∽

He groaned as she tightened and released around him, no longer able to hold back. When their throbbing stopped, he lay against her for a moment, careful not to put too much of his weight on her. Her back moved under his chest.

Getting women into bed had never been a problem for Chace. He'd never even had to try. But he'd never been with someone like Whitney. The way he felt inside of her, making love to her, was different. If he hadn't been sure before, now he was. Whitney was all he wanted.

He rolled off her, and she turned to her side. He looked down at her, stroking her hair away from her face.

"Amazing," she said.

He'd never heard her so inarticulate, yet he knew exactly what she meant because he felt it, too. He never wanted to be without her again. His arm instinctively went around her. He hugged her to his chest. He wanted to protect her even though he was the one she probably needed protection from. After all, the only thing between them now was his lie.

She curled her head against his chest and ran her hand up and down his side.

He kissed the top of her head.

"I feel so open and vulnerable to you. But for the first time? That thought doesn't scare me," she said.

Immediately, he felt badly about the fact that he still hadn't told her about Kelly. But he just hadn't found the right time and way to do it yet. It certainly wasn't after what they'd shared. He couldn't risk losing her forever after that. Not when she was finally letting him in. He just needed a little more time to show her he was serious. To make sure she wouldn't run when he told her. He had to make sure she was completely his before telling her something like Kelly might be having his baby.

"You're so quiet. You okay?" She kissed his cheek.

"I'm better than I've been in a long time," Chace said truthfully. "I'm just thinking." That was mostly the truth.

"About?" She trailed kisses over his jaw.

"Us." Again, mostly the truth.

"I was thinking, too," she said.

"About?" He kissed the top of her head.

"Us making love all night long." She ran her fingers up and down his arm.

"Don't you have to work in the morning?" But he was already nibbling at the lip she brought within reach.

"Well, if you don't want to…"

Chace grinned, sitting up in the bed and pulling her onto his lap. "Hold on now. I never said anything crazy like that."

༄

After what could barely be called a nap, Whitney was glowing even if she had to be tired.

"I want you again. Before work. But I don't think I can. After last night, I'll be lucky if I can walk straight," she said, winding her arms around his neck after he kissed her good morning.

"I'll be here when you get home from work." He kissed her cheek. "That is, if you want me to be."

"Of course I do. You better be."

"You're so gorgeous," he whispered, running the backs of his fingers over her cheeks. "Especially in this light. And you're just—perfect right here right now. Do you have time for me to shoot you? Just a few shots before you go get ready for work."

She blushed. "Sure. As long as you keep it PG."

He grinned. "Of course. Only shoulders and up. Everything else," he said and kissed the top of her breast to emphasize his point, "is for me and me only."

She moaned wistfully. "If only I weren't so sore…"

"Don't worry. We have lots of days and nights ahead of us." He was already out of bed and headed for his camera bag as he spoke.

"I hope so," Whitney called after him.

"Me, too," Chace muttered when he was in the living room and out of her hearing range. Especially after he found a way to tell her about Kelly. And it had to be soon. After all she'd shared with him the night before, it was even more wrong than before to keep this huge secret from her. Still, the thought that she might never share it with him again made it clear that he couldn't tell her yet. No, he couldn't say a word until he was sure he wouldn't lose her because of it.

Chapter 24: Sugarcoated

After her deliciously sleepless night with Chace and a very good morning with him, the prospect of her eval with Kim seemed a little less scary. She was so gone over him, and there wasn't even any point in trying to deny it anymore. She smiled all the way to the office and knew that everyone on the metro that morning must have thought her a fool. Her demeanor, so different from the day before, seemed to throw everyone at work off.

Her good mood held up all the way until she entered the somber atmosphere of Kim's office and shut the door behind her. Kim sat at her desk with her hands primly folded together on top. She looked like she was about to inform Whitney that one of her closest relatives had just died.

"Good morning, Kim." Whitney smiled. She was determined to have a good attitude about this even if she had to force it.

Kim nodded, dismissing the greeting without a word. "We have a lot to talk about this morning."

"Okay." Whitney started to feel shakier about the evaluation as Kim's eyes bored into hers and a small frown creased the corners of Kim's mouth.

"Whitney, compared to your work at your last evaluation, I have to wonder if you're the same person." Kim pointed to a folder on her desk which looked like a personnel file and shook her head. "The word 'atrocious' comes to mind. That may be a bit harsh, but I find it's better not to sugarcoat these things."

She knew she'd been a little distracted lately, but she hadn't thought she'd done badly enough to warrant words like "atrocious." She was still turning in a decent work product. The settlement negotiations in the Bevyx case were going well. She had two copyright cases briefed and expected to win one with little sweat on a motion to dismiss, and the other had a promising counterclaim that she'd come up with all by herself. Well, with a little unwitting inspiration from Chace.

"You've been flitting about the office like some absent-minded child." Kim shook her head. "Barely professional. Not carrying your weight at all."

Lies. All lies. She wanted to tell Kim that, but she knew saying anything would only make the situation worse.

"If I didn't know any better, I'd say you don't even want to be a partner any longer. Do you?"

"Of course I do." Whitney's heart lurched in her chest and her throat burned.

"Well, you're certainly not acting like it. What have you given me to take to the committee? Work ethic? Substandard. Team effort? Substandard. Work product? Poor at best. You've even started coming in on your own schedule."

Whitney had been late one morning. And so she'd stopped coming in early. So what?

"Andersen is very disappointed in these changes in you."

Her heart lodged in her chest. "Can I say something?"

"Whatever it is, is it really going to help your case?" Kim raised an eyebrow.

Not with Kim evaluating her, it probably wouldn't. Still, she had to try. "The Bevyx case is going well and—"

"Thanks to me." Kim sniffed. "Left up to you, who knows what shape it would be in right now?"

Whitney couldn't believe what she was hearing. She'd carried the weight on that case from moment one. Her, not Kim—her.

Kim splayed her fingers in front of her, inspecting her fingernails as she spoke. "There's been a marked change in you. I've heard rumors of a new man in your life." Kim looked up at her. "Now I know your personal life is none of my business."

No. It wasn't. But Whitney wasn't in a position to say so.

"Still, let me give you a little piece of friendly advice, mentor to mentee." Kim leaned back in her seat. "I used to be like you. Young and full of unrealistic dreams. I thought I could have a relationship with a man and still give everything to this job that it required. Thankfully, I realized I was wrong before it was too late. Let me pass along a free piece of advice. Whatever this distraction is, get rid of it. If you want to be a partner at this firm, that is."

Whitney didn't say a word. She was too busy trying not to show her anger at Kim's butting into her business.

"Regardless, right now? I cannot recommend you for partner. You've done nothing to show me you can handle the challenge."

"But you won't let me—"

"You've been missing deadlines, I've found you unprepared for court, assignments have been half the quality of what you used to produce."

"When have I ever been unprepared for court? And—"

"Are you calling me a liar?" Kim shook her head. "It's bad enough that you've become a substandard lawyer. Throwing around baseless accusations as an attempt to mask your mistakes? That is truly in poor taste."

Whitney was too stunned to mention that Kim had started giving her more and more ridiculous deadlines, she'd repeatedly given Whitney misinformation and it'd been up to Whitney to find out what the right information was before she could even begin her projects, and once she'd even given Whitney the wrong court date.

"I've already shared this information with Andersen and the committee, but you're welcome to talk to them, of course. It's well within your rights to do so."

With Kim in their back pockets? What would be the point? Sure, Whitney might have changed her work habits to resemble those of an actual human being more lately. She was no longer a Gibson and Grey robot, but she was still doing her job. She'd made a couple of mistakes lately, with a lot of "help" from Kim, but she couldn't see why Kim was taking partner away from her. It was like Kim was sabotaging her.

She'd heard Andersen compliment Kim on a memo or two that Whitney had written or seen Kim take credit for her work in other respects over the years, but she'd never thought of it as malicious. She still didn't want to think that even Kim was capable of sabotaging her partner prospects just so that Whitney could stay under her and do her work for her. Had Kim taken the opportunity of Whitney's distraction from work over the past few months and used it to derail Whitney's future for her personal gain?

She had to get out of there. She couldn't think in that room with Kim. She could barely keep herself from screaming.

"Okay," Whitney said. "Okay." It was all she could say.

"Then, we're done here. Right?" Kim started straightening stacks of papers on her desk.

Whitney nodded and moved toward the door.

"Oh, and Whitney?" Kim called as Whitney put her hand on the doorknob.

Whitney turned to face her.

"Consider what I said about not letting a man take you off-course. Consider it very seriously," Kim said.

Whitney nodded and left the office. Was Kim right? As an underling with no life, she'd certainly had plenty of time to do Kim's every bidding in the past. Was Chace too much of a distraction? Had she caused herself to lose partner? Had Chace? Had Kim? A combination of the three?

When she got back to her office, she mumbled something to Bettina about being sick and taking a half day. The sick part was right even if she wasn't coughing or running a fever. That evaluation had made her nauseous. She couldn't be at Gibson and Grey one moment longer. The only Grey she wanted to see right then was Grey Goose.

She sent Kim an email, letting her so-called mentor know that she was taking the rest of the day off. After calling Abbott and seeing if she could meet for lunch, Whitney grabbed her coat and her purse, leaving her laptop in the office. She left Gibson and Grey in drastically lower spirits than those with which she came in a mere couple of hours earlier.

The fatigue from the sleepless night before was settling over Whitney now that her Chace high was fading. She slumped over in the booth where she and Abbott sat.

"Bad, huh?" Abbott asked.

Whitney nodded without even looking up. "I don't think I'm going to. Um. I don't think I'm going to make partner." If she were to have any chance, she would have to fight Kim tooth and nail to do it. She wasn't sure she was up for that.

Abbott reached over and rubbed her shoulder. "Whoa. That's huge to you, Whit. Everybody knows that. Are you okay?"

Whitney shrugged. Abbott's hand was still on her shoulder.

"You wanna talk about it, hon?"

"What's the point?" She looked up. "Why am I doing all of this? Everything was for that—for partner. If I don't get partner, all of this has been for nothing."

"You can't believe that job's the only thing in life that matters. Maybe you're trying hard at the wrong thing, if that job's making you so miserable."

"What am I supposed to be trying at, then?" Whitney tapped a fingernail against the dark wood of the table.

"I just meant that—your job shouldn't consume your life. You've been happier than I've seen you in a long time since you stopped letting it do that."

She toyed with the edges of her napkin. "You're talking about Chace, aren't you?"

"Maybe."

She sighed. "What if he's part of the problem? I never even thought about falling in love before him, and now maybe love is ruining my life."

"What are you talking about? How can love ruin your life? Ruin anybody's life?"

Cradling her head in her hands as she spoke, she told Abbott everything. All Kim had said in the evaluation. All about Chace. Even about her suspicions regarding Kim.

"That's horrible," Abbott said. "You know, I never did like that Kim." She moved to Whitney's side of the booth.

"Yeah."

"So what are you going to do?" Abbott rubbed her shoulder.

Whitney looked up. "I have no idea." She'd made lots of plans for lots of different things in life, but she had no plan at all for a situation like this one.

"Are you going to the partners?"

"She has them all wrapped around her finger, and I haven't done a great job of making myself look like the model employee lately." She heaved a huge sigh. "If I go to them, and go over her head, I have to be in for a long, ugly fight."

"Are you going to give up on being a partner at the firm?"

"I didn't say that."

"Do you still want this, Whitney? Are you sure this is really something you want?"

A few weeks ago, Whitney would have answered that question without hesitation. Of course it was. She'd spent her whole life working toward her dream of making partner. But was it something she wanted, or something everyone else wanted for her? Was it just something she thought she should want?

"I don't know," Whitney said. "And I'm not even sure how to go about figuring out the answer to that question."

"I think you should think this thing through, too, and not for the reason Kim wants you to." Abbott put an arm around her. "Chace seems to bring you so much happiness. And you were kind of in a funk ever since Kim suggested that you cut way back on the pro bono work because it was cutting too much into your productivity as an associate. I dunno." Abbott smoothed her hair away from her face. "Is being at the firm for you? If it keeps meaning you have to keep giving up the things that make you happy?"

"Being successful makes me happy. Being at Gibson and Grey? Means success. Being a partner there? Means fulfillment."

"Really?" Abbott stared her down.

At that moment, the server brought Abbott's ginger tea and Whitney's cocktail. She didn't often drink her lunch, but she didn't often get all her dreams crushed in less than an hour, either. Whitney toyed with the glass filled with ice, vodka, and cranberry juice, trying to decide how to answer Abbott's question, or if she would at all.

Abbott put her hand over Whitney's. "I just want to see you happy."

Whitney looked up into Abbott's compassionate pale blue eyes.

"There's an opening at One Justice For All. Why don't you at least drop off a résumé? Go over there and tell them I sent you. Talk to my friend, Gracie, about the opening and about the organization. You wouldn't have to make any moves to leave Gibson and Grey yet. Maybe not at all. Just check out the opportunity."

"Even if I'm not happy at Gibson and Grey. Let's say for the sake of argument I'm not, what about making the people I love happy? Isn't that worth something? A lot? What if I'm even less happy disappointing them than I am being Kim's footstool?" She looked away from Abbott as she said this.

"All I know, Whitney, is if you keep lying to yourself, you risk losing more of yourself. Already, there's so much of the person I knew and loved in law school missing from you."

"Things change. I got realistic. Learned how the world works."

"You saying I'm naïve?"

"I'm saying it's different for you. It always has been. It's easy to walk away from the money and the lifestyle when you've had that chance. I grew up with nothing. I watched my mother suffer. I never want to see that again." Whitney said more than she'd meant to.

Abbott leaned toward her. "What are you talking about?"

"Nothing. Just forget it."

"You never would say much about your family and your childhood, but let me say this. I've met your mother, and she's a beautiful person inside and out. She seems happy with her life, and, to me, nothing matters more to her than her children's happiness. I think what would make her happier than anything is seeing you happy. Not how much money or the amount of material things you can give her."

She smiled. Abbott sounded just like Jo. Abbott always had been good at reading people.

"Now I can tell you all the things you've heard before about money not being happiness, but why bother?" Abbott shrugged. "You need to make this decision for you. Just you. Not for anyone else. Decide what makes you happy. And what you're willing to sacrifice. Is the big law firm lifestyle for you? Is being with Chace what you want? A real life? Is it possible to have both?"

Whitney stared into her glass.

"At One Justice For All, you'll have a real chance to make a difference. I know how much that means to you. Or at least, I know how much it used to mean to you."

She sat back in the booth. Abbott had always had a negative view of big law firms, big business, and so on. So her opinion was probably a little biased.

"You say family is important to you, but how much time do you really get to spend with them when Gibson owns you?"

Good point.

"You know, you're one of the few people from law school I still talk to who went the big firm route. Because you're one of the few who I could tell didn't buy into the whole scheme even though you tried your hardest to do so." Abbott rubbed her shoulder. "Don't give up on who you really are. Don't give up on getting what you really want. It's within your grasp. Not everyone gets that second chance. Don't ruin yours."

Whitney stared down at the plate the server had put in front of her and the salade niçoise occupying it. Even though it was normally one of her favorite meals, she didn't have much of an appetite for it. Everyone was living out their dreams except for her.

Abbott enjoyed her work with the non-profit world aid organization for whom she was general counsel. Rob's T-shirt business was taking off. He finally had the brick and mortar store he'd been fighting years to get, and business was already booming thanks to word-of-mouth around the city about his crazy shirts.

Erika had gotten rid of Old Stupid and was having the time of her life. She always seemed to be going out, almost every night. She invited Whitney, but Whitney never went. She never seemed to have time. What little time she had went to Chace. And even they didn't go out because she was so busy with work. Her compromise to not being at the office was staying home with him where she was close to her laptop and she could watch her BlackBerry like a hawk without the interruptions of life.

Chace was getting somewhere with his photography. There was even going to be an article in a photography e-zine focusing on young artists in the city featuring Chace as an up-and-comer on the D.C. photography scene.

And then there was the question of what she wanted. Her dream had allegedly been the partnership track, but that was probably over now. And was it really her dream anyway? Or had that dream always belonged to others in her life?

She picked up her fork before glancing at Abbott. "I guess I have a lot to think about."

Abbott nodded. "Good. So will you at least consider talking to Gracie?"

Whitney took a deep breath. "Sure."

Abbott grabbed her hand. "I'm glad to hear it. You owe yourself the opportunity to let go of this pseudo-life and be who you really want to be. Live the life you deserve. Live life, period."

Whitney smiled before forcing down a forkful of her salad.

She couldn't see herself leaving Gibson and Grey, but she'd humor Abbott. Plus, it wasn't like handing over a résumé would irrevocably change her life.

Chapter 25: The Rapids

"Wake up, Whitney."

"Huh?"

"We're here."

She looked out of the windshield of Chace's SUV. She could only see as far ahead as the headlights cut through the darkness. Trees, for as far as the eye could see. Nothing but trees.

It was five-thirty in the morning. And she wasn't asleep in her bed. At home. The trip was already starting to seem like a bad idea. Was seeing the sunrise over the valley really worth the lack of sleep?

She yawned. She'd slept the whole way there, but it still hadn't been enough.

"You awake over there?" he said.

"Not really." She climbed out and shut the door after her.

Erika and Ethan got out of his jeep. Erika jogged over to them. She hugged her fleece jacket close to her body. Ethan followed. Rob careened into the parking lot and skidded his car to a halt next to Ethan's jeep. Delaney got out and slammed the door. She looked a little wobbly, a little grim.

"C'mon." Rob laughed. "It wasn't that bad, was it?"

"This is why I like to drive," she said.

"It's not my fault that really slow guy cut me off right before we got on a two-lane road," Rob said. "I had to catch up with these guys."

"No." Delaney threw him a look of death. "You didn't."

Whitney turned back to the SUV to help Chace unload their equipment. He'd wanted to take her on an overnight camping trip to help her get her mind off what had happened with her eval. She hadn't been able to bring herself to tell him that she probably wouldn't make partner, but she'd told him the rest. He wanted to help. And she did feel better being out of the city, away and with people she cared about. She smiled at Chace as she hoisted her backpack onto her shoulders.

He slung his camera bag around his neck. "What?" He grinned.

"Nothing."

He strapped on his pack and grabbed a hibachi grill with one hand and a small cooler with the other. She closed the rear door on his truck.

"Let me help you with some of that stuff."

"Nope," he said.

"No really, let me just—"

"We gotta hurry or we'll miss the sunrise." He nodded in the direction of the trail, and the five of them started down it with their gear.

She pulled her light jacket closer to her body as she walked down the path. It was windy and chilly out, but not too bad. The crisp, cool air felt good against her face, actually. She breathed in deeply. Their footsteps crunched over the gravel path as they made their way up the mountain to the lookout point that Chace had marked on a map earlier that morning. GPS didn't work so well in the mountains.

They made it just as the sky was lightening from dull grays to real colors. The peach-red glow rose over the valley as they watched. Chace put down their gear and snapped some pictures.

After setting his camera down, he put his arms around her.

"Was it worth getting up so early?" he said before kissing her cheek.

She smiled. The trees were still dark with shadows as the first rays of the sunrise hit them. "Yes. It's beautiful here." Peaceful, too. She felt lighter than she had in days. "Thank you."

He squeezed her more tightly to him.

∽✤✑

They made camp and had breakfast once they were done watching the sunrise. Then Whitney went down to look at the river. She regretted it as soon as she got close enough to hear the raging water. Chace must have followed her because he walked up next to her as soon as she stopped moving.

She looked down at the frothing rapids. The white caps on them were a little intimidating. "You sure it's safe?"

Chace laughed and put his hands on her shoulders. "Yeah. I do this all the time."

"Huh. You do lots of things I wouldn't even think about trying all the time."

"Don't worry." He kissed her cheek before hugging her from behind. "I won't let anything bad happen to you."

She smiled and sank into his arms. She knew. And there was a warmth and security that came with that knowledge that she'd always wanted. "Let's go back and get ready."

After lunch, Chace, Rob, and Ethan got the kayaks and everything else they would need ready. The group headed down to the river. Whitney hung back with Erika, watching the guys toss life vests and paddles around.

When they'd gotten everything ready, Chace jogged over to where she stood with Erika. "You ready?"

"Yeah. Let's do this." She turned to Erika. "You said this was fun, right?"

Erika nodded. "I only did it once—with the trainers I hired. It was a team-building thing. We had a good time."

"I'm trusting you." She turned back and looked up at Chace. "And you."

"You're in good hands. No lie," he said. He asked Ethan for a life jacket and Ethan tossed one over to him. He held the vest out for her, and she put her arms through the arm holes. He then fastened the straps on it.

"Where's yours?" she said, looking around.

"That's the last one. I guess we miscounted."

"You need one, too. You can't just get in like that." She glanced at the churning water.

He shrugged. "I've done this hundreds of times. I'll be fine."

"Have you ever done it without a vest?"

"I promise not to die."

She laughed. "Okay, if you promise."

He grinned, kissed the tip of her nose, and then jogged over to Ethan, calling out a question that had to do with some kayaking term she'd never heard before.

She murmured to Erika, "Kayaks don't really...roll over, do they?" She shuddered, thinking of something she'd read on her BlackBerry before she'd fallen asleep in the SUV earlier.

Erika squeezed her shoulder and said with a grin in her tone, "Only if you want them to."

"Great," Whitney said, staring down at the turbulent water again.

297

Erika laughed and tugged at her hand. "It'll be fun."

She sure hoped so.

❧

Once they were done with the river and back at the campsite, Whitney sat by the fire Ethan and Chace had started with a blanket wrapped around her shoulders. She'd really had a great time. Chace had been right. Being out there had been kind of exhilarating, and she definitely hadn't thought about the firm at all while she'd been tucked into a kayak with Chace, out on the rapids.

Chace had hiked down to the cars to get something. Some of the others were napping. Ethan came out of his tent and sat next to her.

"You know, I never really thought he'd get over Kelly this quickly, but it seems he has," Ethan said. "He's really crazy about you."

"You think so?" Whitney smiled, remembering how sure and solid Chace had felt behind her in the kayak earlier. She'd felt so safe in there with him. That was saying a lot, considering how formidable kayaking the rapids had seemed before they got out there. Chace had been so capable and confident the whole time.

Ethan nodded. "I've known him for a long time. Trust me."

Whitney stared at the bright orange and yellow flames, listened to the crackle of the wood.

"He's like a brother to me. I want to see him with someone who makes him happy." He rubbed his hands together and held them out toward the fire. "You seem to do that."

"I care about him. A lot." Her heart jumped a little after admitting that. It was true, but she hadn't said it aloud to anybody. Not to Erika or Rob. Not even to Chace—not really.

"Yeah. I can tell. I'm glad."

"You think he still cares about Kelly?" She turned to him. "You'd know. You're his best friend."

Ethan swallowed hard and kept his eyes on his hands. "I think you have nothing to worry about when it comes to her." He turned and looked directly at her. "I mean that."

He seemed so desperate for her to believe him. Hopefully, it was just concern for Chace that made him seem that way.

❧

That night Whitney and Chace lay next to each other in their sleeping bags. He turned on his side and propped his head up with his hand so that he could look down at her.

"Did you have a good time today?" he asked.

"Great time," she said, reaching for his hand. He gave it. She pulled it to her chest and interlocked their fingers. He rubbed his thumb over the back of her hand. "You've been kind of quiet this evening." She'd noticed him arguing with Ethan earlier. Ever since then, he hadn't said much.

"Yeah," he said.

"Everything okay?"

"Oh. Yeah."

"You sure?"

He leaned close and kissed her neck. "It's gonna get cold tonight."

"Is it?"

"Yeah. And I don't think you want to be in there all alone when it does." He unzipped her sleeping bag.

"What are you doing?"

"We should share our sleeping bags with each other." He climbed out of his sleeping bag.

"There are people right outside."

He chuckled. "They aren't 'right outside.' Besides, the tent's not see-through." He reached under her shirt, touching her bare skin. She shivered with pleasure.

"I guess you're right about that." She let him slip her shirt over her head.

"I'm definitely right about that." He rubbed his thumb over the fabric of her bra, teasing her nipples.

She moaned and moved closer to him.

"This is all I've been thinking about all day," he said.

"But you still haven't told me...oh. That feels good," she said. He slid her pants down her legs and pulled her panties aside. Then, after pushing his own pants down, he was inside of her, pushing hard against her. She needed him, and he seemed to sense that, going harder and deeper until she had to bite her lip to keep from crying out for him. Hoping he would never stop, she dug her fingernails into his shoulders, grabbed the fabric of his T-shirt in her fists.

His breathing was ragged in her ear. She wrapped her legs around him, wanting to pull him as close as possible to her. In that moment, she forgot about everything except for the fact that she had to have him.

Chapter 26: Not in a Million Years

Whitney had a great weekend in the mountains, but the week following was a rocky one. Of course, there was the disaster of having to work with Kim after that horrible eval. Her mom was embroiled in drama with Aunt Cheryl. Apparently Jo needed some plumbing work done in the guest bathroom, and Aunt Cheryl's boyfriend was a handyman. Jo didn't want him to do it, and that was causing trouble between Jo and Aunt Cheryl.

Thank goodness the work week was over because it had been a particularly heinous one. She'd noticed several subtle but unmistakable snubs from partners who'd generally been friendly to her before. She was one of the few senior associates going for partner who hadn't been invited to the Nationals game that afternoon, for one thing. And there'd been other things, too—missing lunch invites, meetings she found out about after the fact, and cold shoulders. Plus, Kim always had a discouraging word for her.

She hoped Chace would be there when she got home. He spent more time at her place than he did at his lately. Seeing him was getting to be the only bright spot in her life, even though Kim's words about not having time for relationships constantly nagged at the back of her mind.

With heavy steps matching her morose thoughts, she trudged home from the metro stop.

When she opened the front door, she spied Chace in the kitchen. He was making chicken salad out of leftover rotisserie chicken she'd brought home the night before.

"Thank goodness you're here," Whitney said, going straight into the kitchen without even taking off her coat and wrapping her arms around him.

"Hey, you okay?" He hugged her back and kissed the top of her head.

"I just had a crappy day. Week. Everything." Whitney murmured her words into his shirt, breathing in deeply the scent of his cologne mixed with that of the spices and herbs that still hung in the air.

"I'm sorry," he said, rubbing her back through the coat.

She reached up and kissed him fiercely. She led him to the living room without ever separating their lips. She tossed her coat aside and pulled him down to the couch with her.

"I need you so much. When I'm with you, nothing else matters. And I need that," Whitney whispered, holding him close. He kissed her. She deepened the kiss, hungry for him. She pushed him back on the couch and pressed her body to his.

He caressed her neck and then the tops of her shoulders, but his mouth remained on hers. She pressed her body to his, needing to feel how much he wanted her.

She pulled back a little. She traced his lips with her fingers, letting them migrate across his jaw line, back to his ears. He was always there for her. He was always what she needed. She thought back to the past weekend in the mountains. To what she'd shared with Chace and to what Ethan had told her. She couldn't hold herself back from saying it any longer and wondered why she'd done so for so long in the first place. "I love you, Chace. So much."

Chace's Adam's apple worked wildly in his throat, and a panicked look grew in his eyes. For one horrible moment, she thought she'd said the wrong thing. Then he said, "I love you, too."

She kissed him, and he didn't kiss back as fully as he had earlier. "Is something wrong?" She smoothed his hair back from his temple with her finger as she spoke.

Chace sat up and pulled her onto his lap. He gave her a troubled look. "I have something to tell you. I should have told you a long time ago." He put his arm around her waist, but he averted his eyes. "I'm sorry I didn't. But after what you just said…it can't wait any longer."

Whitney tried to get off his lap, but he tightened his hold on her. Panic swept over her. She couldn't take

NICOLE GREEN

more disappointment that day. She was at maximum capacity. He was scaring her. "What is it?"

Chace took her hands in his. "Kelly's pregnant. And it might be mine."

Whitney pulled her hands from his. "What?"

"She got pregnant before we broke up. She was— with both of us during that time. I didn't know about him. We were having unprotected sex. She was supposed to be on the pill." He took a deep breath and relaxed his hold on her waist. "She told me right after New Year's. I was afraid that if I told you then, it would scare you off."

"That was my decision to make." Whitney got off the couch and started pacing the living room. "She's— she's pregnant? You've known for two *months*? And you didn't say one word to me?" She wanted to scream, but she repressed the urge. "Not one word."

"She goes to the doctor next week. She's gonna have a test so we know whose it is." Chace ran his hands through his hair.

"And you were going to tell me when? Were you just going to show up one day at my door, bouncing a baby on your hip and say, 'surprise, I'm a father?'" She'd almost risked everything for him. What a fool she'd been.

"I was looking for a way to tell you, but nothing ever seemed right."

"Well, hiding it from me sure wasn't." She walked across the room. "Why would you do this?"

"None of this changes how I feel about you."

"How do you know how you'll feel once that baby's born if it's yours? How do you know you won't want to be a happy family?"

"See? This is what I wanted to avoid." He jumped up from the couch. "Kelly and I are done, and I knew you'd start this dumb stuff about me supposedly having leftover feelings for her."

"It's not dumb. You were together for—"

"Two years. Yes. I know. Do you know how often you say that? I should start keeping count." He laughed bitterly. "That doesn't matter. I only want to be with you."

"You still shouldn't have hidden this. You should have let me make the decision."

"And risk losing you forever over some idea you've concocted in your head that has absolutely no basis in reality?"

"It was selfish of you to decide what I should know and what I shouldn't."

"And it's selfish of you to always put your job first. That job comes before everything in life for you. Including me or—well—anyone else. Besides, you're short-sighted when it comes to Kelly. Maybe if you ever listened instead of assuming you know every thought I'm going to have before I have it, I wouldn't have been so hesitant to tell you."

"So now it's my fault?"

"I'm just saying you should listen to somebody besides yourself sometimes."

What right did he have to judge her? "Get out. I don't want you or your babies or your lies. Any of it." She held the door open and pointed into the hallway.

"You know I'm right. That's why you're so pissed." Chace grabbed his camera bag and coat as he spoke.

"I know you're an ass." She slammed the door after him.

She refused to feel bad about it. She'd almost ruined her life because of him. Now she knew the right decision to make. He was no longer clouding her judgment.

She had to work harder. Of course she wanted to be a partner. Her job was what mattered. That and the people who depended on her. Not some lying, stupid man who didn't even live in the real world.

She couldn't stay there. She couldn't stand the sight of her condo. Plus, if she wanted to get back in Kim's good graces, she had a lot of work to do.

She gathered her things, including a pillow for the cot she kept in her office and a change of clothes. She would shower at her firm's gym. She would get in a good workout, too. Between that and pulling an all-nighter, she should feel much closer to her old self and have a much better outlook on life soon.

Chapter 27: The Test

Kelly asked Chace to go with her to the doctor. She didn't want to go alone. Even Amy didn't know—no one knew except her, the doctor, and Chace. And of course she couldn't ask Hank. At first, Chace had said no. But after his blow-up with Whitney, he decided he might as well.

It would probably be kind of cruel to let Kelly go through that alone anyway. She really had seemed scared the few times he talked to her on the phone. And he guessed he was scared, too. At least they could be scared together. Plus, he had to get his DNA to the doctor somehow. It seemed stupid to make a separate trip down there just to do that.

They met in Richmond, since that was where her doctor was. He parked, checked in with the nurse, and sat tensely next to her until he was called back to give his DNA sample.

The waiting room was drab, full of browns and grays. Two other women were there. One wore a hoodie and the hood kept her face from view. The other one was obviously pregnant and she kept yelling at her two kids to calm down. They ignored her and wreaked havoc in the waiting room instead.

After getting his cheek swabbed, Chace went back into the waiting room and sat next to Kelly. She was wringing her hands in her lap. She wore a loose-fitting sweater and baggy jeans. He'd never seen her in anything that wasn't slim-fitting and designer. It was kind of jarring.

"So, what have you been telling him? He's had to notice by now," Chace said.

Kelly shrugged. "That it's winter weight and I need to get my butt back in the gym. I've been faking my period. Now that we live together, it's an issue, I guess. I don't know if he pays attention to such things, but just in case."

"So how are you going to explain it if you are? Surprise, I'm not fat, I'm pregnant? Just kidding?"

"I mean, I'll just tell him I didn't know I was, I guess. I'll worry about that later," Kelly said, rubbing her hand over her chin. "Right now, I just want to get through taking the test." She looked tired. Faded.

Chace sighed, pressing his hands to his eyes.

"And what did you tell your girlfriend about you being here?" Kelly asked. She sounded a little bitter when she said the word "girlfriend."

"She doesn't know. She doesn't care. We broke up. Happy?"

Kelly put her hand on his knee. "Despite what you want to believe about me, Chace, I really do want you to be happy. You deserve it."

Sure she did. He grumbled a reply. Luckily, the nurse called them back at that moment, and he didn't have to worry about her pestering him for a real response. The doctor was very nice. He explained the test to them before performing it. Chace held Kelly's hand when he inserted the needle, because she'd always hated those.

Afterwards Chace took her to McDonalds, which she'd always hated before but now claimed to crave. She devoured more food than he'd ever seen her eat in her life while he watched, sipping on a cup of coffee. He'd mostly lost his appetite ever since his fight with Whitney.

Kelly looked at him after polishing off her third Big N' Tasty. "It's pretty late. And it's cold and raining and you look exhausted. I don't think you should drive back to D.C. tonight."

He hunched over and finished his coffee with one long gulp. "I wasn't planning on it."

Kelly gave him a look similar to the one she'd given her meal a little while ago. "We could get a room together. I could go back to River Run tomorrow."

Chace raised his eyebrows. "I don't think that'd be a good idea. In fact, I think it'd be a really, really bad one."

"We wouldn't have to do anything. Unless you wanted to. You know, for old time's sake. I just want to spend some time with you. I miss you." She touched his arm.

He moved out of her range and slipped out of the booth, getting to his feet. "Uh, no. That's not going to happen."

"Don't you miss me?"

"Not like that, I don't. You made your decision. In retrospect, it's probably the best one for both of us."

"Nobody'll have to know. I mean, you broke up with her anyway."

"That's not the point. Besides, you're still in a relationship. And anyway, that's not the point. That part of our relationship? Over." Chace put extra emphasis on both syllables of the last word he spoke.

"We might have a baby together. You can't get rid of me completely."

"I explained to you already that, if it's mine, the baby is the one and only link I have with you."

"But we were so good together." She pouted.

"Key word being 'were.' "

"So you're going to stay all alone at a motel tonight?"

"No. I'm going to Ethan's."

"Ethan." She rolled her eyes.

"Yes, Ethan. My friend." He saw why Ethan had never liked Kelly. He began to wonder if she had ever made a move on his best friend. She was quite the poly-amorous type, apparently. Or maybe it was the pregnancy hormones. Either way, he had to get away from her.

"Well, fine. I guess I'll let you know when I get the results," Kelly said, glaring at him.

"Okay." He grabbed his jacket from the booth and shrugged it on.

"I hope it's Hank's so I never have to see you again, you asshole."

"Me, too."

"Why are you so hateful, Chace?"

Chace snorted, toying with his keys. "I'm the hateful one?"

"You're going to regret turning me down. Probably as soon as you get in that car."

"There's nothing that could make me regret turning you down. Trust me. The thought of us together is revolting to me now."

"Screw you!" She stomped off to her car without giving him a chance to respond. He walked over to his own car. Kelly being angry at him didn't matter. Whitney being angry at him, however, was different. No matter who had been in the right and who in the wrong, it was devastating.

He drove to Ethan's and parked on the street in front of his building. He sat in the car and waited for Ethan to get home. When he saw a guy with black hair wearing a corduroy jacket jump out of a beat-up Jeep Wrangler with a battered canvas cover, he got out of his car and walked over to the jeep. He clapped a hand on Ethan's back.

"Hey, man. How you been?"

"Chace." Ethan grinned and slapped his back. "Where did you even come from? Aren't you supposed to be in D.C.?"

"Long story." They headed for the front door of Ethan's building. Chace blew onto his gloveless hands and rubbed them together. "I came down to see Kelly. We did the paternity test."

"Well?"

"What?"

"Is it yours?" Ethan opened the door, and they walked into the building.

"We won't know for a couple weeks, man. You can't just get the results for these things instantaneously. It's not like peeing on a stick, you know."

"Well, you should have called, dude," he said as they jogged up the stairs. "You're lucky I'm here. I'm leaving for Mexico in a few days, and I would have hated to miss you. You know I'm a traveling man."

"You didn't say anything about that the other day," Chace said.

"That's because I just got the assignment."

Ethan unlocked the door to his apartment and pushed it open. As usual, it looked like a war zone. Clothes and takeout cartons were strewn everywhere. Ethan's parrot, Polly, greeted them. The name might have seemed unoriginal, but it was better than those of Ethan's first three birds — Parrot, Parrot the Sequel, and Parrot the Third. Needless to say, Ethan wasn't much into naming things.

"Hey, Polly," Chace said to the bird.

"Man, that thing is so lame. She's just old and blind and mean now. I think I'm getting a cockatiel next. Or a cockatoo. Or something else, you know, not lame."

He laughed. "You're being too hard on Polly." Chace turned back to the bird. "Isn't he?"

"Asshole," Polly said.

"Ethan. Please don't tell me that's the only word she knows."

Ethan snorted. "One of, like, three. I tried to teach her more. She refuses to learn. I told you she's mean."

"Right," Chace said. He walked over to the couch and cleared a space to sit. He blew a breath straight up, temporarily lifting his hair from his forehead. "So. I screwed up. Big."

"Yeah?" Ethan was sorting through an array of takeout menus that he kept on his kitchen counter as he spoke.

"Whitney and I broke up."

Ethan stopped sorting. "What, really?"

Chace nodded. "I finally told her about Kelly. And everything fell apart, as I was afraid it would. She accused me of keeping something from her she had a right to know. I told her she was selfish. The next thing I knew, I was on my way out of the door."

"You try to talk to her since?"

"I'm pretty sure she hates me." Chace mumbled the words through his fingers since he had his hands pressed to his face.

"Ah, Chace. You're so good at getting yourself into huge messes and just kind of enjoying drowning in them. I wish I could say I'm surprised."

"Hey. This one isn't entirely my fault. She was wrong, too. I told you. She could be impossible sometimes. It's hard to come between her and that job."

"But obviously, she's worth the work to you."

"Is she? I mean, she blew up at me all crazy because I didn't tell her about this Kelly thing. It's not like I hid the fact from her that I had an actual baby or something."

"Man, that's a heavy thing to lay on a person. Think about it. You had weeks to get used to the idea—"

"I never got used to it. I'm still not."

"Regardless. The point is, she only had a few minutes."

Chace considered this for a moment. "She won't return any of my calls. I've tried to give her a chance to talk it out. She's so stubborn. I should just give up."

"All I know is you've seemed happier talking about this girl than you have about any of the other ones.

Even Kelly, who was allegedly 'the one' at some point in your life before you found out she's a huge skank."

"Thanks for reminding me."

"Any time." Ethan laughed and ducked the half-hearted punch Chace directed at his arm. "But seriously. You and Whitney are good for each other. I can tell."

"I don't know. I just don't know. I mean, I think she's worth it. But if the baby turns out to be mine, there's a huge chance we'll end up falling apart anyway. That she won't be able to handle it." He sighed. "Why go through all of that for nothing?"

"If it's meant to be, it'll all work out." Ethan walked back over to the counter and picked up the menus.

"Ethan. The walking, talking fortune cookie."

"Quit your bellyaching." Ethan threw a chopstick at him, and he caught it. "Are you admitting defeat? You, the one always talking about love and getting married and all that other crap?"

"I'm not admitting anything."

"You hungry?" Ethan asked.

"Yeah, I guess." Chace stretched out on the sofa and turned on the television.

"Good. 'Cause I'm starving."

"What are we having?"

Ethan fanned the menus out and held them in Chace's direction. "Pick one."

Chace rolled his eyes. "With you? I should have known."

"Unless you feel like cooking?"

Chace yawned. "Hell, no."

"Luck of the draw it is then." Ethan closed his eyes and selected one of the menus he still held fanned out in one hand. He opened his eyes and looked down at the menu he'd selected. "Ah. Looks like Jewish Mother for us."

"Sounds great," Chace said.

Ethan walked away to place the order.

Chace groaned and sank lower on the couch. Ethan had to ask three times what he wanted for dinner before Chace heard him. He was lost in memories of Whitney's attempt to cook him dinner.

❧

The next morning Ethan and Chace sat on the sofa with their microwaved breakfast burritos. Chace had decided to hang out with Ethan for a few days until Ethan left for Mexico. He'd called work to let them know, and they'd been okay with it. His boss at the catering company had told him that they didn't have very many contracts for the next few weeks. They'd been slow recently and had started sending him home early a lot, so he hadn't worried about them having a problem with him taking a few days off.

He needed to be away from D.C. for a while. Everything there reminded him of Whitney. And living with her best friend definitely wouldn't have helped him get his mind off her.

"So you've had a night to sleep on it," Ethan said. "Feel any different from how you felt last night?"

"Not really." He chewed on his rubbery burrito.

"Maybe this is driving her just as crazy as it's driving you."

"I doubt it."

"Man, I've never known you to be so negative," Ethan said.

Chace took another unenthusiastic bite of his breakfast.

"You know, I talked to her that weekend we went kayaking."

"I know. You told me, but you didn't tell me what you two talked about." He stuffed down the rest of the burrito. "What did you talk about?"

"She really cares a lot about you. She's good for you." Ethan stood and stretched. "I've never known you to give up on the things that really matter to you. Don't start that crap now."

"But maybe I don't want to be with anybody that stubborn and quick to jump to conclusions."

"Lie."

"I wasn't the one in the wrong. She was."

"Nope."

"Huh? Who's side are you on, anyway?"

"Love's side." Ethan played air guitar and sang the words in a tone-deaf voice. "Since you're too busy feeling sorry for yourself to be the love-struck sap out of the two of us, I have to pick up your slack."

"You're an idiot." Chace laughed.

"I learned from the best, teacher."

"Seriously. What do you want me to do, apologize to her? For her blowing up at me?"

"Don't start painting yourself as the patron saint of wronged lying boyfriends, okay? You weren't exactly honest with her."

Chace closed his eyes and lay down on the sofa.

"What are you doing?"

"Going back to sleep."

"No, you're not. Get your lazy ass up from there."

Something light and plastic bounced off Chace's side. He opened his eyes and saw a plastic cup that Ethan must have thrown at him. "For what? Why should I get up?"

"Because we have to help Mom haul all her junk out of the attic for some huge spring cleaning yard sale she wants to have this weekend."

" 'We?' "

"Yeah. I volunteered us. So get up."

It would be nice to see Ethan's mom again. He hadn't seen her in a long time. "Okay. Fine. I'm up."

"No you're not."

Chace groaned and dragged himself up from the couch.

"C'mon, Papa. Before I get old and gray."

"Say it again, and I'll sic your own bird on you." Chace said. "She doesn't seem to like you very much anyway."

"I tend to have that effect on people, Papa."

"That's it. Polly, get him."

Polly gave Chace a doleful look and said, "Asshole."

"Fine. Be on his team, traitor."

They laughed. He elbowed Ethan in the side and then ducked Ethan's attempt to put him in a headlock.

Ethan disappeared to his room. Chace ran his hands through his greasy hair before letting them rest at the back of his head. He needed a shower, but the bathroom was so far away. Every step took real effort at that moment.

Having a baby wouldn't have been such a bad thing. Only he wanted it to be with Whitney, not Kelly. Thinking of Whitney and Kelly made the bathroom seem even further away. That test had to come back saying Hank was the father. He wanted Kelly out of his life forever. She caused problems whenever she was around.

Chapter 28: Not Worth It

Whitney needed to get back to her brief, but she couldn't cut her mother off. Not when Jo was in the middle of a rant and needed her support. She'd never been able to say "no" to her mother. That was part of the reason she pushed herself so hard at her thankless job.

Her mother had a brand new problem with Aunt Cheryl.

"Free is the worst thing in the world when you're trying to get somebody to do something for you," Jo said. "If you get them, you better pay them or else not get them to do it at all."

"Mom, will you please let me do something about that fake contractor?" she said. Aunt Cheryl's boyfriend had screwed up the plumbing job that Jo had finally agreed to let him do in the guest bathroom. "It's no problem at all for me to take care of it, and I would feel better knowing it's fixed," Whitney said.

"I swear, that woman gets me in more than enough trouble."

Aunt Cheryl's boyfriend had botched the job. So not only had Jo and Shorty wasted a lot of money on materials, but now a real plumber had to be paid to do the job correctly. Luckily, the guest bathroom didn't get used too often, so it wasn't an emergency situation. However, the mess still needed to be fixed.

Jo paused for a long moment. Then, she said, "I'll think about it."

Whitney closed her eyes briefly. "Please, Mom. Think hard. I only want to help."

"I let you do too much of that already."

"Really. I can help, and I want to." She didn't mention that she didn't feel like she could ever do enough to give her mom all she deserved. Her mother didn't like to hear things like that.

"I'll talk to Shorty and get back to you," Jo said.

"Well, I gotta go now, but I'll call you tonight, okay? Ask him by then."

"That's not enough time for us to discuss this thing."

"At least start by tonight. At least bring it up with him."

"Okay, honey. I'll talk to you later."

"Bye." Whitney tapped her phone against her chin and leaned into the file cabinet. Back to work. She had to drag her way through the rest of the day somehow.

❧

Apparently Whitney had messed up yet again. Kim didn't like the brief at all that Whitney had turned in as a final product, and there was no more time for revisions before the document had to be turned in to the court. The brief was fine. Kim was picking with her yet again, but there was no way of proving that.

Kim didn't want her to make partner because then she would no longer have a footstool. Despite the fact that she was back up to her highest work level and had maybe even surpassed it, Kim was still riding her. She wanted to say something to Andersen, but every time she started to go to his office, she made up a new excuse to put off talking to him. The moment she said something, she had to be ready for a war with Kim. She was already at a disadvantage, considering how Kim had skewed the partners' perception of Whitney's job performance.

The Bevyx settlement had come out in a way to make their client happy, Whitney had written an excellent brief in support of their motion to suppress due to the court that morning on another case, and she was three steps ahead of Kim on the new case they'd been assigned. And Kim was becoming more and more of a terror to her daily.

That morning, she sat in Kim's office while Kim prattled on and on about expectations. She didn't know the words were coming until they were already out of her mouth. But she didn't regret them. "I don't give a damn."

Kim was stunned into silence for a moment. When she recovered, she said, "You don't what?"

"You heard me."

Kim's eyes narrowed. "That's insubordination. I'm telling the partners about this immediately. About this mediocre brief and about what you just said to me."

"Tell them. You have no right to treat me the way you've been treating me lately." She sat forward in her chair. "Then again, you've been treating me like that since you became my mentor. And I've been working like a dog for you. For the past couple of weeks, I've been working maybe harder than I ever have. I've been doing half of your job and twice mine for years, Kim, and I am sick of it. Just plain sick."

"What did you say to me?" Kim's mouth, painted with her ugly trademark red lipstick, dropped open.

"A job should be a part of your life. It shouldn't take over the whole thing. I hope you figure that out one day. It might help you become less bitter and small. But regardless?" She stood. "I'm not going to stick around here and I'm not going to take this crap off of you any longer." She started for the door.

"You think anyone's going to miss your pathetic attempts at lawyering around here? I've been covering for you for years anyway."

"Oh, and I know you've been passing my work off as your own even though you tell me it's horrible and you need to make all kinds of corrections before you turn it in to Andersen. And that you've been passing off your mistakes as mine and making me look like a clueless, worthless idiot to the partners." She glanced over her shoulder at Kim. "I figured it all out. Some of it I've known for years and some of it I found out about recently. But you know what? That all ends now. I'm leaving, and all I ask of this soul-sucking, mind-curdling place is a recommendation letter. That's all I want."

"I wouldn't give you one now if you begged for it."

"That's fine. Because I hope I'm smart enough not to ask you for one." She'd already decided to ask Brent for one. She'd worked with his group for a year. Even though that'd been over four years ago, anything was better than using Kim as a reference.

"And what about court this morning?"

"Ulrich is on the case and he has co-counsel. They know it as well as I do. I'll check in with all my clients and talk to Andersen to see what I need to do to tie up loose ends here. But with how you've tried to make me look to everybody, I'm sure it won't be hard to get out of here."

"No one will ever believe you. I'll deny every word you just spoke."

"Oh. I'm not worried. Even if you don't have a conscience to get you, people will figure out what's going on when the quality of your briefs goes way down. You never were that good of a writer." She wrapped her hand around the doorknob. "That's enough for me. For you to be exposed as a phony."

Whitney slammed Kim's door after her and a smile spread across her face. Sure, she would miss Bettina and Ulrich and a few other of her co-workers. And some of her clients. But she wouldn't miss the office politics or the pressure. She knew she was making the right move. She was going to drop by One Justice For All as soon as she left the office to give her résumé and cover letter to Abbott's friend, as she should have a long time ago.

When she told Bettina she was leaving, the woman was horrified.

Her green eyes widened and she latched onto Whitney's arm. "No. You can't go. I can't be at this place without you, Whit."

She laughed. "You'll be fine."

"Well, you have to at least promise me we'll keep in touch." Bettina hugged her.

"We will."

"Oh, and I'm so proud of you for standing up to Kim." Bettina looked around and lowered her voice before saying, "Nobody likes her."

Whitney smiled. "Thanks."

Bettina flashed her a smile. "Of course."

"I'm going to my office. I have some calls to make. I'll call you into my office soon to talk about helping me wrap things up here. Oh, and if you see Ulrich walking around, can you send him in?"

"Sure."

Whitney made some calls and sent some emails before getting down to the gritty business of typing up her resignation letter. She was halfway through writing it, after having deleted several hundred words. She kept deleting what she typed. She couldn't find the right words. Her palms were sweaty and her hands unsteady even though she knew she was doing the right thing.

Ulrich knocked on the door before poking his head in. "Whit?"

She sat back from her desk and swiveled her chair toward him. She waved him into her office.

He walked into the room and slid into a chair across from her, in front of her desk. "What's this crazy mess I hear about you quitting?"

"Word travels fast around here."

"Don't act surprised."

She laughed. "I guess you're right about that." She twisted her thin gold bracelet around her wrist before looking at him. "Sorry. I wanted to be the one to tell you."

"So. You're really going to leave me to fend for myself in this place, huh?"

"You'll be fine. Really," she said. Ulrich was going to make partner. There was no doubt about that. Andersen had invited him out golfing with some of the other unofficial partners-to-be the previous weekend.

"Why are you doing this?" Ulrich leaned forward in his chair. "You want partner as bad as I do. You're not really going to let Kim run you off, are you?"

Whitney shook her head, tapping a pen on her desk top and looking between it and Ulrich several times before she spoke. "No. I'm not. I thought this was what I really wanted, but I was wrong. Really, really wrong."

"I don't get it. You've worked your ass off around this place for the past few years. For all the time I've known you. No matter about Kim. The partners have noticed. And I'd be willing to vouch for you. Lay down on the line for you."

"I appreciate that. I really do. But this life isn't for me. I had a wake-up call recently. One I really, really needed without ever realizing that I did."

"Is this about that Chace guy?"

Her heart beat faster at the mention of his name. "Parts of it." She smiled weakly. "And most of it is about me. And being happy. And not dreading where I'm headed when I wake up in the morning."

"Well, as long as you're sure leaving is something you really want to do." Ulrich looked skeptical even as he spoke. "Is it really what's best for you?"

"It is."

"I guess I'll have to accept that," he said. "You have something lined up?"

She told him about Abbott's friend and the opening at her non-profit.

"I guess there's not much else to say. Except…I'll give Kim hell for you."

She smiled. "Thanks."

"Be good, Whit."

"Good luck with partner, although you won't need it."

"Thanks."

"We'll stay in touch, right?"

"Of course." He walked out of her office and shut the door behind him.

Everything suddenly felt new and scary all over again, but she wouldn't let herself give into that. Instead of banging her head on her keyboard like she wanted to, she went back to working on her resignation letter.

∽⚬∾

There was something Chace loved about a darkroom. It was the main reason he couldn't give up using his one last film camera, even though he'd converted over almost completely to digital. He couldn't leave film behind completely—especially black and white.

Being in the darkroom surrounded by photos and trays and nothing else. The dim red light. The photo paper. Developing photos, making the images arise from blank sheets of glossy paper. The whole process was therapeutic.

When Chace had gotten back to D.C., he'd gone to see Archie at his camera shop. Archie had agreed to let Chace use his darkroom. He'd converted the shed in his backyard into one. Archie lived over the Maryland line, just outside of D.C. in Takoma Park. It was nice out there. Quiet. Peaceful. Suburban. And in that darkroom, Chace could lose himself in another world.

Chace insisted on disturbing his own peace, though. He'd finally decided to develop some photos of Whitney he'd put off developing ever since that last time he'd seen her.

A sad smile creased his face as hers began coming into relief. Whitney laughing so hard she was doubled over. She'd been crying out that her stomach hurt from laughing so much when he took that one. Whitney with a smudge of flour on her forehead, trying to look cross with him even though she couldn't stop smiling. That one was from the night she'd tried to cook for him.

A small frown of concentration on her face. Her laptop had been inches away from her face when he'd snuck up on her and taken that one. A close-up. He'd nearly gotten himself killed over that one. He chuckled at the memory.

Walking down the street with her hands stuck in her pockets, her scarf blowing in the breeze. He was amazed that some of his shots from that day had come out so well. The wind had been so crazy and they'd been walking down the street so he hadn't had his tripod with him. It was like it'd been meant to be.

Meant to be. What about him and Whitney? Was that meant to be? Every time he thought of her, he hurt. He hadn't asked Rob about her since coming back to D.C. He'd stopped asking when he realized Rob didn't like talking about it because he felt trapped in the middle. He knew that she'd stopped coming to their place—Rob always went over to hers. And he hadn't tried to call her since he'd left Ethan's place. He would pick up his phone and realize he had no idea what to say. Then he started telling himself that he wouldn't even bother until Kelly told him the news. That was no excuse, but it felt good to make a decision—especially a decision that allowed him to put off something he wasn't sure he even knew how to do.

Chace dipped a sheet of photo paper into a tray filled with a chemical-based solution. He had no idea what to say to her anyway. He loved her, sure, but were they good for each other? She was the professional, structured life, high-stress type. Him? Pretty much the exact opposite. He'd tried that high-stress corporate lifestyle, and he knew it didn't work for him. Then, if there was a baby, that was a whole new level of complication.

Chace had secured a show at a local gallery. He should have been more excited. Maybe he would be once he actually had an idea of what he wanted to show. And if he could get the bitter taste of losing Whitney out of his mouth. She was all he wanted, but he had no idea how to get her or get through to her. Why did everything always have to be so complicated with her? Why couldn't anything ever be clear-cut?

"That's it," Chace whispered, removing a picture of Whitney with the saddest expression he'd ever seen on her face from the tray. "It's not so black and white," Chace said to the picture. He looked up at one of the pictures hanging above him drying. One of the few featuring both himself and Whitney. She was turned toward him and their fingers were entwined. They'd kissed a few moments after that shot. He'd set the timer on his camera. There was an intensity between them. Not happiness. Not sadness. Just an intensity. Love.

That was it. His collection. His wonderful even if brief time with Whitney. It had been anything—everything—but black and white. He had a title. It's Not So Black and White. Because it never was when it mattered. He thought back to Ethan's words. Ethan had been right. He'd been an idiot, and he had to make it up to her—in a huge way.

He was anxious to finish developing his photos and get home. Whereas he'd been taking his time, dreading leaving the darkroom earlier, he picked up the pace. He had to get home and sort through the rest of his photos.

He had to call June, the gallery owner, as soon as he got home. He was ready for his first show. He wanted her to know she had nothing to worry about, and he wanted to thank her again for the opportunity. Everything was coming together at the right moment and in the right way. His brain was already working overtime with fresh ideas flitting through it.

Chapter 29: A Dreaded Phone Call

She wanted to call them first and get it over with, but her stomach twisted at the thought of the people she had to tell about her decision. She stared at the phone, hoping that would somehow help her get her nerve up to call her grandparents. It wasn't going to get any easier. She just had to pick the phone up and call them. So she did.

"Hello?" Her grandmother's voice came through, cold and crisp, after the second ring.

"Hi. It's Whitney." She put the phone on speaker so that she could set it next to her on the sofa. She drew her knees up to her chest.

There was a short pause before a drawn out, speculative-sounding response. "Yes?"

"I called because I have something important to tell you."

"And it is?"

Whitney took a deep breath. "Is granddad there?"

"He's upstairs."

"He should hear this. Can you get him to pick up on the line as well?"

"Whitney, what is it you're talking about? I'm getting concerned."

"I'm here," her grandfather said. Apparently he'd picked up on his own. "What's going on?"

"Okay," her grandmother said, her voice strained. "We're both on the line now. What is this important news?"

Whitney rushed the words out before she could lose her nerve. "I quit Gibson and Grey." She pulled her knees closer to her body. "Yesterday."

There was complete silence on the other end.

"Grandma? Granddad?"

After a heavy sigh, her grandmother said, "Weren't you going to be up for partner soon?"

"It's a long story, but I realized that's not what's important to me. There are things more important in life than so-called prestige and titles." She thought of Chace and felt a brief pang of sadness.

"Like?"

"Doing something I'm passionate about." She told her grandparents about One Justice For All.

"What is this nonsense?" her grandmother asked. "You've quit a perfectly good job to squander away your life and your legal education on a career path—if you can even call it that—that is beneath you. If you want to help people, donate to charity, but don't throw away your career. What has caused you to derail your entire life?"

Not what. Who. But she wasn't going to tell her grandparents about Chace. They would only put him down. And what was the point? He was out of her life now anyway. She tried to ignore the sadness that came with that thought. "It's just time I do this. Make this change for myself."

"Is this some sort of crisis? Perhaps you should seek professional help."

"It's not a crisis. It's part of who I really am. I'm not going to live a false life any longer." The words had sounded better in her head earlier, before she called her grandparents.

"You have too much of your father in you."

"Whether or not that's true, I'm tired of living my life for everybody else. I'm sick and tired of trying to pay for my father's mistakes. I know you've never told me I had to, but I've always felt like I had to make up for what he did." She took a deep breath. "You've never hesitated to pull that guilt card, though. You drop little hints about him whenever you feel like things aren't going the way you want them to."

"What makes you think you can talk to us this way?"

She closed her eyes and pinched the bridge of her nose. "I'm sorry. My tone was a little out of line. But I meant what I said. I'm finally happy." Talking to her grandparents, she was starting to feel unsure about her decision. Maybe after all her option weighing, she'd still made the wrong decision. Had she acted on a stupid impulse because Kim had made her angry and Chace being gone was making her crazy?

"And how happy will you be when you realize you've been a fool and it's too late to get back the important things in life?"

"That's not going to happen. Not now that I've finally realized what's truly important." She hoped that was true anyway.

"You're being irrational." Her grandmother sounded completely disappointed in her. "I don't know what I did to deserve this."

"I care about you, and I know you think you know what's best for me." She ran her hands through her hair and tugged at the ends of it. "But I also now know that trying to please others isn't worth being miserable. There needs to be a balance. A balance that allows me to actually live life instead of watching it pass me by. Or worse, being too busy to even watch it."

"We'll talk again after you regain your senses." Her grandmother hung up before Whitney could say anything else.

❧

Whitney asked Erika to come over after she closed the gym for the night. She could always count on Erika. She hadn't been able to sit still or think straight since she'd gotten off the phone with her grandparents earlier that night. When Erika arrived Whitney practically dragged her into the apartment.

"Whoa, what's going on?" Erika said. She wore sweats because she'd come over straight from the gym. She took off her jacket to reveal a red tank top.

"I may have done a very stupid thing." Whitney paused for a moment, but before Erika could speak, she said, "I quit Gibson and Grey."

"Oh." Erika walked over and hugged her. "Whitney, that's huge."

"Okay, I'm really freaking out here. I have no idea what to do. For the first time in my life, I'm completely lost," Whitney said. She pulled back from the hug a little. She bit her fingernails as she waited for Erika's reply. That was a habit she'd supposedly quit in the seventh grade, but it never failed to resurface when she was extremely stressed.

"So you want to be at Gibson still?" Erika raised her eyebrows. Whitney had told her friend about One Justice For All and about the fact that she was thinking about leaving the firm. However, at the time, she hadn't been considering it too seriously. Then, yesterday, something had snapped while she sat in Kim's office.

"Yes. No. I don't know. I think more than anything, I'm afraid. It's not like I have a definite job at One Justice. Right now, I'm jobless. I've let go of the only thing that has propelled me forward for years. And now I have nothing. No career. No Chace."

"Chace?"

"Oh. I didn't say that."

"Yes, you did."

"Yes." She sighed. "I did."

They laughed.

Erika leaned her head back and gave Whitney the you're-not-fooling-me look. "This is about him, too."

She shrugged. "A little. I guess."

"Meaning, you've come to your senses?" Erika put an arm around her. "I still can't believe you kicked him out over something like that." She'd told Erika and Rob what had happened the day Chace left.

"He's the one who was wrong. He hid something big from me—something huge. How am I supposed to trust that I'm the one he really wants? Do you know he almost asked Kelly to marry him? Right before she screwed it up?"

"That's the key. She screwed it up. He couldn't be more done with her and into you. Only a fool can't see that."

"Are you calling me a fool?"

"Right now, I think the shoe fits," Erika said.

Whitney leaned against the side of the sofa. She'd finally allowed herself to fall for someone. And she'd fallen, completely and totally. That was scary enough. She didn't think she could handle it if the person she fell for—the one she finally let in—betrayed her. What would happen if Chace turned out to be just like her dad? What if he disappeared without warning, too?

NICOLE GREEN

Even if Erika was right about Chace's feelings for her, that didn't mean she could trust him to stick around forever. She didn't know how much she could trust him period. It was best to just not take that chance.

"Maybe I'm scared," Whitney said.

"Of?"

"The women in my family haven't had the best of luck with men, you know."

"Shorty and Jo. Are you kidding me?"

"It took Jo three tries to get there." She couldn't help it. All she could see was the negative.

"What about Brenda and Glen?"

Her lips twitched with a smile. She had to give Erika that one. "They really make each other happy, huh?"

"Seems like it," Erika said. "There's one thing you can't allow yourself to do."

"What's that?"

"Well, two things. You can't talk yourself out of embracing the things that'll make you happy. Or, conversely, talk yourself into believing the things that make you miserable are things you need." Erika patted her back. "Take it from A.J.'s ex-girlfriend. I know a little something about these things."

Whitney nodded and looked down at her phone. She was still unsure about a lot of those things, but she certainly knew one thing. She missed Chace. A lot.

Chapter 30: Starting Over

Whitney dropped off her résumé and cover letter with Gracie, Abbott's friend, at One Justice For All the day after she finished cleaning out her office at Gibson and Grey. She was ready for her fresh start. Not only that, but she didn't want to lose her nerve, either.

As soon as she walked into the office, she could tell she would like the place. The atmosphere was so much more relaxed than that of Gibson and Grey. And when Gracie walked up to her wearing dress slacks and a blouse—no tailored suit or hose—she smiled. This woman was a far cry from Kim and a welcome change.

"Hi. You must be Whitney," Gracie said, extending her hand for Whitney to shake. "I'm Gracie, the CEO."

"Yes. We spoke on the phone. I'm Abbott's friend." Whitney shook her hand and then handed her the résumé and cover letter.

"Great. Listen, I'm heading out for a lunch meeting in a little while, but if you have a few minutes, we could duck into my office and have a little chat," Gracie said.

Whitney forced herself to keep her composure. She couldn't believe things were going so well. "I have a few minutes." She walked with Gracie to her office.

Gracie shut the door once they were inside. She perched on the corner of her desk and gestured, indicating that Whitney should take a seat in one of the chairs in front of it. When she did, Gracie said, "Abbott tells me you two went to law school together. I've heard a lot from her about you. All good things. Very good."

Whitney sat up straighter in her chair. "Abbott is such a great person."

She nodded emphatically. "She certainly is. She says that you're interested in civil rights law."

"Definitely. I quit my job at Gibson and Grey. I'm ready for a change of pace and a shift of focus away from the corporate world."

Gracie's eyebrows shot up. "You've already quit Gibson?"

"Well, I'm working a little while longer at the request of the partners. My last day is next Monday. But I'm basically done with them." That was true in every way possible.

"And you know that things will be pretty different from what you're used to here, right? We're no Gibson, that's for sure." She crossed her arms across her cranberry-colored blouse.

"I'm counting on it." She was depending on it with everything she had inside, actually, but no need to make herself look as desperate for change as she was.

"Well, you'll be playing two roles like our other two lawyers," Gracie said. "I'll introduce you to them before you leave. You'll be helping us with the transactional side of the legal work as well as the litigation side. For instance, our lawyers just walked us through the incorporation process, which is quite interesting for a 501(c)(3). But for anything out of your capabilities we'll bring in outside counsel." Gracie flipped her dark hair over her shoulders. "We're usually able to get some pro bono help now and again. In fact, I think we've gotten some from Gibson before. Anyway, we also have quite a few litigation issues coming in from the community. Our lawyers can tell you more. They've been here just as long as I have and they're the ones down in the trenches, so to speak." She stood. "Are you ready to meet them?"

"Yes." Whitney sprang up from her chair and smoothed the wrinkles out of her skirt. She had a good feeling about this. Gracie seemed to like her. She didn't know if this was an interview of sorts or not, but she knew it had to be a good sign that Gracie was taking so much time out of her busy morning for her.

She thought with a pang of sadness that she probably wouldn't have even been there if it weren't for Chace. He'd brought so much joy into her life. And she considered for all of a second calling him. But he'd been wrong.

He'd shown her a lot of wonderful things, and she'd never regret their time together, but she needed to be with someone more predictable. He'd shown her that carefree was good, but maybe he was a little too carefree. Whitney's father had been carefree, too, and that had caused Jo to get burned.

Chace had probably forgotten about her and moved on with his life anyway. Most likely with Kelly. She didn't dare ask Rob. She couldn't bear to hear the answer if he was with someone else.

She didn't want to know about it or think about it if he was with someone else. Because it would still hurt. Despite everything, she still cared about him. The fool had wormed his way into her heart over the few weeks that she'd known him. And she hadn't figured out how to get him out yet.

She forced thoughts of Chace aside and plastered a smile on her face. Gracie was introducing her to the two lawyers she hoped would be her co-workers soon. It was time to make a good and lasting impression.

∽✍∾

Whitney had told her mother about quitting her job a few days ago, and her mother had supported the decision. She was happy whenever Whitney was happy. She called her mother that evening to tell her that things had gone well at One Justice.

"I think I have a good chance at getting the job," she said as she pushed open the door to her condo and walked inside. She couldn't help but notice that no meal was cooking. Nobody had been in the place since she'd left early that morning. It was going to be another sad, lonely takeout food night.

"That's good, baby," Jo said. "Now that you're between jobs, I don't want you to worry about this foolishness going on with the plumber."

Before Whitney had quit Gibson, she'd finally gotten Jo to agree to let her pay half the amount it would cost to redo the plumbing job.

"No, Mom. I still want to help. I have a lot of money in savings, I'm pretty sure I'm getting this new job, and the firm is even letting me have a severance package despite the clause in my employment contract that would let them get out of it." Andersen had been sad to lose her after all. To show there were no hard feelings, he'd given her a generous severance package.

"I don't feel right taking the money," Jo said.

"Please. Just let me do this one thing for you. I can't do anything right anymore. I can at least do this. Give you this."

"What are you talking about, honey?"

Before she knew it, Whitney was pouring out all of her feelings of guilt—irrational as she knew they

346

were—about Jo having to raise her alone for several years. Then, she started going on about her dad, her grandparents, and all that she'd felt she owed to others for so long. She even told her mom about Chace. About her brief relationship with him and how messy the end of it had been.

When she was done, Jo said, "You stayed at a job you hated for my benefit?"

"I didn't know I hated it at the time. But yeah. That was part of the reason."

"Whitney." Jo's tone was scolding. "You know all I want for you is for you to have everything you want and be happy."

"Making you happy makes me happy."

"Well, then make yourself happy. You being happy is all I need to be happy. I didn't bring you into this world so that you could pay me back something you never owed me in the first place. You act like you went into a store and bought a mom on credit."

She laughed. "When you put it that way, it does sound kind of stupid."

"Because it is," Jo said without a trace of doubt in her voice.

"I just feel like I don't even know what the 'right thing' is anymore. And my grandparents—"

"Don't you dare let those people tell you what to do. Or let you feel inferior. I never have, and why should you? You're my daughter. A Jones. We don't let people push us around, even if they are family. Most of the time."

Whitney thought of her Aunt Cheryl and sighed. "Yeah."

"And what's this about Chace? I had no idea you two were serious. You've mentioned him once or twice, but that's about it."

"That's another thing I don't know." She kept feeling less and less sure she'd made the right decision about Chace. He'd made her feel like no one else ever had. She'd fallen in love for the first time in her life. Did she want to give up on that so quickly? Even though he'd been wrong, he'd done what he did in a misguided attempt to protect her. Erika had been right when she'd said that the other day.

Maybe letting go of him wasn't the answer.

∾⟊∾

Chace sat on the sofa, staring at the blank television screen. Rob had turned it off, and Chace made no move to turn it back on.

"I'll turn it back on if you stop pretending like I'm not here." Rob tapped the remote against his open palm.

"Huh?" Chace continued to stare at the screen. He knew what Rob was talking about, but he didn't want to.

"You've been moping around this place ever since you came back from Richmond, man. I thought you said you had a good visit there."

He had. It had been good to hang out with Ethan for a few days. That wasn't what was bothering him. Being in D.C. again, in that apartment again, so close to her yet so far away, was what bothered him. After his initial excitement about his new collection, reality had sunk in again. Whitney probably didn't want anything to do with him. He had no idea how to make her understand how much she meant to him.

"It's about Whitney, huh? That's why you're like this?" Rob said as if reading Chace's mind.

He shrugged.

"You should talk to her, man."

"What makes you think that? Wait, did she say something?"

"You know I try my hardest to stay out of the crazy you two have created. We don't talk about you two just like you and me don't talk about it. But let's just say I think that if you called her, she'd talk to you."

"You think she misses me?"

Rob flopped onto the couch. "I think she's not any happier about the situation than you are."

"You know what? I don't want to call her," Chace said. He held up his hand when Rob started to protest. "Hold on, hear me out. I don't think that's enough. You think you can convince her to come to my show?"

"This mysterious show you won't tell me anything about hardly besides the gallery's location?"

"Yeah."

"I guess. I'm like the official go-between for you guys, huh? First her with the cooking disaster, and now you."

"You'd be doing me a huge favor."

"I know." Rob grinned. "Sure. For the two of you? And the chance of not seeing either of you mope anymore? I'd do almost anything."

"Thanks, man."

"Yeah, well, I'm just tired of you moping around here, always on this couch." Rob walked into the kitchen, singing "Matchmaker" from *Fiddler on the Roof*.

Laughing to himself and feeling a little better, Chace went to take a shower and get ready for work since he had the nightshift. They were catering some sort of awards ceremony that evening.

When Chace walked back into his room, still rubbing excess water out of his hair with a towel, his phone was vibrating on his desk. It was Kelly calling.

"Great," he muttered. "Wonderful."

He'd been working all day with June to get things together for the show, and he was going to have to spend all night at work. He really wasn't in the mood to deal with nonsense. She'd better actually want something.

"Yeah, Kelly?" Chace sighed into the phone.

"Somebody's in a mood."

"I'm tired. Did you actually call to say something or you just want to babble?"

"Oh, I think you'll want to hear what I have to say."

Chace held the phone to his ear with a shaking hand. He didn't know whether to laugh or cry.

∽≳∾

Rob and Erika thought Whitney had made a good decision when it came to her career change. They told her she was already starting to look less miserable on a daily basis. She did feel a lot better.

However, they thought she'd made a really bad decision about Chace. She was having trouble convincing herself that they were wrong. He hadn't even tried to call her, though. Calling him was out of the question. He'd lied to her. He'd been in the wrong, not her. She wasn't even sure she wanted him to call. The fact that he hadn't called was probably a good thing.

She sat on her couch between Rob and Erika. They'd come over saying they wanted to watch a movie, but they had ulterior motives. The whole time they'd been making little hints about Chace. When she'd asked them to please stop talking about him, they dropped the bomb—they told her the real reason they were there. As subversives for Chace.

They wanted her to come to his show at a downtown gallery. Admittedly, she was impressed that he'd gotten the show and gotten an "in" with June—an heiress and up-and-comer in the photography world who'd recently opened her own gallery.

But she refused to go. There was no reason she wanted to see him—well, there was no way she would go see him, anyway.

Rob groaned and sank lower on the couch. "What would it hurt to come to his show? He really wants you there."

"Yeah, Whit," Erika said. "You haven't even seen the guy in weeks. If you do this and you decide it's the worst most horrible idea ever, you can leave. It's a huge, public place. We'll be surrounded by lots of people. You don't even have to talk to him if you really don't want to."

"Yeah, and it's not like my apartment, which you've been avoiding like the plague, and don't think I haven't noticed," Rob said. "It wouldn't have to be awkward and just you two. There's going to be a lot of people at this thing. I mean, did you see that spread that June was able to get for him in the *Post*?"

She had seen it. She wondered darkly if he'd done anything special for that spread in the Arts section. Then she was ashamed of herself for thinking it. Chace would never even consider something like that.

"I'm glad he's doing well," she said. She stared at the movie she hadn't been following at all instead of looking at either of them.

"Then why don't you show your support, if nothing else? If the two of you happen to talk…you talk," Rob said.

"Okay. I'll go. To support his art. Because I think he's a good artist. And that is the only reason I'm going." She looked at her friends.

Erika and Rob exchanged looks.

"What?" she asked them.

"Huh?" Rob said.

"What was that?" she asked, crossing her arms over her chest.

Erika turned innocent eyes on her. "What was what?"

"The look business. What were those looks you two were giving each other?"

"Oh, nothing. Stop being paranoid," Erika said.

Whitney leaned back against the couch and looked at the two of them again. They had turned back to the movie and turned the conversation back to it as well. She didn't know what they were up to, but if they expected anything to come of her going to Chace's show, they were going to be sorely disappointed.

Whatever that craziness with Chace had been, it was over. She didn't regret it, but it was over. She didn't blame him anymore for what she'd known at heart had never been his fault, but she couldn't get past him keeping the fact that he might have had a child secret, no matter why he'd done it. Besides, there was always the chance that he would want to be with the mother of his child — even if he didn't think so yet. What if he changed his mind after the baby was born?

And if he did abandon the baby, he wouldn't be any better than her father had been. She didn't want to be with a man like her father.

Chapter 31: Beautiful Whitney

Rob drove. Whitney sat in the backseat of the car, glaring at the backs of Rob's and Erika's heads. Although she'd agreed to go, that didn't make her any more enthusiastic about it. She'd trudged around the apartment as they attempted to get her out of the door. Finally, they'd had to almost pry her fingers from the door frame and push her downstairs.

The gallery was near Chinatown. She, Rob, and Erika walked up to the door after parking in a nearby lot designated that night for special guests of the artist.

Whitney wore a simple knee-length dress with a scoop neckline under her coat. She'd paired it with black knee-high boots that had three inch heels. She wanted to keep it simple and tasteful, not look like she was trying too hard, but also make Chace know what he was missing and regret losing it.

Whitney put a hand over Rob's as he started to pull open the door to the gallery. "You said we could leave the moment it gets awkward, right?"

Rob nodded emphatically. "Absolutely. I promise."

"Let's go in. Do y'all not know it's freezing out here?" Erika said, brushing both of their hands aside and opening the door to the gallery.

Whitney's heels clicked against the shiny hardwood floor and her eyes swept over the white walls featuring black and white photographs. Rob handed her a brochure and she saw the title, "It's Not So Black and White," but didn't pay attention to anything else about it.

Rob and Erika mumbled about having a look around and slipped off before she could say anything. They weren't slick. If things didn't go well, she would find them, grab them, and be out of there before they could say "cheese." Tapping the brochure in the open palm of her opposite hand, she scanned the crowd until her eyes landed on him.

Breathtaking, hurt-her-heart gorgeous. What had she expected? Chace wore a black shirt unbuttoned at the throat under a tan blazer that seemed to have been made for him even though she doubted he would have something tailored. His dark wash designer jeans were pressed and creased. And he wore the loafers she remembered from Valentine's Day. He was talking and laughing with a woman Whitney recognized as a mutual friend of Rob and Ulrich's. Ulrich knew her from college and Rob from his super secret double life.

Sometimes it seemed as if Rob knew everyone in the city, which was clearly impossible. Except maybe for someone like Rob. The woman was part socialite, part local art critic. Her opinion was highly respected in the city and beyond. Even a bad review from her was good news. And Chace's charm alone was probably enough to make the review go well. Besides that, he had real talent.

Speaking of his talent, she moved further into the room and took her first real look at the photographs. What she saw froze her to the spot in shock. That was because what she saw was herself.

She put a hand over her heart. It was her. Everywhere. Crying. Laughing. Frustrated. In love. Every single photograph was beautiful. She'd never seen a better photograph of herself anywhere. She wouldn't have considered herself art until that moment. But the best photos—even though there were only three in the whole collection—were the ones with Chace. The two of them in bed together. Holding each other on her balcony. And him trying to shove a disgusting hotdog piled with relish, mustard, and other unsavory things into her mouth, both of them laughing. Her watery smile broadened. That was the best one.

"Oh, Chace. If only—why?" She reached out to touch the glass of the frame, catching herself just in time after forgetting where she was and what she was doing. She pulled her hands back and placed them on either side of her neck.

"I don't know. But I want things to go back to the way they were," Chace said. "I want you."

She gasped and turned around. She'd had no idea he'd been standing right behind her. "You heard that? I was talking to myself."

He took a step closer. "It sounded like you were talking to me."

She smiled. "I quit Gibson and Grey. I'm happier. You were right."

He nodded. Then he reached for her, coming within inches of her arm before dropping his hand back to his side. "I'm sorry for hurting you. And lying to you."

"I'm sorry for jumping all over you like I did. And for hurting you, too." The words tumbled out of her mouth before she could think them through properly. "But you were still wrong for not telling me."

"I know. But I want you to know that the baby's not mine."

Whitney looked down at her hands as he wrapped his around them. Then she looked up into his ice blue eyes. The place where she'd fallen in love for the first time. And the only time she wanted to. Ever. "It's not?"

"Whitney, all I want is you. That would be true even if it was mine. I haven't been able to think of anything else. Maybe you can tell that if you have a look around this place." He gestured around the room at the photographs.

Her eyes filled with tears. He slipped his finger between her skin and the gold necklace she wore. He traced a pattern over her collarbone. She'd never wanted anything more than she wanted to be held by him. Relief overcame her as he pulled her against his chest and squeezed. Hard.

"I'm so sorry I pushed you away," she said.

"Shh. We're together now. And that's all that matters."

She smiled up at him and continued smiling as he brushed his lips against hers. "You're right. It's the only thing that does."

"I want to put a ring on this finger." Chace kissed the ring finger of her left hand.

"And what's stopping you?"

"I guess nothing now." He leaned in close. "Whitney Jones. Will you marry me?" He brushed his thumb against her ear.

She looked up at him, feeling like her face would crack if she couldn't wipe the grin off for at least a few seconds. But she couldn't. "Chace Murphy. How could I say 'no' to that?"

His whole face brightened with his smile. "Good. My brother and his family are coming tonight. So are my parents. They're all stuck in traffic right now. You can meet them. We can tell them tonight."

She rested her head against his shoulder. "Good."

"So are going to call your family?" he asked.

"In a minute. This is your night. This show is amazing, by the way. You really have a gift."

"None of this would exist without you, Beautiful Whitney." He put a hand behind her neck, pulling her close, and kissed her. "And you're wrong. It's our night, not mine. I want to call them. Right now." His hands slipped to her shoulders.

"Okay." Blushing and beaming, Whitney dialed her mother's number and handed the phone to Chace. "You're going to have to do it. I can barely speak right now."

Chace took the phone from her and kissed her cheek. "Hi. Ms. Jones? Oh, sorry, this is Chace Murphy. Yeah, exactly, that's me." He laughed at something and hugged Whitney close. "Sure did. I'm calling to tell you that you have the most wonderful daughter in the world. But of course you already know that. But there's another reason I'm calling. I've asked this wonderful daughter of yours to marry me and you know what she said? I still can't believe it. She said yes."

Whitney hugged him close, tears of happiness in the corners of her eyes. He brushed them away while still talking to her mother.

"She's right here. Yeah. But before I go, the important question. Can I start calling you Mom now or do I have to wait?"

Laughing, Whitney took the phone from him. "Hi, Mom."

"You're engaged? Oh, lordy. Really? You?" Jo said.

Whitney laughed harder. "Yes, Mom. Me."

"Then this Chace must be something else. You bring him home for me and Shorty to meet as soon as you can, hear?"

"Of course."

"Whitney, this isn't like you. Getting engaged. And I haven't even met the boy. For you to be so impulsive? He must be something special. I had a good feeling about him, though, from the way you talk about him."

"He is. Something really, really special," Whitney said, staring up at Chace as she spoke.

"Okay. You bring your something special home to us soon. You hear me?"

"I will."

Whitney slipped her phone back into her purse and reached up to kiss Chace. "Let's go find Erika and Rob."

When they did, the two went nuts over the news.

"This is awesome!" Rob cried.

"I'm so happy for you two." Erika hugged them both in turn.

"Ugh," Rob groaned. "You know the only bad thing about this is Delaney's going to be looking for the old proposal now. Thanks a lot, buddy."

Chace laughed. "You're welcome. Speaking of, where is Delaney tonight?"

"She had this charity auction thing for work. She had to go with her boss."

"Oh, okay."

"Oh, yeah. I forgot. She said to tell you congrats and good luck," Rob said.

Chace nodded. "Great. Tell her I said thanks."

"You're getting married!" Erika hugged Whitney again. Whitney was relieved about her reaction. She'd been worried marriage would be a sore spot with Erika after what had happened with A.J. Erika pulled back and clasped her hands. "I can't wait. Seriously, and I can say this now that you're going to, but I was afraid this would never happen for you. Really afraid, because you deserve to be happy. So much."

"Thanks, Erika." So did Erika, but no point in bringing up anything negative at the moment. Erika would find love. Whitney kept wanting to ask about Gi, but Erika got weird every time she did.

"Have you guys set a date yet?" Erika asked.

Whitney looked at Chace.

He shrugged, kissing her hand before pressing it to his cheek. "The sooner the better."

She put her arms around his neck. "This summer?"

"Perfect." He kissed her cheek.

"Why so quickly?" Erika asked.

Whitney shrugged, looking at Chace while speaking to Erika. "Why wait to spend the rest of our lives together when we both know it's all we want to do?"

"I'm going to call Mom. She's going to have a fit."

"Okay."

"I'll be back." Erika took her cell phone out of her purse and hurried outside.

Chace hugged her close. She wrapped her arms around him, glad to have his arms around her again.

❧

Chace heard Emma's voice before he turned around to confirm it was her. "Well! I'm flummoxed. I thought Ms. Jones hated your guts." He turned and sure enough, there she stood, gold hair in its usual curls, next to Cliff. Behind them stood his parents. "That's what you told your brother, right?"

"Your family?" Whitney whispered into his ear.

He smiled, took her hand, and pulled her forward. "Whitney, meet my brother, Cliff, and his wife, Emma." Chace waited until hands were shook and greetings were exchanged. Then, he gestured to the two people standing behind them. "And my father, also Cliff. And my mother, Belinda." He smiled at his tanned parents, who'd flown to Pennsylvania from their winter home in Florida. Then they'd ridden down to D.C. with Cliff and Emma for the show. "I'm glad you guys made it."

"Of course we did," his mom said, hugging him. "Whitney, we've heard so much about you." Belinda stuck her hand out and Whitney shook it.

"Yes. We have." Chace's dad shook Whitney's hand.

"Mom, Dad, Cliff, Emma, I have some news for you. While you were on your way here, I asked Whitney to marry me and she said yes." He grabbed Whitney's hand. "We're getting married."

"Oh. Oh dear. You're getting married?" Belinda put a hand over her heart. "What a surprise!"

"Our son. You always were…impulsive," Cliff said, clapping Chace on the back. His dad had long ago accepted that Chace wasn't going to follow anybody's path but his own. He'd learned to go with the flow. Dad engaged in a little bit of what he liked to call "good-natured ribbing" from time to time, but that was it.

"Oh. Sister-in-law," Emma crooned over Whitney before hugging her and kissing her cheeks.

"Congrats, bro." Chace's brother shook his hands. "And Whitney, to you, too. Although, I'm sure you'll want to give him back before long." Cliff winked before hugging Whitney.

"So. This is his career." Cliff the elder swept his hand across the open space, indicating Chace's photos. "And he's getting married." His dad chuckled. "Made any other life decisions lately that we don't know about?"

Chace stopped himself from telling his dad he'd almost had a kid. No need to give him a heart attack or anything. "Nope, Dad. You're all caught up on what's going on with me."

"Your, uh, pictures. You're pretty good at this, huh?" his dad said, looking around the gallery. "And I see your future wife's the star of the show."

His mom grabbed Whitney's hands. "And what a good star she makes." She pulled Whitney aside and began chatting with her in a confidential yet excited tone.

Chace turned to his brother and Emma. "Where's my nephew?"

"He's in Pennsylvania with our sitter. We didn't feel he was up to traveling such a distance in this weather. Especially since he's getting over a bit of a cold," Emma said. "Okay. We're stealing her. Mum, Whitney, let's go."

He watched Whitney walk off with Emma and Belinda. Before long, Erika walked up to them. The three women did a lot of jumping and squealing. His show, once something he couldn't imagine anything topping in terms of giving him a sense of fulfillment, faded into the background next to Whitney.

When June and the art critic found him again, he had to force himself to pay attention to what they were saying so he could answer their questions. All he wanted was to have his arms around Whitney again.

Later that evening Chace and Whitney stood near the back of the gallery. The women left Whitney alone after hogging her all evening. His family, Erika, and Rob had all left. It was getting late. The crowd was thinning out, and he wished it would get thinner. He couldn't stop thinking about having makeup sex with Whitney, and plenty of it.

Whitney reached up for a kiss. "I love you. So much."

"I love you, too." He pulled her close. "I'm surprised and impressed that you didn't need rescuing from my crazy family tonight."

Whitney laughed. "Nobody's family is crazier than mine."

Chace raised his eyebrows. "Let's see if you're still saying that by the time they go back to Pennsylvania."

"Just wait until I take you to meet mine."

"Looking forward to it."

"That's what you say now."

He laughed and kissed her hand. "Let's find June and ask her how much longer we have to stay."

"I can't believe how anxious you are to get out of here. This is huge for you."

"I got big plans tonight."

"Bigger than this?"

"Way bigger." He whispered to her all the things he wanted to do to her when they got home.

She grabbed his hand. "Yeah. Let's find June."

Chapter 32: Everything to Me

Whitney walked into her apartment and smiled at Chace sitting on her couch, toying with his cameras and doing something with his computer. A little over a week had passed since his opening. He'd gotten a permanent exhibit at June's gallery, and he was working on his next project. He kept most of his stuff at her place. He was moving in after the wedding. All of his camera stuff was there.

"Guess what?" She dropped her bag by the door and walked over, kissing him on the cheek.

"What, baby?" He moved a couple of his lenses out of the way so that she could sit next to him.

"I got the job." She'd gotten the job at One Justice For All.

"That's great." Chace set his laptop aside and pulled her close, kissing her.

"Thanks." She kissed him again. "So you ready to meet my fam this weekend?" They were going to Jo and Shorty's house that weekend. Her grandparents still wouldn't talk to her about her engagement or anything else. They would find a way to get over it, or not. Either way, she was marrying Chace and she was working for One Justice.

"Sure."

"I had a good time with yours." Chace's brother and Emma had to leave the day after the opening, but his parents had stuck around a few extra days before renting a car and driving back to Pennsylvania. Whitney and Chace had shown them around the city. She'd gotten a chance to know them a little better. His dad was hilarious, and his mother was very sweet.

"I'm glad. They love you. I knew they would."

"Good." Chace's family was great. Especially Emma. She could already tell she was going to enjoy having that woman for a sister-in-law.

She reached up, pushing his hair out of his eyes. "Yep."

Chace grinned.

"What?"

"I'm so happy to be right here, right now. That's all."

Whitney put her head on his shoulder. "Me, too."

∾

That weekend, at Jo and Shorty's house, when Jo threw open the door and saw them, she grabbed them both and told them how happy she was. Then she called out to Shorty, telling him to come to the door because his daughter and future son-in-law were there.

Aunt Brenda and Uncle Glen were there as well. Whitney noticed them after the initial excitement with Jo calmed down.

"I told you it would happen," Aunt Brenda said. She held out her arms and smiled.

"Yes." Whitney threw her arms around her aunt and squeezed tightly. Then she hugged Glen.

After Chace took their bags upstairs, everyone went into the living room so that Whitney's family could get to know Chace a little better. They were also waiting for Devon and Alicia to get there before they ate dinner. Jo had insisted on cooking even though Whitney had wanted to take everyone out to celebrate.

Chace acted very naturally with her family. It was as if he'd been one of them all along. They sat next to each other on the couch. He reached for her hand, and she slipped it into his. This was her perfect life.

She was thankful that Chace had elbowed his way into her life while she'd had her mind and heart turned to stone and set on blind ambition. How could she have lost sight of the most important thing in life? Love was everything, and she didn't know how she'd thought she could live without it. Now that she knew what she was missing, she never wanted to miss it again. She'd learned that the hard way.

Her grandparents had reluctantly agreed to come to the wedding. At least they were trying to be reasonable. That was progress.

After Devon and Alicia arrived and met Chace, everybody headed to the dining room. Whitney and Chace lagged behind the rest of the group. He put his arms around her, and she rested her head on his chest.

"Do you believe in love at first sight, Chace?" she said.

He took her hand and kissed each of her fingertips individually. "I do now." He put her hand over his heart.

Epilogue

Whitney had her back to the crowd, holding the bouquet in her hands. She turned her head, calling to them over her shoulder. "Ready, ladies?"

There were cheers and squeals behind her. She took that to mean that they were indeed ready.

"Here we go!" Whitney tossed her bouquet in the air and then turned around to see the mad scramble for it, laughing at her unmarried bridesmaids and female wedding guests all grabbing for the flowers. Erika, Alicia, and Abbott wore the gold strapless dresses she'd picked out for her bridesmaids and maid of honor. Alicia was maid of honor. Her other bridesmaid and now officially her sister-in-law, Emma, stood off to the side, cheering them on.

Delaney stood apart from the crowd, pumping one fist in triumph and holding the bouquet up with the other.

"No. Why?" Rob moaned from nearby. She turned to face him, laughing.

"Aw, man up, bro," Gi said to his brother, clapping Rob on the back. Gi had come down to be Erika's date to the wedding. Erika wouldn't let Whitney make a big deal about that fact.

"Yeah. Easy for you to say. No one's breathing the word 'marriage' down your neck every day." Rob rolled his eyes and gave Whitney a teasing grin. " 'Cause some people just have to go and get married. Geez."

Whitney laughed. "Thanks, Rob. I'm glad you're happy for me."

"No, seriously? I really am. Congrats. I can't say that enough. You two are great people and I'm glad to see you both happy."

"Thanks." Whitney hugged him.

Jo and Shorty were thrilled as were most of Whitney's family members. Even Aunt Cheryl was having a good time at the wedding. Only Whitney's grandparents separated themselves from everybody else. They sat at a table in the back of the reception hall and ignored all the other guests.

At least they were there. They'd flown in that morning, and they were flying out the next day. She would have a talk with them before they went back to New York. Maybe things would go better in person than they had over the phone.

Chace walked up and slipped an arm around her waist at the same time that her bridesmaids and Delaney materialized. Delaney hopped over to Rob and started chattering about catching the bouquet.

"How does it feel to be Missus Murphy?" he said before squeezing her shoulders and kissing her forehead.

"It feels pretty wonderful so far." She smiled, thinking back to their first dance. She'd let him surprise her with the song and he'd done a good job. He'd chosen "What's It Like" by Jagged Edge, taking her right back to Valentine's Day. And the wonderful night they'd shared at the restaurant. "I think I'll be in love with you forever. Is that going to be a problem?"

"I don't think so considering I'll never stop falling in love with you."

She grinned against his lips. "Good."

He kissed her. "Good."

"So what do we do now?"

"Dance the night away with me," Chace said, grabbing her hands.

"More dancing? Aren't we supposed to leave soon or something? After all the bouquet and garter stuff?"

"No leaving. Yes. More dancing."

"Okay, let me ditch these shoes." Whitney kicked her shoes off and let Chace pull her back out onto the dance floor. She smiled up at him, thinking that she had everything she needed in life right there on that dance floor. What a good feeling to have.

About the Author

Nicole Green is a graduate of the University of Virginia. She is also a graduate of the College of William and Mary's law school. She currently resides in Falls Church, Virginia. She works as an attorney for the federal government. She is a member of the Virginia Romance Writers chapter of RWA and of SCBWI. You can visit her online at: www.nicolegreenauthor.com. She would love to hear from you.

2011 Mass Market Titles

January

From This Moment
Sean Young
ISBN-13: 978-1-58571-383-7
ISBN-10: 1-58571-383-X
$6.99

Nihon Nights
Trisha/Monica Haddad
ISBN-13: 978-1-58571-382-0
ISBN-10: 1-58571-382-1
$6.99

February

The Davis Years
Nicole Green
ISBN-13: 978-1-58571-390-5
ISBN-10: 1-58571-390-2
$6.99

Allegro
Adora Bennett
ISBN-13: 978-158571-391-2
ISBN-10: 1-58571-391-0
$6.99

March

Lies in Disguise
Bernice Layton
ISBN-13: 978-1-58571-392-9
ISBN-10: 1-58571-392-9
$6.99

Steady
Ruthie Robinson
ISBN-13: 978-1-58571-393-6
ISBN-10: 1-58571-393-7
$6.99

April

The Right Maneuver
LaShell Stratton-Childers
ISBN-13: 978-1-58571-394-3
ISBN-10: 1-58571-394-5
$6.99

Riding the Corporate Ladder
Keith Walker
ISBN-13: 978-1-58571-395-0
ISBN-10: 1-58571-395-3
$6.99

May

Separate Dreams
Joan Early
ISBN-13: 978-1-58571-434-6
ISBN-10: 1-58571-434-8
$6.99

I Take This Woman
Chamein Canton
ISBN-13: 978-1-58571-435-3
ISBN-10: 1-58571-435-6
$6.99

June

Inside Out
Grayson Cole
ISBN-13: 978-1-58571-437-7
ISBN-10: 1-58571-437-2
$6.99

2011 Mass Market Titles (continued)

July

The Other Side of the
Mountain
Janice Angelique
ISBN-13: 978-1-58571-442-1
ISBN-10: 1-58571-442-9
$6.99

Holding Her Breath
Nicole Green
ISBN-13: 978-1-58571-439-1
ISBN-10: 1-58571-439-9
$6.99

August

The Sea of Aaron
Kymberly Hunt
ISBN-13: 978-1-58571-440-7
ISBN-10: 1-58571-440-2
$6.99

The Finley Sisters' Oath of
Romance
Keith Thomas Walker
ISBN-13: 978-1-58571-441-4
ISBN-10: 1-58571-441-0
$6.99

September

Except on Sunday
Regena Bryant
ISBN-13: 978-1-58571-443-8
ISBN-10: 1-58571-443-7
$6.99

Light's Out
Ruthie Robinson
ISBN-13: 978-1-58571-445-2
ISBN-10: 1-58571-445-3
$6.99

October

The Heart Knows
Renee Wynn
ISBN-13: 978-1-58571-444-5
ISBN-10: 1-58571-444-5
$6.99

Best Friends; Better Lovers
Celya Bowers
ISBN-13: 978-1-58571-455-1
ISBN-10: 1-58571-455-0
$6.99

November

Caress
Grayson Cole
ISBN-13: 978-1-58571-454-4
ISBN-10: 1-58571-454-2
$6.99

A Love Built to Last
L. S. Childers
ISBN-13: 978-1-58571-448-3
ISBN-10: 1-58571-448-8
$6.99

December

Fractured
Wendy Byrne
ISBN-13: 978-1-58571-449-0
ISBN-10: 1-58571-449-6
$6.99

Everything in Between
Crystal Hubbard
ISBN-13: 978-1-58571-396-7
ISBN-10: 1-58571-396-1
$6.99

Other Genesis Press, Inc. Titles

Other Genesis Press, Inc. Titles (continued)

Blindsided	Tammy Williams	$6.99
Bliss, Inc.	Chamein Canton	$6.99
Blood Lust	J.M. Jeffries	$9.95
Blood Seduction	J.M. Jeffries	$9.95
Blue Interlude	Keisha Mennefee	$6.99
Bodyguard	Andrea Jackson	$9.95
Boss of Me	Diana Nyad	$8.95
Bound by Love	Beverly Clark	$8.95
Breeze	Robin Hampton Allen	$10.95
Broken	Dar Tomlinson	$24.95
Burn	Crystal Hubbard	$6.99
By Design	Barbara Keaton	$8.95
Cajun Heat	Charlene Berry	$8.95
Careless Whispers	Rochelle Alers	$8.95
Cats & Other Tales	Marilyn Wagner	$8.95
Caught in a Trap	Andre Michelle	$8.95
Caught Up in the Rapture	Lisa G. Riley	$9.95
Cautious Heart	Cheris F. Hodges	$8.95
Chances	Pamela Leigh Starr	$8.95
Checks and Balances	Elaine Sims	$6.99
Cherish the Flame	Beverly Clark	$8.95
Choices	Tammy Williams	$6.99
Class Reunion	Irma Jenkins/	$12.95
	John Brown	
Code Name: Diva	J.M. Jeffries	$9.95
Conquering Dr. Wexler's Heart	Kimberley White	$9.95
Corporate Seduction	A.C. Arthur	$9.95
Crossing Paths, Tempting Memories	Dorothy Elizabeth Love	$9.95
Crossing the Line	Bernice Layton	$6.99
Crush	Crystal Hubbard	$9.95
Cypress Whisperings	Phyllis Hamilton	$8.95
Dark Embrace	Crystal Wilson Harris	$8.95
Dark Storm Rising	Chinelu Moore	$10.95
Daughter of the Wind	Joan Xian	$8.95
Dawn's Harbor	Kymberly Hunt	$6.99
Deadly Sacrifice	Jack Kean	$22.95
Designer Passion	Dar Tomlinson	$8.95
	Diana Richeaux	

379

Other Genesis Press, Inc. Titles (continued)

Other Genesis Press, Inc. Titles (continued)

How to Write a Romance	Kathryn Falk	$18.95
I Married a Reclining Chair	Lisa M. Fuhs	$8.95
I'll Be Your Shelter	Giselle Carmichael	$8.95
I'll Paint a Sun	A.J. Garrotto	$9.95
Icie	Pamela Leigh Starr	$8.95
If I Were Your Woman	LaConnie Taylor-Jones	$6.99
Illusions	Pamela Leigh Starr	$8.95
Indigo After Dark Vol. I	Nia Dixon/Angelique	$10.95
Indigo After Dark Vol. II	Dolores Bundy/	$10.95
	Cole Riley	
Indigo After Dark Vol. III	Montana Blue/	$10.95
	Coco Morena	
Indigo After Dark Vol. IV	Cassandra Colt/	$14.95
Indigo After Dark Vol. V	Delilah Dawson	$14.95
Indiscretions	Donna Hill	$8.95
Intentional Mistakes	Michele Sudler	$9.95
Interlude	Donna Hill	$8.95
Intimate Intentions	Angie Daniels	$8.95
It's in the Rhythm	Sammie Ward	$6.99
It's Not Over Yet	J.J. Michael	$9.95
Jolie's Surrender	Edwina Martin-Arnold	$8.95
Kiss or Keep	Debra Phillips	$8.95
Lace	Giselle Carmichael	$9.95
Lady Preacher	K.T. Richey	$6.99
Last Train to Memphis	Elsa Cook	$12.95
Lasting Valor	Ken Olsen	$24.95
Let Us Prey	Hunter Lundy	$25.95
Let's Get It On	Dyanne Davis	$6.99
Lies Too Long	Pamela Ridley	$13.95
Life Is Never As It Seems	J.J. Michael	$12.95
Lighter Shade of Brown	Vicki Andrews	$8.95
Look Both Ways	Joan Early	$6.99
Looking for Lily	Africa Fine	$6.99
Love Always	Mildred E. Riley	$10.95
Love Doesn't Come Easy	Charlyne Dickerson	$8.95
Love Out of Order	Nicole Green	$6.99
Love Unveiled	Gloria Greene	$10.95
Love's Deception	Charlene Berry	$10.95
Love's Destiny	M. Loui Quezada	$8.95
Love's Secrets	Yolanda McVey	$6.99

Other Genesis Press, Inc. Titles (continued)

Mae's Promise	Melody Walcott	$8.95
Magnolia Sunset	Giselle Carmichael	$8.95
Many Shades of Gray	Dyanne Davis	$6.99
Matters of Life and Death	Lesego Malepe, Ph.D.	$15.95
Meant to Be	Jeanne Sumerix	$8.95
Midnight Clear	Leslie Esdaile	$10.95
(Anthology)	Gwynne Forster	
	Carmen Green	
	Monica Jackson	
Midnight Magic	Gwynne Forster	$8.95
Midnight Peril	Vicki Andrews	$10.95
Misconceptions	Pamela Leigh Starr	$9.95
Mixed Reality	Chamein Canton	$6.99
Moments of Clarity	Michele Cameron	$6.99
Montgomery's Children	Richard Perry	$14.95
Mr. Fix-It	Crystal Hubbard	$6.99
My Buffalo Soldier	Barbara B.K. Reeves	$8.95
Naked Soul	Gwynne Forster	$8.95
Never Say Never	Michele Cameron	$6.99
Next to Last Chance	Louisa Dixon	$24.95
No Apologies	Seressia Glass	$8.95
No Commitment Required	Seressia Glass	$8.95
No Regrets	Mildred E. Riley	$8.95
Not His Type	Chamein Canton	$6.99
Not Quite Right	Tammy Williams	$6.99
Nowhere to Run	Gay G. Gunn	$10.95
O Bed! O Breakfast!	Rob Kuehnle	$14.95
Oak Bluffs	Joan Early	$6.99
Object of His Desire	A.C. Arthur	$8.95
Office Policy	A.C. Arthur	$9.95
Once in a Blue Moon	Dorianne Cole	$9.95
One Day at a Time	Bella McFarland	$8.95
One of These Days	Michele Sudler	$9.95
Outside Chance	Louisa Dixon	$24.95
Passion	T.T. Henderson	$10.95
Passion's Blood	Cherif Fortin	$22.95
Passion's Furies	AlTonya Washington	$6.99
Passion's Journey	Wanda Y. Thomas	$8.95
Past Promises	Jahmel West	$8.95
Path of Fire	T.T. Henderson	$8.95

Other Genesis Press, Inc. Titles (continued)

Other Genesis Press, Inc. Titles (continued)

Soul to Soul	Donna Hill	$8.95
Southern Comfort	J.M. Jeffries	$8.95
Southern Fried Standards	S.R. Maddox	$6.99
Still the Storm	Sharon Robinson	$8.95
Still Waters Run Deep	Leslie Esdaile	$8.95
Still Waters...	Crystal V. Rhodes	$6.99
Stolen Jewels	Michele Sudler	$6.99
Stolen Memories	Michele Sudler	$6.99
Stories to Excite You	Anna Forrest/Divine	$14.95
Storm	Pamela Leigh Starr	$6.99
Subtle Secrets	Wanda Y. Thomas	$8.95
Suddenly You	Crystal Hubbard	$9.95
Swan	Africa Fine	$6.99
Sweet Repercussions	Kimberley White	$9.95
Sweet Sensations	Gwyneth Bolton	$9.95
Sweet Tomorrows	Kimberly White	$8.95
Taken by You	Dorothy Elizabeth Love	$9.95
Tattooed Tears	T. T. Henderson	$8.95
Tempting Faith	Crystal Hubbard	$6.99
That Which Has Horns	Miriam Shumba	$6.99
The Business of Love	Cheris F. Hodges	$6.99
The Color Line	Lizzette Grayson Carter	$9.95
The Color of Trouble	Dyanne Davis	$8.95
The Disappearance of Allison Jones	Kayla Perrin	$5.95
The Doctor's Wife	Mildred Riley	$6.99
The Fires Within	Beverly Clark	$9.95
The Foursome	Celya Bowers	$6.99
The Honey Dipper's Legacy	Myra Pannell-Allen	$14.95
The Joker's Love Tune	Sidney Rickman	$15.95
The Little Pretender	Barbara Cartland	$10.95
The Love We Had	Natalie Dunbar	$8.95
The Man Who Could Fly	Bob & Milana Beamon	$18.95
The Missing Link	Charlyne Dickerson	$8.95
The Mission	Pamela Leigh Starr	$6.99
The More Things Change	Chamein Canton	$6.99
The Perfect Frame	Beverly Clark	$9.95
The Price of Love	Sinclair LeBeau	$8.95
The Smoking Life	Ilene Barth	$29.95
The Words of the Pitcher	Kei Swanson	$8.95

Other Genesis Press, Inc. Titles (continued)

Things Forbidden	Maryam Diaab	$6.99
This Life Isn't Perfect Holla	Sandra Foy	$6.99
Three Doors Down	Michele Sudler	$6.99
Three Wishes	Seressia Glass	$8.95
Ties That Bind	Kathleen Suzanne	$8.95
Tiger Woods	Libby Hughes	$5.95
Time Is of the Essence	Angie Daniels	$9.95
Timeless Devotion	Bella McFarland	$9.95
Tomorrow's Promise	Leslie Esdaile	$8.95
Truly Inseparable	Wanda Y. Thomas	$8.95
Two Sides to Every Story	Dyanne Davis	$9.95
Unbeweavable	Katrina Spencer	$6.99
Unbreak My Heart	Dar Tomlinson	$8.95
Unclear and Present Danger	Michele Cameron	$6.99
Uncommon Prayer	Kenneth Swanson	$9.95
Unconditional	A.C. Arthur	$9.95
Unconditional Love	Alicia Wiggins	$8.95
Undying Love	Renee Alexis	$6.99
Until Death Do Us Part	Susan Paul	$8.95
Vows of Passion	Bella McFarland	$9.95
Waiting for Mr. Darcy	Chamein Canton	$6.99
Waiting in the Shadows	Michele Sudler	$6.99
Wayward Dreams	Gail McFarland	$6.99
Wedding Gown	Dyanne Davis	$8.95
What's Under Benjamin's Bed	Sandra Schaffer	$8.95
When a Man Loves a Woman	LaConnie Taylor-Jones	$6.99
When Dreams Float	Dorothy Elizabeth Love	$8.95
When I'm With You	LaConnie Taylor-Jones	$6.99
When Lightning Strikes	Michele Cameron	$6.99
Where I Want to Be	Maryam Diaab	$6.99
Whispers in the Night	Dorothy Elizabeth Love	$8.95
Whispers in the Sand	LaFlorya Gauthier	$10.95
Who's That Lady?	Andrea Jackson	$9.95
Wild Ravens	AlTonya Washington	$9.95
Yesterday Is Gone	Beverly Clark	$10.95
Yesterday's Dreams, Tomorrow's Promises	Reon Laudat	$8.95
Your Precious Love	Sinclair LeBeau	$8.95

Order Form

Mail to: Genesis Press, Inc.
P.O. Box 101
Columbus, MS 39703

Name _____

Address _____

City/State _____ Zip _____

Telephone _____

Ship to (if different from above)

Name _____

Address _____

City/State _____ Zip _____

Telephone _____

Credit Card Information

Credit Card # _____ ☐ Visa ☐ Mastercard

Expiration Date (mm/yy) _____ ☐ AmEx ☐ Discover

Qty.	Author	Title	Price	Total

Use this order form, or call 1-888-INDIGO-1	Total for books	
	Shipping and handling: $5 first two books, $1 each additional book	
	Total S & H	
	Total amount enclosed	
	Mississippi residents add 7% sales tax	